Human And Freakn'

(Freakn' Shifters, Book Four)

Eve Langlais

Copyright © October 2012, Eve Langlais
Cover Art by Amanda Kelsey © October 2012
Edited by Brandi Buckwine
Edited by Amanda Pederick
Copy Edited by Brienna Roberston
Produced in Canada

Published by Eve Langlais
1606 Main Street, PO Box 151
Stittsville, Ontario, Canada, K2S1A3
http://www.EveLanglais.com

ISBN-13: 978 1988 328 22 5

ALL RIGHTS RESERVED

Human and Freakn' is a work of fiction and the characters, events and dialogue found within the story are of the author's imagination and are not to be construed as real. Any resemblance to actual events or persons, either living or deceased, is completely coincidental.

No part of this book may be reproduced or shared in any form or by any means, electronic or mechanical, including but not limited to digital copying, file sharing, audio recording, email and printing without permission in writing from the author.

Prologue

Somewhere in the Lacandon jungle, a few days before Christmas ...

Nothing screamed 'Wake up, dumbass!' like regaining consciousness to the fluttery warmth of something breathing moist air into her face. A living, breathing entity, which smelled both earthy and spicy – covered in tickly fur. In other words, something that didn't belong in the shelter with her.

Panic took complete control of her body. Despite knowing it was the middle of the night and pitch black, her eyes flashed open to see the intruder. In retrospect, she perhaps should have feigned slumber, given she now stared into a pair of glowing eyes – one golden, the other a clear blue. Had she forgotten to note they glared – probably with murderous intent – a few paltry inches from her face? Not a good distance when it came to wild animals, especially with no bars to separate them.

Should she freak? *There's a plan. Scream my face off, get eaten, and become a tiny blurb in the paper.* On to option two. Scream for help. *Sure, because high, piercing shrieks won't piss it off and send it into a murderous frenzy.* Skipping that route seemed prudent. What else did that leave? Peeing her pants? Seeing that Carlie held the control to her bladder only tenuously at the moment, it was almost a foregone conclusion. As for closing her eyes and pretending nothing stood over her, eyeing her like a tasty tidbit? *No way am I letting that creature out of my sight.*

Choices. Choices. To act or not to act? Maybe later she'd choose a route of escape. For the moment, it didn't truly matter what she wanted to do as terror froze her from head to toe. She couldn't utter a sound, not when her vocal cords refused to co-operate.

Paralyzed by fear, she just concentrated on breathing – without any whimpering or reciting of Hail Mary. Funny how staring death in its mismatched eyes could make a girl find religion. Lying like a wax statue seemed best considering any sudden motion or sound might startle the jungle cat staring intently at her.

How did she know a giant kitty hovered over her? She'd watched enough documentaries about the Lacandon jungle region to recognize those distinctive orbs of what she'd wager was a jaguar. The massive golden eyes and round pupil shape gave it away, even if the fact the cat possessed a blue one was an anomaly.

How did I not hear it enter the tent? How did it get in? She'd drawn the zipper tight and snapped it shut so nothing could sneak in and snuggle with her. It only took waking to one fist-sized, hairy spider – with a scream to wake the dead – to realize the merit in making her sleeping area as secure as possible.

A damp nose nudged her cheek. Carlie bit a threatening shriek into submission.

Did the how-it-got-in matter? Only one simple fact mattered. A big ass cat stood over her, and judging by the glint in its narrowing, mismatched eyes, the feline was damned hungry. A raspy tongue emerged and swiped across her cheek, then back, leaving a wet trail.

Oh dear God. She waited for the jaguar to follow with a great big bite, and held her breath as her whole body tensed. It rubbed a furry head against the wet spot. Soft, silky fur did not distract her from the fact this wild creature wasn't a domestic pet. Out came the tongue again, trailing over her cheek to her chin and then across her lips. Oh, no way.

"Gross!" she exclaimed, finding her voice. "That was so uncalled for. If you're going to eat me, then just do it already. No need to torture me with slobber and bad breath." She wanted to slap herself for the outburst as soon as she uttered the last syllable. So much for staying calm in the face of death.

Expecting to get her face chewed off, she waved her hands around for a weapon – didn't find one of course, unless her hand lotion counted. She did locate the small pencil flashlight she used at night if she needed to visit a bush for a late night pee. Brandishing it, she flicked it on, the feeble beam reflecting off the eyes of the predator.

"Get away," she said in a wobbly voice, pointing it at the feline. "Or I'll poke you with my stupid weapon." A human would of course laugh at her threat, but she hoped the words and menacing wave with her object would … What? Make the giant cat suddenly tremble in fear?

The jaguar, of course, didn't run away. It cocked its head, and darn it all if it didn't seem as if it smiled. Wait, could cats smile?

A paw landed on her wrist, immobilizing her arm. A moment later, her other arm got pinned, as well. The tip of its tongue peeked again for a quick swipe at her chin. It tickled. She squirmed, arms held flat, the sleeping bag trapping the rest of her limbs and torso under the caging legs of the cat. Forget escape.

The jaguar lowered its body and squished her flat, its weight impressive enough to force the air out of her lungs. The head moved to the side, the disturbing eyes – showing too much intelligence and misplaced humor – left her as the feline sniffed her skin, nuzzling the bare flesh between shoulder and neck, then lower.

Lower? Wait a second. The damned creature was pulling the blanket in its teeth, the unzipping sound loud in the tent. Carlie wiggled madly to no avail. It seemed Mr. Kitty wanted its food unwrapped. The only good thing was it released her arms, and then her body, as it wiggled back, taking her sleeping bag with it.

Prey exposed, the jaguar proceeded to sniff its way up her body. The brush of a damp nose, too close to her girl parts, made her pull up her legs. "Perv. Stay out of there. I've sworn off men for this trip, and that goes for big kitty cats too."

It ignored her and leaned forward to smell again. Before she could stop herself, she tapped it on the head. "No. Bad kitty."

A low growl rumbled and mismatched eyes flashed in her direction.

Okay, perhaps she shouldn't have smacked it. Still, though, it wanted her to lie still while he sized her up for dinner? Not freakn' likely. Yet, what else could Carlie do? Her pale, human flesh would prove no match to a creature that not only outweighed her, but sported a set of nasty teeth and claws. Doing nothing, though, seemed dumbest of all.

I am not going to sit here and let the darned thing eat me. Not without a fight. She kept her legs up to her chest when it occurred to her she was no longer frozen. Nor did she camp alone in the jungle. If she shouted out, then some of her expedition's members would surely come to her aid. *If they haven't been mauled already.*

Nothing like optimism to brighten a girl's night. She opened her mouth, closed her eyes against the possible violence about to erupt, and prepared to let loose the mother of all yells.

Great plan, except a hand slapped over her lips, stifling any sound.

A hand? Who was in the tent with her and the cat? How did they all fit?

She opened her eyes, but even with her flashlight still feebly shining, the shadows were too thick for her to see anything with clarity.

An arm snaked around her upper body, and she reacted, thrashing against an iron band that didn't budge. Of the cat, she saw and heard no sign. But at least now she knew how it got in. *Someone let the jaguar in my tent.* But why?

The hand over her mouth loosened a bit as her attacker shifted her body. Carlie used his lapse to make her move. Biting down hard, she heard a sharp hiss, and she kicked out, glad for once of her extra size. She broke free and scrambled for the opening of the tent.

"Help m—" She didn't finish her yell because a heavy body landed atop her, squashing her flat. Pinned to the ground, just like one of Roberson's bugs, she could barely lift her head. Her poor vantage point didn't stop her from taking stock of what she could glimpse. In the moonlight filtering down, what she saw made her groan. A new set of eyes, both golden this time, perused her. A new tongue licked her.

"What is it with the cats around here?" she grumbled, too annoyed at her aborted attempt of escape to show proper fear. Besides, her mind had already surmised the felines weren't wild, killing machines, not if they worked with humans. However, she might have preferred a quick, if painful, death to the other possibilities. Slavers. Indigenes who believed in human sacrifice. Cannibals. Why couldn't she ever imagine something nice, like that Ed McMahon guy and a giant check? Or that cute Ashton fellow and one of his famous pranks?

Hands yanked her body upright, snapping her back to the moment. She staggered at the abrupt motion. The damp evening air kissed her skin, her nighttime attire of shorts and a tank top leaving generous swaths of flesh exposed, an important thing to note because she fully felt the extent of taut, heated skin pressed against her rear. Very naked skin, garnished with an erection that poked her in the lower back, not an easy feat given her almost six foot height, which made the guy behind her pretty freakn' tall. And horny. *Let's not forget horny.*

Sucking in a shocked gasp, she went to lunge forward, but another bare chest hemmed her from the front, not that she saw it in the pitch dark outside her tent. She couldn't avoid feeling it, though, when her hands touched a hot and hard male upper body. For a second, she stood frozen but not cold. Not anything close to cold with the naked, heated flesh sandwiching her. Under other circumstances, she might have even enjoyed it. But common sense prevailed, and she shoved at the male in front of her.

"Get away." She didn't think her words would do anything, but she had to try.

A guttural cough sounded behind her, and the body in front took a step back. Spun around, she didn't wobble as strong hands gripped her upper arms, holding her steady. Carlie peeked up, and things went hazy as soon as she met the impossible gaze of her captor. The blue and gold gaze of a cat, which now stared at her steadily from the face of a man.

What the freakn' hell is going on? was her last cognizant thought before she inhaled something powdery and her mind went blank.

Chapter One

To Kendrick's surprise, his sister Naomi bawled worse than one of her babies at the airport when she came to see him off. Talk about out of character. Even worse? Hers weren't the only tears. Ma cried too, although, hers were thankfully silent. The big shocker? His gruff father showed a hint of moisture, which he of course blamed on nonexistent dust.

Weight shifting from one foot to the other, Kendrick wondered how to escape the waterworks. "Geez, guys, it's not like I haven't gone away before."

"But never so far," sniffled his sister. "And where there's so much danger."

Good grief. Who took his snarky sister and left this emotional mess in her place? Sure, Kendrick appreciated the break from her acerbic tongue and strong-for-a-girl fist, but still ... The Naomi he knew didn't cry because her brother went on a trip. She celebrated because she got more of Mom's cooking to take home as leftovers. "I'll bring you back a present?" He asked this hopefully.

Ow. He'd take the shot to his gut as a no.

Violence beginning – not unusual in his family – Joel, his best friend, weighed in to help. "Don't worry, Naomi. Kendrick won't be alone. I'm going too, and promise to keep his furry ass safe." Joel volunteered his declaration with bravado, his bright smile withering under Naomi's glare.

"That is not reassuring, Joel. I've seen your idea of protection."

Uh-oh. When his sister got that glint in her eye, it didn't bode well for anyone. Kendrick jumped in to save his friend. "Not that again. No harm was done. I knew the Saran Wrap couldn't take the place of a condom."

"What?" his mother yelled. Forget saving his friend. With Ma involved, it was every wolf for himself. Joel wisely shuffled sideways until he stood behind Kendrick. "Do I have to worry about strange women showing up with pups?" his mom demanded, hands on her hips.

"I don't think so. But then again, the ladies were pretty sad last night at the bar to hear I had to go, and they were eager to show it." Kendrick grinned as his mother snapped her mouth shut, speechless.

His dad chuckled. "Now you've done it."

He sure had. With his mother busy tracking down his ex-girlfriends and one-night-stands, to make sure they were child free, she wouldn't have time to worry as much about him. His distraction, however, didn't work on his sister.

Naomi sniffled. "I don't understand why you have to go. You've never even been out of Canada. And the Lacandon jungle is so far. Who will come over and drive Javier nuts if you're not here?"

"Oh please, Stu does that better than me, and you know it."

"But Stu doesn't give Mellie the best belly zerberts, and he doesn't know how to get Mark to eat his mushed peas."

"So get your mates to do it."

"But I want their uncle Kendrick to do it." Naomi pouted.

"This has nothing to do with my niece and nephew. Admit it. You're going to miss me."

"Am not."

"Naomi's gonna miss me. My baby sister loves me," he sang.

"Do not."

"Do too."

"Do not, you jerk." She hit him in the arm and then burst into tears before throwing herself at him, again, wetting his plaid shirt. Kendrick gave his dad a desperate look.

"Leave your brother alone, baby girl. He's going adventuring. Lucky bastard." His dad dragged him into a bear proportioned hug. "Bring me back some images of the local ladies. Naked ones if you can," he whispered.

"You'd need eyes to look at those, Geoffrey," his mother retorted.

While they argued about his dad's interest in the human body as art, Naomi clutched his tear soaked shirt in her fists and shook him.

"Be careful."

"Aren't I always?"

"No. Especially when you have dumbass with you."

"Hey," said the dumbass in question.

"Don't *hey* me, Joel," she snapped. "I am fully aware of the trouble you two get into. I'm going on the record now as saying this is a bad idea."

Ma stepped in front of her. "Oh stop your belly aching, Naomi. Your brother is going because it's the right thing to do." His mother's quiet spoken praise almost made Kendrick scuff his feet and say, *Aw shucks, Ma*. He hugged her instead, inhaling the scent of home on her, feeling the frailty of her frame.

When had she become so small? Since when did he get so maudlin?

Stepping away and putting on a stoic face – before he started crying like a baby too – Kendrick gave his family one last wave then left them to enter the boarding area for the flight, Joel at his heels – but only after he got away from the hugs of Kendrick's family.

"Sheesh, man. Talk about waterworks." Joel lengthened his stride until they walked side by side.

"Jealous?"

"Yeah," his best friend quietly admitted. "When I told the old man I was going on this trip and that it might be dangerous, he just grunted."

"I'm sure deep down inside, he gives a damn."

"Really, really deep. But who cares? We're going on an adventure."

"A rescue mission," Kendrick corrected.

"Whatever. I am not going to let the fact my dad already cleared out my room to turn it into a study bother me."

Kendrick slowed as they neared a check-in area. "Did you spike his rum with a laxative before you left?"

"Damned straight. And the whiskey too." Joel grinned.

"Think a violent case of the shits is going to send him to AA?" Kendrick asked as he slid off his shoes and began the pirouette as the agent at the gate scanned him for weapons. As if he needed something so paltry as a knife or a gun. His deadly inner wolf didn't set off any alarms. The joy of being his own weapon.

"My dad, go to AA? Only if they serve alcohol."

Despite the fact Joel would punch him if he knew, Kendrick felt sorry for his poor buddy. His mother, a human who never found out she'd mated with a shifter, left when Joel was just a pup. Unlike a shifter, humans were immune to the mating bond. Not so for the unlucky mate left behind. Devastated at her abandonment, Joel's dad turned into an alcoholic who refused all help. There was no cure for a mate who lost the other half of his soul, even a human one. Poor Joel suffered the consequences.

Kendrick wondered sometimes what would have happened to Joel if his parents hadn't opened their home and hearts to him, giving him a place to crash when his dad went on one of his binges. They'd built a strong friendship over those hard years, hard years that Joel prolonged by staying at home, worried his father would hurt himself during one of his excessive moments. Despite himself, Joel couldn't help but love his father, a man whose psyche never healed from the loss of his mate. A fate Joel swore he'd never suffer.

For his sake, Kendrick hoped his friend would one day find a woman, a shifter woman, to love and trust. In the meantime, Kendrick decided Joel needed a break from the emotional nastiness of his life. Some time away from his father, a bit of R&R for himself, maybe some playtime with exotic girls. While the reason proved serious, the timing of the mission worked. When he got the call, Kendrick couldn't think of a better partner to have on this trip, a rescue mission in the heart of the Lacandon rain forest, and home to a tribe of legend, the Luunnaa Xtaabay Jix, more commonly known as the Moon Ghost Jaguars.

Boys grew up on stories of their prowess as warriors, how they survived in the wild, the last Mayan survivors, hidden from the real world. Of special intrigue, the rumors that the Luunnaa Xtaabay Jix stalked and kidnapped their brides, choosing from the most beautiful village girls and then spiriting them away from under their families' and village's very noses. These abductions were valued rather than feared or guarded against because of the riches left in the girl's place. Gold. Jewels. Wealth enough to make a poor family celebrate their daughter's good fortune.

It sounded dashing and dangerous. Kendrick, once upon a time, wished he could have belonged to the Luunnaa Xtaabay Jix. Or, as Ma liked to call them, 'those women stealing perverts'.

But this time, the Moon Ghost Jaguars took the wrong girls. A botanical expedition of university students ended up the victims of a bride raid, or so the clues indicated. Three of the girls on that trip – one American and two Canadian girls, all pretty and under the age of thirty – disappeared into thin air. Left in their place? The most ridiculously sized emeralds and diamonds. Chaos erupted in the news before anyone could stop it.

White slavers kidnap students on fieldtrip, but in an odd twist, leave payment.

Virgin sacrifices have begun again deep in the ancient Mayan jungles. Pray to the gods for aide.

Wild cat men are just one of the rumors behind some kidnappings in the rainforest. Villagers say it is the Moon Ghosts, men disguised as big cats ...

Usually, missing human girls wouldn't make a person bat an eye, but when the news speculated on shifters? Action was required, along with damage control. And that's where Kendrick, Joel, and a few other specially chosen shifters came into play.

"How long is this flight again?" Joel asked as they took their seats on the plane and buckled in for takeoff.

"Long enough for you to read the file instead of skimming it."

"Who says I didn't memorize it?"

Kendrick didn't bother to smother his snort. "I know you."

"Can't I get the cliff notes?"

"Not from me, you won't. Read. It will be good for you. Might wake up that brain of yours. And when you're done studying the mission, I've got a book on the different species of plants and animals we can expect on our trip."

A prolonged groan rumbled out of Joel. "Way to suck all the fun out of this adventure. I thought this was supposed to be a hunt and rescue? Us against nature. Men in shining fur coming to the rescue."

"It is. I don't know about you, but personally, I'd rather know which leaf not to wipe with given some of the foliage in that area can give even our tough skins a rash. Not to mention, I'd like to know what critters to avoid. Did you know there's a bug in some waters that can climb up your tool and cause havoc?" Just the thought made his dick shrivel in an attempt to hide.

A big sigh escaped Joel. "I hate it when you tell me shit like this after the plane has already taken off. Would it kill you to warn me ahead of time so I can tell you no freakn' way?"

"And have you miss out on the adventure of a lifetime? Buddy, have you seen the images of the three girls we're supposed to rescue?"

"Hot?" Joel queried, his blues eyes lighting with hope.

"Very. And grateful. Don't forget very, very grateful when we rescue them from the wild men who took them."

Lips stretched in a wide smile, Joel sat up. "Dude, you just said the magic words. Now shut up. I've got some reading to do."

Holding in a snicker, Kendrick turned to look out the window, the fluffy duvet of clouds he flew over almost anathema. Wolves traveled on land and by foot when possible, unless the drive spanned days and time was of essence, then flying would do. But no true shifter enjoyed it.

What he could admit, however, was his appreciative male enjoyment as he watched the flight attendant bend over when Joel dropped his straw, the slacks pulling taut over her slim ass.

It's a long flight and I've never applied to the mile high club. No time like the present, he thought, flashing the stewardess a grin.

A smart man, Kendrick would take what he could now because once they entered the jungle, they wouldn't see any women until they managed to rescue the missing ones. Even then, traumatized by their experience, forget any fun time in the sack despite his words to Joel. He and his buddy would probably have to deal with a hysterical bunch that would require counseling – and severe hypnotism by the secret shifter council who kept their kind safe. Only once the council got through with them, would the human girls return to the normal world with no memory of their time in the jungle and any trauma they might have suffered.

Despite knowing there would be no women, no real recognition, but lots of danger, Kendrick couldn't wait for the adventure of a lifetime. A man and his wolf against a primitive jungle on a quest to find a tribe of legend.

Totally freakn' cool.

*

I'd give anything to feel cool again. Ruth fanned herself and wondered, not for the first time, what the heck she was doing traveling thousands of miles from home. Her family warned her not to go, her mother pleading with her to stay so she wouldn't lose another child. The authorities cautioned against it as well, but with her sister Carlie missing in the jungle and no clear answers from the people investigating, she couldn't sit still. So on a plane she hopped, traveling way out of her comfort zone, with her nerves strung taut, hoping that somehow, someway she might make a difference.

Forget making a difference. I'm more likely to faint from dehydration. Not a breeze stirred the humid and heavy air at the airport, and the stench of hundreds of bodies – sweat and perfume blending with the aroma of cooking food – made her wish for the crisp cleanness of her garden at home. *My oasis.*

People often joked they possessed a green thumb, but Ruth possessed more than that, or so people claimed when they saw the miniature jungle she'd managed to create on the rooftop deck of her apartment building. To say she loved plants put it mildly. From an early age, she'd developed a fascination for nature and the things that grew as a result of the earth's bounty. When it came time for a career choice, botany seemed the most natural course.

Had she arrived in the southern part of the Yucatan Peninsula for any other reason, she would have delighted in exploring and taking samples of the local fauna. But she had another purpose, and she wouldn't allow herself to be deterred.

Peering around, she managed to decipher where her baggage would arrive and scooped her suitcase without mishap. Lugging it behind her on squeaky wheels, she weaved and dodged, heading toward what she hoped was the exit.

What a chaotic place. Ruth tried not to flinch as a wave of sound enveloped her. Used to quiet places and small groups of people at a time, this pushed the boundaries of her comfort levels. But she couldn't turn back. Not with her sister's wellbeing possibly at stake.

As she fought to remember her bits and pieces of Spanish to relay to the taxi driver where she wanted to go, she heard the bellow of an irate passenger. "What do you mean you lost my freakn' luggage?" For some reason, it caught her attention and she turned her head only to see the broad back of a man, more like a giant, gesturing wildly.

It sucked to be him, she thought as she handed her own meager set of bags to the driver who piled them into the cab's trunk before taking her on a hair-raising drive to her hotel. It seemed speed limits and road rules were the choice of the driver. Thankfully, hers must have trained with some stunt-devils because she'd never seen someone slide into so many tight spots at high speeds, and without even a scratch.

Despite having lost about ten years off her life, she checked in without mishap. The place she'd chosen, found on the Internet and not as pretty as the images on the site suggested, appeared clean, if worn out by time and the passage of people. The flowered bedcover on the sagging double bed hung over the sides, thin and faded from many washings. Artistic prints framed in brass rectangles hung on the painted – salmon pink and peeling – cement walls. As for the window, it didn't open, and even if it did, thick bars were bolted outside of it. How reassuring.

As for the teeny, tiny bathroom? It did possess one saving grace. It smelled of lemon scented cleaner and had toilet paper.

Not bothering to unpack, Ruth headed into the tiny bathroom to wash her face. In the chipped mirror, she caught sight of her reflection – wan with dark circles under her eyes, a result of too many sleepless nights since her sister's reported disappearance. How could she rest when as soon as her eyes closed, the nightmares descended, horrible dreams that woke her crying for her lost sibling?

Splashing more tepid water on her face, she changed the blouse sticking to her skin to a fresh one and reapplied some antiperspirant, which worked all of two seconds before the pervasive heat made her skin sticky again. But by then, she'd already headed out again with instructions to find the local police station.

She returned an hour later frustrated beyond belief.

How can they not tell me anything? It was her sister lost in the jungle. Kidnapped, or so the evidence indicated. Never mind the naysayers and those with averted eyes saying she'd be found. She knew they lied to placate her. Ruth knew better than to listen to them. Carlie was alive. She could feel it.

"What are you doing to find her?" she'd asked the officer in charge of her sister's case.

"Do not worry. We are looking into it."

The generic answer echoed around her as other people inquired about their own personal problems. It didn't reassure. Frustrated, she left the police headquarters and headed back to the hotel.

If the police won't help me, then I'll just have to do something myself. Easier said than done. Finding a guide was easy; finding a guide who would take her into the jungle to find her sister's last location? An exercise in futility.

But she wouldn't give up. Not while she knew in her heart of hearts that Carlie was alive.

I will find her.

She just didn't know how. Dragging her feet back to the hotel, wondering if she should invest in a good night's sleep before tackling the police again, an employee of the hotel waylaid her.

"Package for you, miss."

A package? She took the small box addressed to her in boldly printed letters and frowned. No one in her family had time to send her anything and no one else knew she was here. So what the heck was in the box?

She took it up to her room and stared at it for a moment, wondering if it contained something dangerous. A white girl, alone in a strange country, ripe picking for criminal sorts – or so her mother wailed at the airport – she had to wonder if opening it would prove dangerous.

Maybe it's booby trapped and I'll release a gas that will render me unconscious until I wake up in some harem as a sex slave to a handsome prince. Wrong country. She didn't think the Yucatan had royalty. And speculating wouldn't open the mysterious package. Slitting it open with a nail file she had stashed in her luggage, she flicked the lid open and jumped back just in case. Nothing sprang out so she leaned forward and peered at the contents.

No way. Did she dare believe what she beheld? Did she dare hope? *Can I be so lucky?* She sure hoped so.

Chapter Two

Haven't I had my share of bad luck yet?

"What do you mean the group started without us?" Kendrick growled, not that the wizened old man before him seemed to care.

"You were late. They left." Gnarly shoulders shrugged.

"Because the bus from the airport got a flat."

"Still late."

"But I'm supposed to lead the damned expedition."

"Then you should have set a better example and arrived on time," the old geezer announced all too smugly.

"Well that's just freakn' great." And getting mad at the guide, the only other one available, unfortunately, wouldn't change a damned thing.

It seemed things went downhill the moment after they stepped on the plane. Or as Joel joked, they must have offended Lady Luck because since their departure, they'd encountered nothing but problem after problem, which translated into delay after delay.

It began with turbulence midflight. Forget joining the mile high club, despite the overt invitation from the cute flight attendant. Who could think of screwing when his stomach spent most of the rocky flight in his throat, reinforcing his belief that four-legged creatures should keep their damned paws on the ground? The roughness eventually passed, but then they got held for hours at some airport. Not allowed to leave the plane, he could only watch with great concern as men in grey jumpsuits swarmed one of the wings with tools and even a blue-flamed torch. So reassuring.

The plane lifted and nothing caught on fire or fell off. They made it to their destination in one piece – without a single antacid left on board. Things continued to go wrong. Landing should have ended his woes, the bouncy, inflatable slide off the plane was especially fun. So what if a few people stared at him funny when he dropped to his knees and kissed the ground? Did his problems end there?

Nope. It seemed they'd offended someone with a higher power as their luggage didn't appear as scheduled, and only after they hunted down an airport staff member and threatened to feed him his balls did they get him tracking the missing bags. Yeah, they found them eventually, mangled and torn, but at least most of his clothes survived, if reeking of Axe body spray. By then, the taxis were gone and they waited a ridiculous amount of time for the next one.

After a shitty night's sleep – a mattress with poking springs, a noisy couple who enjoyed angry sex, and the whine of mosquitoes in his ear – bleary eyed, they set off on the next leg of their trip.

What a nightmare. He should have rented a car because the buses in this Godforsaken place made him want to call his mother so he could tell her one last time he loved her. Okay, he exaggerated. The first few weren't too bad, but the last one to this most remote and hellish of places? Hot, sweaty, jam packed, not to mention late because it drove using wind and prayer, a lot of prayer. All the *Hail Mary*s in the world wouldn't have saved that tire, though.

Then, to top off a marvelous two day voyage? The other team members left without him and Joel. Nice teamwork. If not for the shifter council's insistence they work together because of their individual skills, Kendrick would have said screw them and bypassed their group altogether.

"Who cares if they went ahead?" Joel remarked. "We'll catch up to them, no problem."

"I know." But it still didn't explain his overpowering need to find the group. Sure, he'd kind of gotten assigned leader position, but only because nobody wanted it. Leader meant paperwork. Who volunteered for that kind of punishment? So he if he didn't really care who was in charge, then why the big hurry?

Ever since they'd hit the village, impatience gripped him. Hell, even his wolf woke to pace his mind, urging him to hurry. To get his lazy ass moving. No reason given as to why, but the urgency made Kendrick irritable.

Determined to not let minor setbacks ruin his adventure, Kendrick took some deep breaths, and allowed his senses to open up, to fully embrace and enjoy the wildness surrounding them. *I'm here. In a land man and his modern ways has yet to ruin.* It didn't take long once they left the village to lose all signs of civilization. Inside the dense jungle, nature reigned supreme.

Towering arboreal monoliths stretched high, their thick canopy shading the travelers from the sun. Wild blooms in a rainbow of colors sprouted around them, their scents heady and yet pleasing, their foliage vivid and perfectly displayed against the green. The lush smells of the forest tickled across his nasal passages – rich earth, foliage, the trail of wild animals, and things more exotic.

Nothing like feeling both powerful and humble as he pitted himself against the raw beauty of Mother Earth. With the help of a local guide, of course. Since the first group had already left with the prearranged guide, lucky Kendrick had to settle for second best, the irritable father.

For a few hours, they trekked, Kendrick and Joel lapsing into a comfortable silence while the old guy, more nimble than his appearance would indicate, scrambled ahead, not once looking back to see if they kept up. They did, of course. As if the old coot could lose either Kendrick or Joel with their enhanced sense of smell. Despite his unspoken challenge, Kendrick and Joel clung close to his trail, but after a while, Kendrick stopped and Joel piled into him.

"What's up? Hear something?"

A frown knit his brow as Kendrick peered around. "This isn't the right way."

"Run that by me again."

"This isn't the right way. I wasn't sure at first, but for at least the last hour, we've been following a different path than the first group."

Joel frowned. "You know their scent?"

No, but given his wolf's whining for the past sixty minutes and the fact the scent trail they'd initially followed, the one tickling him all over, vanished, he'd wager his hunch was a good one. "I'm pretty sure I picked it up at the village, or do you know many natives wearing Irish Spring antiperspirant?"

"I don't think they know what deodorant is," Joel muttered with a shudder. "Maybe the old guy is trying to catch up via a shortcut."

"Possible, but my gut says no."

"Good enough for me." Placing his fingers in his mouth, Joel let out a whistle, a piercing noise that caught their guide's attention.

Branches thrashing, the old man returned to them with a scowl. "Why do you stop? We need to move if we wish to catch up before nightfall."

"This isn't the right way." Forget stating it like a query. Kendrick mentioned his suspicion as a certainty.

"Of course this is the right path. I know the forest better than you," said the guide in a belligerent tone.

Watching for it, Kendrick noted the shift in the fellow's eyes when he lied. "Bullshit. Where are you taking us?"

"Short cut."

Again with the flickering eyes. Kendrick growled. "I can tell you're lying. What are you doing? Is this some kind of scam to take outsiders off track and kill us for our money?"

"If I wanted you dead, I would not have to lead you into the jungle to do it."

Finally a truthful claim, if one Kendrick rather doubted the old man could keep. He and Joel could handle this cocky idiot. However, he couldn't speak for the others. "What have you done to the other group? If you've harmed them ..." He didn't need to threaten with his fist given his tone held all the menace needed to make the grizzled gent blanch. Not for long though.

"They won't be harmed. They are going exactly where they are needed."

Kendrick wondered at his odd turn of phrase. "What do you mean needed?"

"Bah. I do not need to explain myself to you. Good luck finding your way back, American boy."

"Canadian actually." Not that their guide stayed to hear his rebuttal. In a flash, the old man disappeared back into the jungle. For a human, he moved pretty damned quick and quiet. Neither would protect him, though, from someone like Kendrick and his wolf's developed sense of smell. With a growl, Kendrick made to go after him.

Fingers curled around his bicep as Joel held him back. "While I commend your need to beat up an old human, one step away from needing spoon feeding, shouldn't we instead worry that the first group might be heading into some kind of trap?"

"Aw come on. Just one slap? You know the old coot is asking for it."

"Yes. And he'll get one when we pass through the village on our way back. Imagine the surprise on his face when we show up to say *hello*."

Petty, but Kendrick could admit the priceless look of fear and disbelief when they did return did sound fun.

"Okay, we'll go with your plan and rescue the other team first."

"Or at least find them before trouble does."

"Should we shift for speed?"

"And travel through the jungle with no supplies?"

If they went as wolves, yes, they'd make better time, but arrive with no clothes, food or other amenities in a strange place where even sleep required guarding. "Good point. We'll jog."

Joel hitched his knapsack as he glanced around the jungle and its concealing foliage. "Jog where? I guess we could backtrack to where we last encountered their scent and follow from there."

"Or, we let technology do its thing." As if Kendrick would come on a trip without the latest gizmos. Stu, his brother, might be a lot of things – giant p.i.t.a, crude and foul mouthed – but he also had the latest toys, and even better, shared them with Kendrick for the trip. Dropping his bag, he rifled through the side pocket and pulled out the latest in satellite GPS technology.

Whistling, he powered the sucker up as Joel shook his head. "Whatever happened to using a compass? Talk about taking away from the spirit of the trip."

As if anything they were taught in Wolf Scouts would apply here. The note left by the group contained coordinates for their camp that night. Kendrick could only hope the guide wouldn't spring his trap before then. "You can have spirit while running around in circles in the forest. I, for one, am going to use all the tools in my sack. Impassable jungle, meet the future."

Of course, the future didn't do too well finding him a trail through a wild forest replete with hidden ravines, limb-sucking bogs, deadly snakes, and a thicket of something prickly that made even his tough skin itch.

Yet, despite the setbacks, they trekked quickly and overcame the issues, getting hot and sweaty in the process. It did wonders for their tempers.

"We should be coming across the rest of the team any minute," Kendrick announced as he checked the GPS for their latest position. He hitched his pack higher, wondering not for the first time why innovative camping items of the future weighed so freakn' much.

"I don't know why they couldn't wait for us at the last village," Joel grumbled, his good humor finally lost as he mimicked Kendrick's words of earlier. "I thought this was a team effort."

"Look on the bright side – at least once we arrive, unless they're being held captive, we'll have a chance to relax. I bet you they probably have a camp set up already."

"Does it have a woman, a cold beer, and a plate of nachos?"

Mmm, nachos. Damn Joel for making him hungry. "Probably none of the above, but I sure hope it has water." Not that Kendrick really needed extra moisture, the sweat on his body slick and his clothes wet enough to wring. However, he would have loved to sluice off the powerful stench. His antiperspirant just couldn't handle this kind of heat and his sensitive nose didn't like it at all. The discomfort level was high. And he'd thought braving the Canadian wild would prepare him for the lushness of a tropical forest. Not even freakn' close.

"I'd settle for a glass of water to pour over my head."

"You might get that wish. Good news finally, my friend. According to my GPS map, there should be a lake of some sort at our destination."

"Lovely. I get to swim with the crocodiles and keep the piranhas away from my junk. Why did I volunteer for this again?"

"Because I made you."

"Oh yeah."

And we needed the adventure, Kendrick mentally added. Canada just didn't have the kind of primitive danger still found in some pockets of South America. Actually, not entirely true. It did north of his hometown in the territories, but the weather wasn't as nice, the trees were few and far between, and there was nothing like, say, a legendary tribe to discover.

Treading through a jungle that rapidly thinned as they approached a clearing, Kendrick wondered if he'd recognize anybody in the group that went ahead. Comprised of shifters, theirs was a special ops mission organized by the secret shifter council, a council he'd only recently learned about. Concerned with the events occurring in this stretch of the jungle, namely, disappearing groups of explorers, and more specifically, women, the council wanted answers. His task, with the others in his group, was to find the girls, rescue them if possible and report on the Moon Ghost Jaguars, if they even existed.

The hope was they would find some kind of clue or trail to follow from the campsite the girls were kidnapped from. Missing for many days already, it was a slim hope, but it didn't mean they'd give up.

Stepping free of the foliage, Kendrick blinked as the bright sun momentarily blinded him. Joel seemed to have no such problems adjusting because he whistled then said, "I'll be damned. Someone brought his chubby girlfriend along."

Eyes adjusting to the change in illumination, Kendrick let his gaze rove over the temporary camp until he spotted the woman in question – a lot more curvy than he preferred, and pale-skinned, so pale she'd burn if unprotected by sunscreen. She appeared delicate despite her height and full figure. According to his shocked senses, she was also one hundred percent human, which made her totally out of place on this expedition. Oh, and if the sudden yipping in his mind and the hard-on in his pants were any indication … *She's my mate.*

Un-freakn' real. The adventure he'd looked forward to took an unexpected twist, a fairly rounded one with wavy blonde hair.

*

Oh. My. God.

Yup, that about summed up the hotness level of the two guys who stepped from the jungle. Ruth had thought the current men she traveled with a good-looking lot – Liam with his blond, Ken-doll appearance, Peter with his cocoa skin and beautiful smile, and the all too suave Fernando, his Hispanic heritage evident in his accent and flirtatious dark eyes. But these two guys? Damn! Hot freakn' damn.

It wasn't a pretty boy cuteness that rendered them so appealing, though, but rather their innate ruggedness. From their short haircuts, almost military in style, to their square, bristled jaws, wide, superbly-wide shoulders, and perfect height, these two guys oozed testosterone. Confidence. Swagger. Hot, I-am-the-man, stuff. In other words, all the things that totally turned her on.

Sometimes she hated her hormones. Why did she always find herself attracted to the impossible to attain type? So unfair, given her attraction was rarely returned.

At six-foot-one, Ruth stared most men in the eye – or would if she didn't duck her head from shyness in most cases. Unlike wafer thin models with confidence and pouty lips, Ruth hated her stature. No one wanted to date a girl who, by sheer altitude, could predict an early case of male pattern baldness. Sure, some men enjoyed the fact she towered over them, those whose face came to chest level, but Ruth had gotten better over the years at avoiding this creepy type.

Somehow she doubted her height would provide a source of intimidation with the group she currently travelled with. The shortest one, Fernando, was probably still an inch taller than her. That was a great thing because it made her decision to forge ahead and demand a spot in their group easier. Tall guys tended to prefer short and skinny girls. So what if the rescue operation lacked other females? Given her track record with studs, she figured she was safer with these guys than with a group of short pervs intent on getting a peek. And if the cute guys did decide that tall and chubby was better than nothing at all? What happened in the jungle stayed in the ... Yeah, no – she'd probably enjoy that particular memory for a long time.

It was a tall girl's paradise and a shy girl's nightmare, especially when she had to argue with the cute hunks about letting her join the mission.

"I need to come with you," Ruth had bravely stammered when she arrived at the last village on the beaten path on her quest to find her sister.

Fernando, whom she initially nicknamed Antonio Banderas the Second, turned a chocolate gaze her way and smiled. "You can *come* with me anywhere, darling. That's a guarantee."

The sexual innuendo made her flush red, especially since she doubted he meant it. Good-looking guys did not crave wide-hipped, small-breasted Amazons with a few too many donuts around the middle. Unless they were drunk and at a frat party. "I was talking about your expedition. I need to go with you to find my sister."

A frown marred his smooth, tanned complexion. "How do you know of our quest?"

Because the mysterious package she'd received at her hotel told her. It also gave her instructions on how to get to the village and find these men. Who sent it and why, she didn't know, but given the dead end and run around she'd gotten from the cops, she'd jumped – perhaps foolishly – at the chance to do something, anything to help her sister and best friend.

Despite her usual shyness, Ruth didn't back down from the men's initial refusal. In the end, after a phone call made to some mysterious group in charge of their expedition, Liam announced she could go, but she could tell none of the men were too keen on the idea.

And neither was the newly arrived pair, judging by the glower shot her way by the taller of the two, and by taller she meant six foot almost six behemoth versus his friend at six-four.

After a short, heated, but inaudible meeting with the men in the group, Mr. Tall – and really angry looking – stalked toward her, his handsome friend not far behind.

"You don't belong here," he stated without pre-amble.

Here we go again. Despite the intimidating tone in his voice and stern gaze, she stood straight – and shook inside. She couldn't back down, even if he scared the pants off her. Carlie needed her. "You're going after the missing girls. I need to go with you."

"I don't know what you're talking about."

Denial? Seriously? "Of course you know what I mean. Just like I obviously know or I wouldn't be here."

"Just freakn' great. Who the hell opened their big mouth? Not that it matters. I don't know how you got your information, honey, but just so we're clear, we're not taking you, journalist or not."

"A what? You think I'm a reporter?" She gaped at him. "Why on earth would you think that? I don't even have a camera." Because she'd had it picked out of her hand when she went for a short sightseeing tour upon arriving at one of the stop over villages on her way to the jungle. A very short tour. After that, she kept everything double knotted to her body and a can of mace ready. Lucky for her, a scared-looking, super-sized blonde with a trembling finger on an aerosol can was more than the local thieves wanted to deal with.

"No camera, but you do have a notepad."

"Yes. To take notes. I'm a botany major. You know, someone who studies plants and stuff. I've actually specialized in jungle flora and fauna, which makes me useful as I'm familiar with the vegetation we'll encounter." Ha. She'd throw logic at him and see how he handled that.

"You're a gardener?" He sneered.

Her smile fell. "We prefer the term botanist."

"Splitting hairs, honey. But whatever you want to console yourself with, you still don't belong. This is a rescue operation, not a tea party."

"I'm aware of that, hence the attire." Because seriously, no woman with wide hips would ever wear the totally unflattering cargo pants tucked into black – weighed a thousand pounds – boots.

"Listen, I don't care who you are, what you do, or your reason for insisting on coming. Me and the boys are going to track the missing girls and we'll bring them back when we find them."

"When? You sound pretty sure."

"Because I am. I don't give up." Grim determination etched lines into his face and Ruth's insides tickled, but not just in arousal – because honestly, when a good-looking guy, with obvious strength, made an uncompromising statement like that, she couldn't help but hope he could keep his word. If he did, then perhaps this mission stood a chance. Optimism and hope – Ruth would take it any day, even if it meant putting up with an obnoxious chauvinist, and especially if it meant saving her sibling. Of course, her goodwill to him evaporated as he kept talking.

"Now that we understand each other, why don't you run back to the village and wait like a good girl while the boys and I do our job?"

Look at that. Chauvinism was alive and well in the jungle. In normal circumstances, faced with an order from a domineering male in a position of power over her, Ruth would have ducked her head and maybe managed a weak nod. But not today. Today she had purpose at her back – and a shot of whiskey from a flask Fernando offered her. A sip to give her energy after their long trek, or so he'd explained when he offered it. More like five minutes of coughing with watery eyes as it burned a path down her throat to her stomach. Given she never imbibed alcohol of any kind, it went right to her head. It also loosened her tongue. *Screw this guy and the high horse he rode in on.* How dare he act like only his will counted? She wasn't about to trust her sister's fate to the hands of a stranger. "No. I'm not going back."

His brows drew together. "No? Like hell. Since it seems you haven't heard, you're not in charge of this expedition. I am."

"Yeah right," she scoffed. "If you're in charge, why did they leave without you?"

"That's what I'd like to know," he muttered.

Staring up at him, a novel experience that left her heart racing and palms damp, Ruth couldn't help but shiver, and not just because he scared the panties off her with his grim countenance. Up close, despite his male scent that screamed jungle sweat, he set her nerve endings on fire. Heat curled in her lower tummy. She fought an urge to flatten her hands on his chest, not to push away but to draw him nearer. She really needed that sip of liquor to wear off before she did something stupid, like suck on his stubborn lower lip. "Who are you exactly? Liam didn't say anything about someone else coming."

"I'm Kendrick Grayson and this is my second in command, Joel Marsh. And now that we've met, I'll have my friend here run you back to the last village."

Was this guy deaf? "No."

"Did I say you had a choice in the matter?"

Why did he have to look so sexy when he arched his brow and pulled a Captain Caveman? "I won't go. My sister is one of the girls missing. I have to help."

His expression softened. "I am sorry about your sister. I know you must be worried, but it changes nothing. You can't come. You'd slow us down."

"Why? Because I'm not a skinny fitness model?" she retorted, the words spewing forth before she could stop them.

"Hey, you're the one who said it. Not me. But yes. I'm not going to sugar coat it. This is going to be a physically challenging trip."

"I can keep up." The skepticism in his eyes made her tilt her chin stubbornly. "I can." Hadn't she made it this far already?

"No, you can't."

"Um, in case you hadn't noticed, I'm here. And I got here using my two feet."

"On a well-trodden path at a slow pace so we could catch up."

Slow? Damn. "I can still keep up."

"Doubt it."

"Let me prove it."

"Oh no you don't, honey," he said, a glower crossing his face. "I've seen that look too many times with my sister and fallen for way too many a stupid dare. You can stop it right now. It is not going to work."

"I'm not your sister."

He raked his gaze over her; head to lips, onwards to her chest then lower before coming back to her eyes. "So I've noticed. Which is another problem. You'd be the only woman."

"And?"

"And we're all guys. It's not right."

"Excuse me, but chaperones went out in the dark ages, you know, right after we burned our bras and got the right to vote. Or are you implying you'll all turn into uncivilized animals once we're alone? That you'll ravish me?" She should be so lucky.

How odd. His eyes almost seemed to flash for a moment. She took a step back.

"No one would dare lay a hand on you. But what will other people think when they find out?"

"I really don't care. I'll know the truth." And really, once women got a look at the troop of men, she'd end up envied more than likely, not reviled.

He sighed and tugged at both sides of his scalp, his short hair still managing to appear mussed. "You wouldn't last a day out there."

"I have so far."

"Yeah, but that was before, during the still relatively tame part of our trip. Where we're going, very few men have gone before. It's not a place for a girl."

"So think of me as a guy. I'm the same size as one. Normal ones at any rate," she muttered as she continued to crane her neck. Damn he was tall. Did he fall in a vat of radioactive waste as a child?

"I doubt any idiot could mistake you for a male. Too many curves for that."

He meant it like an insult. She could tell he did. It still didn't halt the heat from rushing to her cheeks, or the quiver further below. "I am fully aware of my ample deficiencies." He opened his mouth, but she rushed in to speak before he could. "I might not look tough. Or perfect, but I won't give up. Insult me all you want. I'm not changing my mind."

Kendrick sighed loudly and ran fingers through his short hair. "Why me?" he said to no one in particular. "Of all the things I expected on this trip …" Trailing off, he stared at her.

Looking away seemed too much like giving in, so despite the fact she shifted from foot to foot, she held his gaze and chewed her lower lip.

"You aren't going to change your mind, are you?"

She shook her head.

"Stupid, stubborn girl. This isn't a place for a lady, especially not one as delicate as you."

Delicate? Ruth almost looked behind her to see if another woman stood there. "I'm not some fragile flower. I can keep up."

"I'm sure you'll try, but it's still a no. Joel, gather her things and take her back to the village. Leave your stuff here so you can run back."

Run back? Was this Kendrick guy crazy? The village was five or six hours behind them. No one could just run back. A hand grabbed her arm in a gentle grip. Awareness slammed into her, a tingling heat that brought her entire body alive. Startled, her gaze met that of Joel's.

Oh my, what pretty eyes. A light blue with a dark center, they totally mesmerized her and went great with his lightly tanned skin and jet black hair.

It took her a moment of walking like a zombie in his grip before she snapped back to herself and dug her heels in. "No. I won't go."

"You will because I say so," snarled Kendrick, his eyes flashing. For a moment he looked feral. Animal like. Savage.

She shivered as fear and desire raced through her body. Despite how he tried to dominate and impose his will, she refused to give in. If only she owned this much fortitude at other pivotal moments in her life. "You can try, but it's a waste of time. Even if you get your friend here to drag me, the moment he turns his attention, I'll just turn back around and follow. You can't stop me."

"You'll get lost."

"Maybe. Or maybe not." Time to play her pivotal piece. "I have a map."

*

In the silence following her words, Kendrick could have heard his brother Stu fart from thousands of miles away. "A map?" Kendrick said. "What the hell are you talking about?"

Cheeks pink, her gaze finally not challenging him, the Amazon-sized blonde – with the most amazing scent – dug a hand in the front pocket of her pants.

"Hold on. It's not in that one. Let me try this one." She muttered to herself as she rummaged through her many partitions. Kendrick almost offered to pat her down, not to help but because his hands itched to touch her. Not a good idea. He tucked them behind his back as he watched her yank various odds and ends from her pockets before she finally pulled a Ziploc bag forth with a sheepish grin. "Got it."

"Got what? Start explaining."

"Not long after I got here, a package arrived at my hotel, addressed to me." She waved the plastic bag. "Inside was a note, bus tickets, directions to the last village, and a map."

"What note?" The more she talked, the more confused he became. Not just because of her surprises – her damned scent kept throwing him off track, sending such inappropriate thoughts through his mind, most of them involving his tongue and a certain part of her body.

"This note. Here. Read it for yourself."

Kendrick snatched the thick vellum from her hand, square in shape, cream-colored, with four perfect creases, he unfolded it to find a typed missive. He read aloud.

"Dear Miss Anderson, we regret the unfortunate taking of your sister. Rest assured, she is unharmed and safe. However, we cannot just release her. Arrangements are being made to send an extraction team. We would like you to be a part of that group, to act as a familiar buffer with your sister and her friends. The group you'll be joining has no idea you're coming. We think it best that way lest they attempt to leave you behind. But you must come. It is very important for the wellbeing of your sister and the others that you join this expedition. Time is of the essence."

Kendrick read it again silently before raising his head to peer at her anxious face. "On the basis of this, you hopped a plane, by yourself, to the middle of nowhere with a bunch of strangers."

"Not exactly. I'd already arrived when I received it. I went to the police first, but they wouldn't help me. Actually, I couldn't get anyone to tell me anything so when this got left for me at the front desk of the hotel, I took it as a sign."

"And on the basis of it, decided to go hiking in the jungle?"

"Yes."

"Are you freakn' nuts?" he yelled.

Funny how his words mirrored that of her mother's. It straightened her spine and her lips flatted into a thin, mulish line. "It's *my* sister lost out here."

"This is crazy!" He waved the note in her face. "Your sister and her friends were kidnapped. As in taken by force. Did you really believe for one second those responsible would send you a letter and a map so you could rescue them? Seriously?"

"Well, when you put it like that, it sounds kind of farfetched," she mumbled. "But what else was I supposed to do?"

"Wait by a phone like everyone else."

"I tried that for a few days and just about went nuts."

"Patience is a virtue."

"So are manners. I guess we're both screwed in those departments."

Joel snickered behind her. Kendrick almost smiled himself. But he couldn't give in, not when his wolf growled about the danger she put herself in.

"Nice note. You should have given it to the authorities so they could search it for clues."

"I tried. They laughed and said it was a hoax."

"And yet you still came."

She scuffed her feet. "But I have a map." A feeble excuse and he could tell she knew it.

"Ooh, a map," Kendrick mocked as he grabbed at the second item she handed him from the bag. The hand drawn map contained very little detail. The name of the village they departed from. A giant N for north. A few landmarks like the lake they currently camped by, but he frowned as he began to recognize the longitude and latitude codes scribbled in beside the landmarks. He yanked out his own notepad with its backup set of instructions in case things like his GPS got lost. Sure enough, the woman's codes matched his, right up to the last known position of the missing girls, plus a few extra ones. But her map also had something he didn't. An X.

"What's here?" he asked, stabbing at the spot.

She shrugged. "I assume it's where they want us to meet for the exchange."

"Or ambush."

"Seems like an awful lot of trouble for an ambush."

"Are you always this argumentative?" he snapped.

"No, actually." She sounded surprised.

Like he believed that. Despite her poor judgment – made out of love for her family – he recognized the signs of stubbornness whether she admitted it or not. Worse, he enjoyed the fact she held her ground. Add to that her spectacular height, which he could totally see the benefit of – her lips just the right height for a kiss that wouldn't bend him in half – her skin dewy and soft. He tore his gaze away because the more he studied her, the more he noticed her subtle beauty. Mixed with her assertive nature? His wolf practically rolled on his back it wanted to lick her so bad. Not happening. "Your map and little note change nothing."

"What do you mean it doesn't? I have an actual invitation to be here. And a map. What do you have?"

He took a step and tried to intimidate her. She drew herself straight and met his glare; only the slight tremble in her frame, barely noticeable, let him know she wasn't as brave as she wanted him to believe. He leaned closer. Their noses almost touched. "Only authorized members can be in this group."

"I was authorized."

"Not by me." Why did he care if this human chit wanted to put herself in harm's way? He should just leave her while he and the boys went on. Let her regret the folly of her actions.

"I guess you don't know everything then."

"Um, sorry to interrupt your little spat," an idiot with a thick accent said.

"Who the hell are you?" Kendrick snarled, not taking his eyes from her lest she think he retreated.

"Fernando. I don't think we've had the pleasure of meeting, but I'm Javier's and Alejandro's cousin."

"Seriously?" The claim diverted him long enough to note the similar features the Latino male shared with his brothers-in-law.

"Small world, eh?"

Very. "Can we save the get to you know chit-chat for later while I deal with our departing guest?"

"About that – when she showed up in the village, we contacted those in charge of our jaunt and they confirmed her spot in the group. It was also they who suggested we leave without waiting, perhaps to ensure you could not leave her behind?"

Was there a freakn' conspiracy afoot? Why on earth would anyone want him to take the human into the jungle? "Are you sure you talked to the right person?"

"Apparently, her addition was a recent thing once they were notified of her travels to the area."

"Who do you work for?" the curvy blonde asked, her nose wrinkling adorably. Argh!

"None of your business," Kendrick said in a tight tone, still trying to digest why anyone would expect him to bring her on what promised to be a dangerous trek.

"Are you or are you not a rescue team? How is asking who's running the show none of my business?"

"Only members of the group are authorized to know that information."

"Did you not listen to what Fernando said? I am part of the group."

"We'll see about that." With those words, Kendrick stalked off, his satellite phone in hand to get some answers. Even better, some space from the human who made him want to howl in frustration. Shake her until her teeth rattled. Oh, and strip her so he could lick every inch of her until the blush in her cheeks turned to one of arousal instead of anger.

I need to get her out of here. Before he did something monumentally stupid, say, like claim her human, lily-white ass.

Chapter Three

We'll see about that indeed. Ruth watched Kendrick stalk off and whip out a satellite phone. Darn it all. Did everyone have one but her? Although, who would she call? Carlie wasn't anywhere near a phone and she didn't need to listen to her mother's sobs.

A heavy sigh escaped her as she sat down on a rock. "What's he doing?" Ruth asked Fernando who stuck close by.

"Calling our boss, who will tell him the same thing he told Liam, that you're going. So don't worry your pretty little head."

"Only would a gang of giants think to call me little," she muttered. Seeing Kendrick stalk back, a not so happy expression on his face, she braced herself for his ire. "You can't kill me. There're witnesses." Her quip fell flat.

"I don't suppose you've changed your mind?"

She shook her head.

"Stubborn wench! Of all the stupid, ill thought, dangerous—"

"But necessary," she interjected.

"Did you hear the stupid part?" he yelled.

"Better dumb than worried and wondering later if I should have done more," she hollered back.

Where did this courage to stand her ground come from? She had only to picture her sister to find out. She also made a mental note to invest in a flask of her own whiskey for the occasional liquid backbone she'd always dreamed of.

"You'll never keep up," he snapped as he whirled on his heel and stalked away.

"Watch me!" she ranted at his retreating back. Startled at her own loss of control, she gaped and then flushed at the rude gesture he flung her way. "Well that wasn't nice," she huffed.

A soft chuckle interrupted the daggers she mentally threw at the obnoxious man who thought to refuse her a chance to show her worth. "What's so funny?" she snapped.

The other handsome newcomer raised his hands in mock surrender. "Nothing. Just, you seemed so sweet and shy on the outside."

"I am."

A slow shake of his head and a half smile said he thought otherwise. "If you say so, *querida*. I'm Joel by the way."

"I'm Ruth." Good manners trumped her annoyance.

"And your sister must be Carlie. You both share the same good looks."

Nice line. But she didn't believe it for a second. Ruth knew what the mirror and scale said. Not for the first time, she wished she and Carlie shared more than the same features. If only they shared the same body. Her sister, while almost the same height, tended toward the slimmer side with her hips and ass in proper proportion to her bust. What a cow. Skinny cow, as Ruth liked to tease her.

Despite her slight jealousy at her sister's nicer shape, Ruth loved Carlie, especially since her sister always stood up for her, like when boyfriends tried to stomp on her heart. Take her last beau – dating six months, she'd enjoyed the fact he didn't leave diet pamphlets lying about and didn't drop subtle hints about joining a gym. She'd actually begun to think he was the one. He met her parents. Told her he loved her. Dumped her quicker than a hot potato when something more petite came along. But hey, as he told her, via text message no less, they could still get together to screw if she wanted because he liked how she crushed him with her thighs in bed. As Ruth cried and refused to leave her room, Carlie posted pictures of him in his superman outfit – blue tights and all – on a website showcasing small dicks. A petty pleasure Ruth enjoyed with her double Dutch chocolate sundae. Carlie rocked the role of protective sister and BFF, which was why Ruth now needed to step up to the plate.

I owe her for all the times she brought me ice cream when I needed it and helped me see what losers those guys were.

"Flattering me won't make me change my mind."

"I wasn't trying to. Just stating a fact. Although, Kendrick is right. This isn't a trip for someone delicate like yourself."

Ignoring Joel's compliment – but storing it for later enjoyment – she asked the first question that came to mind. "Why is he so adamant about me staying behind?" she asked.

An enigmatic smile graced Joel's lips. "I'm sure he has his reasons. A sixth sense, if you will, that you'll bring trouble. I can't say I disagree. You'd be much safer in the village than following us into the wilds. This isn't a picnic in the woods, *querida.*"

"I know that, which is why I came prepared. Actually, I'll bet I know more about this jungle than you do since I did my university thesis on the fauna of the Lacandon jungle."

"Words cannot compare to reality, though."

"I've been in the wild before. I know how to take care of myself." Jellystone National Park did *so* count. Or was that Yellowstone? Who cared? They both had bears.

Again, he smiled. "You think you can protect yourself? Even against untamed animals? They're all around, you know. Hungry for a taste of your flesh. Chomping to take a bite."

Cheeks flushed, she fought the heat his warning created because either her hormones were making her hear things or he was coming on to her. "Any animal that comes near me better be prepared to get tranquilized." She patted her hip and the holster slung on it.

Joel laughed. And laughed some more, enough that Kendrick across the camp shot him a dirty look.

"As if your little gun will stop a wild predator intent on tasting your skin."

Odd way of putting it. "Then maybe I'll stand behind you and let him sate his hunger on your carcass first," she snapped, tired of the skepticism.

"Ah, *querida*, what a time and place to meet you. I will admit, though, this adventure is finally looking up. Way up," he chortled. Still grinning, he saluted her and wandered over to the others. Only once she felt their scrutiny veer elsewhere did her shoulders slump and a faint tremor shake her hands.

She'd survived the confrontation. Gotten her wish to stay on the trip. Now, she just needed to back her claims that she possessed the toughness required to survive.

See, she might have lied a teensy tiny bit. Yes, she'd gone on trips – with large groups at well-established sites where the wildest thing was Harry Summerville after a few glasses of wine. Also, while she wore the tranquilizer gun at her hip, she didn't have the slightest clue how to use it. It was just part of the package a village woman handed her when she arrived, along with some camping supplies. It seemed whoever wanted her on this expedition didn't want to give her any excuse to back out.

Several times during the frightening trip out, she'd wondered at her decision. She only had to read the note and look at the hand-drawn map to bolster her resolve. A map she'd hoped not to tell the group about and keep as her ace in the hole. But Kendrick ruined that plan.

Still, all was not lost. His refusal to let her come along stemmed from some ill-conceived notion she couldn't keep up because she was a girl. To be fair, she wasn't sure she could either, but she wouldn't give up. Not only did Ruth have her sister to wonder about, but who she suspected took Carlie. A tickle in her gut told her the rumors of the Moon Ghost tribe, a mysterious group of Mayans with an ancient culture and seeming riches weren't entirely baseless. And what a find they would be. *Are they the ones who sent me the note? Who took Carlie?* The treasure left behind seemed to say yes, but she'd never find out sitting in a dusty hotel room.

So what if she'd had to tell the guys about her map? Safety in numbers, after all, because despite her brave words, she knew she wouldn't survive alone in this dangerous place. *I need to find the mysterious tribe quick – or let them find me. Shouldn't be too hard if it's true they steal women and take them as brides.* So sue a girl for having hope. If they thought Carlie's tall frame was good enough for one of their men, then maybe Ruth stood a chance, too.

What a sick fantasy. Hoping for a kidnapping indeed. She really needed to lay off the romance novels. *You know you need a love life when even the idea of getting kidnapped and forced into marriage with a stranger sounds romantic.*

*

I need a life. Or at least sex. Something to quell his ridiculous hard-on.

Wandering back to Kendrick, Joel's mind spun, and not because of their mission. A scent, *her* scent, clung to him. The touch of her skin when he'd grabbed her arm seared his hand.

Holy hell, the human's my mate. Or at least that was the most likely reason as to why his wolf took up howling in his head.

A mate. A human. A chubby human. A freakn' Amazon of a woman with the waviest blonde hair, the biggest, bright blue eyes, a perfect handful of tits, rounded hips, and a height that wouldn't give him a damned crick in his neck. God, imagining those thick thighs of hers wrapped around him, squeezing …

Joel tripped over a root and went sprawling. His first thought? *Shit. I hope she didn't see that. Wait, why do I care what she thinks?* The fact he didn't want to appear foolish in front of her meant nothing. Blame that on the whole testosterone deal. No guy wanted to look inept in front of a girl. He didn't give a rat's ass what she thought of him because she wasn't his mate. No way. No how. Not in a million years. His wolf gave a snort of disbelief and told him to prove it.

What? Mutiny from his inner beast? He'd show his other half who was boss. Joel let himself glance her way, saw her crouched with her full ass filling out her stretched cargo pants, and his wolf surged with an excited yip. *Ours.*

No way. She wasn't even his type. And she was human. Human for God's sake!

Joel popped to his feet and brushed off. Trying to feign nonchalance, he peeked back in Ruth's direction, saw her luscious buttocks up in the air as she pawed through her bag. Bigger than he usually chased, he couldn't help imagining the white expanse, spread for him as he speared her with his shaft, his tanned skin distinct against hers. His cock, already semi-erect since he'd touched her, went to fully engorged in one second flat. Joel shuffled his bag to hide it.

Ah, freakn' hell. Despite the turgid evidence in his pants, he refused to believe for one moment the human woman was his to claim. Perhaps he'd caught some kind of jungle illness. They'd gotten pretty scratched up during their trek. Maybe some kind of toxin lingered. He did feel kind of hot.

"Dude, feel my forehead."

"What the heck for?" Kendrick asked.

"Because either I'm running a fever or that woman is meant to be mine."

Joel told his best friend the truth because he knew Kendrick would save him from a fate worse than death. Mated to a chubby human? As if he'd repeat the same mistake as his father.

"Impossible," Kendrick snarled, not seeming at all pleased.

"Yeah, I'll admit, it seems unlikely given she is one hundred percent non shifter, but damn it, my wolf is losing its mind inside here."

"It just needs to go for a run."

"I don't know. It seems pretty sure. And it's not the only part of me reacting."

"So go for a swim to cool down or put up your tent and whack off. Horniness does not mean that woman is your mate."

"Why are you so convinced I'm wrong?" Joel asked.

"Why are you determined to think she is? Let's face facts. You're overdue for some sex. You broke up with your last girlfriend about six months ago and haven't gotten close with anybody since."

"Hey, my five friends and I get plenty of exercise," Joel protested, wiggling his digits.

Kendrick snorted. "Like a fisting compares to the real thing. Reason number two your dick is waving like a flag is because she's hot."

His eyes widened. "Hot? Whoa buddy, maybe this illness is contagious, because since when do you think chubby girls are hot? I thought you liked yours short and skinny."

"I do. But we're not talking about me," he growled. "Reason number three, you're feeling protective toward her because she's a girl and you have that stupid chivalrous streak that always gets you in trouble."

"Us in trouble, you mean. And laid. But you're one to talk. You're worse than I am when it comes to protecting women. How many guys did you beat up in school because of your sister Naomi?"

Kendrick grinned. "I never said I wasn't a knight in shining armor, I was just explaining the attraction."

"So you think I'm mistaken?" Joel's query emerged with a dubious lilt.

"Dude, she's human. Fate wouldn't be so cruel to you twice in your life."

God, Joel hoped not. He'd barely survived his mother ditching him as a child, how would he survive a mate doing the same? "Maybe it's this freakn' heat."

"Probably. Drink something to make sure you're not dehydrated. And go for a swim. Clear your head. Get a good night's sleep and see how you feel in the morning."

Despite his friend's reassurance, Joel doubted anything would change. He just had to look at Ruth, struggling to get her tent to pop up, to know. *Chubby or not, she's my freakn' mate.* Question was, what would he do about it?

Nothing, and for many reasons.

First and foremost, Joel doubted he possessed the needed social skills to make a woman happy for life. His ex-girlfriends all said the same thing – 'You're emotionally detached,' 'I don't feel like you give a darn about me,' 'This is just about sex.' Truthfully? They were right.

Raised by his father, Joel knew he lacked some of the manners only a mother could impart, and while Meredith, Kendrick's mom, did her best, only an idiot wouldn't recognize Joel came from a different world than his friend. In Joel's reality, violence, hunger, and shame made him do things he wasn't always proud of.

Then there was his father. *Dear old Dad.* Did he dare bring a woman, any woman, human or not, anywhere near the toxicity known as his father? He could just imagine the things he'd say to the poor girl. "Good for nothing human whore." Imagine that. Dad still held a grudge against Joel's mother, the mate who left him.

Not that it was entirely her fault. Joel's mother was human. One hundred percent, never knew about the shifter secret, human. Mated, if unknowingly, to a wolf, she never got the same overpowering need to claim her man. Never felt the sting of separation when she left his father, screaming, "I can't take the secrets anymore, or your jealousy." Never cared she left a little confused boy behind with a man who went slightly crazy. A man who lost a part of his soul and would never get it back.

Yeah, Kendrick was right. She couldn't be his mate. He wouldn't let her. Wolves and humans should never mate because it hurt too much when they left.

Of course, as he noticed later in his tent, pain came in many forms. Blue balls, while a cute term, didn't feel good at all, but they were preferable to the alternative.

Sinking my cock into her velvety heat and pounding into her flesh. Hmm, he needed a better visual if he was going to stay away. Unfortunately, all his possible scenarios ended up with her naked. It made for a very long – and hard – night.

*

Momentarily distracted by the female, Kendrick finally recalled his initial haste in finding the group.

"Where's your guide?" he asked Liam, having met the other members of their group while setting up his sleeping roll and grabbing a bite to eat.

"Right over …" Liam frowned as he swiveled to look. "Hold on a second. Now that you mention him, I don't recall seeing him since your arrival."

The news didn't surprise Kendrick. "Notice anything peculiar about him? Was he nervous? Did his scent seem off?"

Liam shook his head as his face turned thoughtful. "No, but I'm assuming you have a reason for asking."

"His father was leading Joel and me in the wrong direction. When I confronted him about it, he spouted off some nonsense about your group going where it was needed, then took off. We were worried he was leading you into an ambush, so we high-tailed it over."

"Nothing weird other than his bailing on us. We are in the right spot, though, at least according to my GPS."

"Mine too. Odd. Perhaps it's a language thing and I misunderstood."

"Well at least you made it in time for sunset. Good thing too. It gets pretty freakn' murky out here. I don't know what it is about these woods compared to the ones back home, but damn they're dark. And noisy."

"Where are you from?"

"West coast. Vancouver Island to be exact. Fernando is from the plains and Peter is from Toronto."

"I'm an Ottawa boy. Any idea how we were chosen?"

A roll of Liam's shoulders told him he knew as much as Kendrick.

"What about that whole note and map? What the hell is that about?" Who thought to throw obstacles in their way? For what purpose did someone want Ruth in the jungle? Was it truly about her sister, or was something else afoot? Kendrick didn't like playing games, especially not the type with the potential for a deadly outcome.

Ruth belonged anywhere but here in the jungle with a group of shape-shifters, about to confront who knew what. Did they need to worry about ambush, and not just from bipedal creatures, but wily four-legged ones too? Where had the guide disappeared to? Did he give signal that the foolish outsiders took the bait? Even now, did they prepare to strike? He kept his doubts and questions to himself for the moment.

"We should set a rotating watch," Kendrick said. "Rotating shifts of two hours."

"I take it we're leaving the woman out of the line up?"

Kendrick snorted. "What do you think? She might think herself brave, but she's no match for our kind. Nor would she catch them sneaking up."

"She's pretty though."

Kendrick hadn't even blinked when he found his arm across Liam's throat, his nose almost pressed to his. "Hands off the woman."

"Holy shit, man. Calm down. I didn't know she was claimed."

"She's not. But she's human, and is now our responsibility whether we like it or not. So hands off."

"No hands. Gotcha. What about helping, though? She's kind of clueless."

"She wants to act stubborn and claim she can do it on her own, then let her. No one lifts a finger. Understood? It's time Ms. Anderson learns the jungle isn't a place for a lady."

"No, it's not," Peter agreed as he joined them. "However, she looks damned cute trying to pretend she's not afraid and knows what she's doing."

And that quickly, Kendrick flung another arm over someone's throat and repeated his *no touch* rule.

Peter rolled his eyes. "Oh, this is going to be a great trip."

"What's that supposed to mean?" Kendrick growled, eyeing Ruth as she picked up a rock, saw something she didn't like, and smashed the rock back down. She squealed and hopped around, stamping her feet. A part of him wanted to laugh, maybe mock; however, another part, with his wolf leading the charge, wanted to race over and save her from whatever bug caused her such distress.

"Nothing. It's going to be a blast." Peter smiled.

Eyes narrowed, Kendrick waited for him to expand, or say something about Ruth again. Peter didn't, but his wolf still rumbled, upset these males dared look at her in a carnal way in the first place. While he'd never admit it to Ruth, she was under his protection now, which meant no one would touch her.

Except us, his wolf agreed.

No, not us, Kendrick replied.

Why? whined his wolf. *Ours.*

Not ours. No. No. No. No.

He kept repeating it, but his wolf kept denying it. Over and over.

Some food and a two-legged run later, Kendrick hadn't shaken off his wolf's belief that the stubborn human was their mate. Nor could he do anything about his disbelief when Joel stated he thought she belonged to him too.

It wasn't bad enough the mating affliction confused a human for his mate, it wanted to also drag his best friend along. Sure, ménages existed in the shifter world. Hell, his sister and brother both belonged in committed polyamorous matings, but Kendrick never imagined it as a possibility for himself. Two dicks, one hole? He wasn't crazy about the odds on that one.

Angry, confused, and more than a little aroused, Kendrick stalked off in search of a spot to throw his sleeping bag down, as far away from the chubby blonde as possible. Nowhere was far enough, not with his wolf yipping at him to claim their woman before Joel did.

Maybe both he and Joel were mistaken. Perhaps the air of the jungle messed with their usual senses, or they'd been bitten by some bug that made him think tall blondes with big asses were sexy. Not usually an ass man, Kendrick, nonetheless, couldn't help picturing Ruth's rounded bottom bent, naked of course, the plush cushion of her cheeks welcoming his thrusts.

Damn his dirty mind. Lying on top of his sleeping bag, with no privacy to take care of the problem in his pants, it occurred to him he'd probably feel better after a swim. Despite the greenish cast, the water beckoned his sweaty body. Shedding his clothes – while watching the curvy problem on the shore – he couldn't help but grow harder when her shocked eyes stared at him as he stripped down. His hands hit the waistband of his pants and her cheeks turned pink before she looked away. Her reaction made his wolf toss its shaggy head in amusement.

Glad you think this is funny, my canine side. Blushes or not, the human is not for us. We're on a mission, so get your head in the game. His wolf's reply to his chastisement? An image of a swollen head getting between her thighs.

Despite orders and her wishes, he should have had Joel toss her over his shoulder and march her back to the village. But, he couldn't, not when he didn't doubt her words. She would follow them. She made her determination on that clear. When given the choice between letting her ineptly stumble around in the jungle on her own or keep her under his watchful eye, he chose the route that would torture him most. He kept her close.

But now that meant keeping an eye on her without getting too close, fighting his unthinkable attraction, keeping Joel's teeth to himself, oh, and saving three girls from shape-shifters who'd probably already claimed them.

And to think he'd craved this adventure. Given the mishaps, he renamed Joel and Kendrick's Awesome Adventure to Jungle Misadventure.

Chapter Four

Waking in the morning from dreams rampant with a glowering Kendrick and a smirking Joel – in various states of undress – Ruth crawled from her tent, her hair a tangle of curls, mouth pasty, dry slobber possibly on her chin, and her body much warmer than the climate warranted. Stretching in her tank top and shorts, feet already clad in her boots – because it only took stepping on something squishy once to cure her of the bare feet she enjoyed usually strutting in – she noted her companions already busy at work. Everywhere she looked, evidence of their camp disappeared as they packed up.

"Thanks for waking me," she muttered, shooting Liam, the closest guy to her, a dark glare.

"If it's any consolation, I just woke up too."

Yeah right, she thought, eyeing his clean clothes, bright eyes, and combed hair. No one looked that good before seven a.m., not without prep work.

Letting her gaze rove again as she sucked back a few gulps of water, Ruth caught Kendrick's eye. He smirked at her and glanced pointedly at his watch.

The jerk. He intended to try and leave her behind. Not while she still breathed, he wouldn't. Scrambling, she forewent her usual morning pee as she clumsily pulled down her tent, a tent Liam had put up before Mr. High and Mighty arrived with his orders, while she screamed in the bushes about the spider she almost sat on.

Forget Liam pulling it down, though. Kendrick had spoken. No one was to help her, which suited her just fine. She could take care of herself. How hard could dismantling one small shelter be? Considering she got whacked twice in ten seconds as she yanked on the elasticized rods, it should have come with a dumb ass warning – *Please use safety glasses if the only thing you know how to set up is a PlayStation.*

Bet I could do it faster than a tent, she thought with a grunt of frustration when she couldn't fit the darned thing in its carrying case. But she didn't need Liam or any of the others to help her. She could do it, especially with Kendrick shooting her obnoxious looks and sneers.

"Where's the guide we picked up from the village?" she asked, peeking around. "I haven't seen him since we stopped yesterday."

"Probably because he disappeared," Liam replied.

"What? Ow!" Ruth caught her finger in the zipper of her bag and yanked it out to suck on.

"We think he might have gone back to his village."

"Gone? But why? Who will guide us now?"

"Don't worry. I'll take you anywhere you want to go," Fernando answered as he walked by, the shadow of a beard on his face giving him a more rugged, untamed appearance. Hot. Super-hot. And yet, it didn't give her any of the flutters she got when she looked at Joel or Kendrick.

Didn't that figure? Surrounded by good-looking, tall men, one who kept flirting outrageously, and yet she seemed fixated on the pair who paid her the least attention. *Dream the impossible so there's no disappointment.* Maybe she should take Fernando up on his many offers to show her various heights of pleasure. It would at least scratch the itch she had for Mr. Ornery K. Grayson and his attractive sidekick.

"Better move faster, Ruth, or he might just leave without you," Liam whispered.

"I'm moving as fast as I can," she grumbled, still trying to stuff her belongings back in her knapsack. They'd all come from the stupid bag, the least they could do was return to it in an orderly fashion.

"I'll get her a few extra minutes," Fernando said. "But don't waste them. We should get going."

Engaging Kendrick on a discussion of their disappearing guide, a man who'd seemingly vanished into thin air right after Kendrick's arrival, Fernando aided her by keeping Kendrick turned away and busy. He stalled their leader enough that she managed to pack up her things – if messily – pee, and even wash her face.

She couldn't help a triumphant grin when with a wink, Fernando announced himself satisfied with their plans and ready to go. Kendrick frowned as he peered from her to the handsome Latino. He didn't say anything, but his tight lips said it all. They wouldn't get away with that trick twice. She'd have to make sure she got faster.

When the group finally assembled to leave, she stuck herself behind their leader – and not just because his ass appeared particularly hot in his low-hipped cargo pants. She intended to keep him in sight, no matter what. *You aren't going to lose me, buddy, no matter what you think.*

"Ready?" he snapped.

"Whenever you are, captain."

"Are you sure you want to do this, honey? It's not too late to turn back."

"I wouldn't dream of turning around, *darling*," she replied sweetly in a taunting tone she didn't recognize as her own.

"Anyone ever tell you that you're stubborn?"

"Actually, no. What can I say? You bring out the best in me." And he did. Despite her usual shyness around men out of her league, she couldn't help but stick up for herself, despite his forbidding glares.

"I wish I could say the same."

She resisted a childish urge to stick out her tongue. Barely, and only because she worried a roaming insect would take the opportunity to bite it. As they began their trek, she cast glances at Kendrick's second in command. Joel, so friendly to her yesterday, he seemed determined to ignore her this morning, never once meeting her gaze. When her hand accidentally brushed him, he snatched it away as if she bore the plague. That hurt a little. Kendrick must have gotten to him. No matter. She'd show them she deserved a place in their group.

And show them she did. How to huff and puff as they marched at a quicker pace than the day before. How to fall over roots. Snag herself on branches. Oh, and step on something that squealed, which in turn, made her shriek. The laughter kept her head down, watching her feet for what seemed like hours after that.

Despite her mishaps, she kept up. Barely. Sweated out probably a whole person in water. Discovered antiperspirants did nothing in the jungle but attract bugs. Speaking of which, anything in the Chilopoda family that could not be squished by hand was wrong. So freakn' wrong.

The only saving grace of the moment when the thousand-legged, million-eyed, segmented body dropped onto her shoulder and scurried down her arm while she screamed like the most delicate of little girls? Joel flinched from the centipede too. Kendrick, the jerk, didn't bat an eye when he stomped it flat with his industrial combat boots.

Of the scenery, she noted little other than the fact is was green. Green. And more green. Did she mention green? With some brown. Maybe some flowers. With sweat streaming in her eyes, and her focus on getting one foot in front of the other, she didn't really have time to study the scenery around her. A shame, because the botanist in her would have surely drooled at some of the specimens they passed.

At their third rest stop of the day for water and food – dried meat that took patience to chew, fresh fruit that left her chin sticky, and tepid water – she noted Kendrick and Joel sniffing the air. And not little inhalations, but heads bobbing side to side, constant sniffs. What aroma tickled their noses? And what did they think they were? Dogs?

Inhaling deep, she tried to sift the odors and figure out what caught their attention. Whatever it was proved too faint for her to distinguish. Maybe they admired the perfume of the flowers, flowers she kept clear of given the large insects buzzing around them. Who knew what they did? It wasn't like Joel or Kendrick spoke to her or acknowledged her – caught her up in their burly arms and carried her through the nasty parts of the jungle.

Not that she cared or anything. But she really needed to lay off the romances for a while. Fantasizing about guys who didn't want to give her the time of day said something sad about the state of her love life. *Yeah, that I have none.*

Still, though, she'd not done anything to deserve their cold shoulder. A braver girl would have given them a piece of her mind. Ruth settled for silent, dirty looks done covertly when she didn't think they were looking.

The rest of the group found it entertaining, or so she judged by the snickers.

One in particular, Peter, kept chuckling for no reason and when Kendrick would ask what was so funny, he claimed a fly bothered him. Speaking of which … Fernando plunked beside her on the fallen tree she'd chosen as the safest-looking spot to park her tired ass. "What has you glaring laser beams?"

"Kendrick. He's not very nice. And neither is his friend."

"They seem fine to me," he replied with a wide grin.

Sure, take their side. "That's because you're a man."

"Thanks for noticing." Fernando winked, but she didn't feel a need to duck her head, blush, or swoon. While good-looking and friendly, Fernando didn't set her heart pattering or her blood boiling, not like some other men she knew – and hated at the moment.

"I don't understand his attitude. I kept up."

"I don't think any of us doubted you would. No, his angst comes from an entirely different source."

"So I'm not the reason he's pissy?"

"Oh, you are the cause of his mood, just not for the reason you think. Poor guy. I almost feel sorry for him. But he should know better by now. You can't fight fate."

Forget heads or tails, his words made no sense. "What are you talking about? What do you have to pity him for?"

"Because this trip is going to change his life drastically." Fernando's smile, if possible, got even bigger. "He will never be the same."

"You're obviously dehydrated and delusional. This is a rescue mission. How is that going to change him? Don't tell me he's one of those guys with a hero syndrome?" Not likely, given he let her suffer without offering even one helping finger.

"Oh no, Kendrick would never do anything for fame and glory. Not his style. None of us like the spotlight. We're here because it's the right thing to do."

Wanna-be heroes or adrenaline junkies? She wondered if they were men who lived for danger and adventure, or did they all trek together because of one person, a behind the scenes organizer with an ulterior motive? Once again, her imagination threatened to overtake with wild ideas. "I have a hard time believing you'd go through all this trouble and danger for nothing."

"Oh, we'll end up compensated. Never fear. Kendrick, and I think Joel, more than the rest of us."

So they did expect remuneration of some sort? Did he mean some kind of special salary for people who went on crazy rescue missions? That didn't seem to warrant Fernando's cryptic words. Then the light bulb went off and she could have smacked herself for not seeing it earlier. As mission leader, Kendrick probably had access to all the speculation and facts around the missing women. Including one rumor that for some reason, Ruth thought held the biggest grain of truth. "Is this about the Moon Ghost tribe?"

"You know about them?" Joel's voice from behind surprised her and she almost fell off the log. Sure, now when she didn't expect it, he sneaked up to talk to her.

Big hands – which instantly heated the skin they touched – steadied her as she craned to look back at Joel's frowning mien. "Of course I know of the tribe. Any researcher worth her mettle looking into the Lacandon jungle would."

"What do you know?"

"About the Moon Ghosts, or as the locals call them, Luunnaa Xtaabay? Here's the condensed version. No one is entirely sure if they exist or not. Just as the name says, they're like ghosts. They come and go without being seen. Some say it's because they wear the spirit of the jaguar, borrowing his strength and agility, his skill in hiding within shadows."

Fernando snickered. "Borrow. That's a nice way of putting it."

"Shut up," Joel hissed. "Tell me more of the tribe," he insisted in a softer tone. "What else do the scholars know?"

"Speculation seems to indicate they live deep in the heart of the Lacandon jungle, venturing only rarely to the domesticated parts to find brides. They look for young, unmarried virgins, spiriting them from the house of their parents, unseen, unheard, leaving behind piles of treasure as dowry. Gold, rubies, diamonds. Enough to make the family rich."

"Sounds like a fairytale. What makes you think they exist?" Joel seemed oddly curious about her answer, his head tilted as he regarded her, eyes intent.

Why did she believe in a legend? How about because of a foolish wish that something as romantic as ghostly warriors in search of love could truly exist? "All rumors and legend have a small grain of truth."

"I'll give you that. But this legend sounds old. Real old. What makes you think they've survived the advance of civilization?"

"The heart of this jungle is still untouched. Primitive. Someone, a whole tribe of someones, could live and die unknown and never see the world. It's possible."

"But there's more to it than that?" Joel pressed.

"Here's what I know. My sister and two other girls were taken. The men in the group and the one older woman heard nothing. They slept right through it. But in the morning, they saw the mound of gems left behind in each of the girl's sleeping bags. Someone took them and left a dowry behind. The whole thing fits the legend. Who or what else could it be?" She retorted, then flushed as she realized how heated she'd become.

"I'll admit, there are some coincidences to your story, but that doesn't make the kidnappers automatically this moon tribe," Joel stubbornly insisted. "It could be slavers."

No it wasn't, because Ruth refused to entertain that possibility. If she did, she'd have to admit her sister was gone. "Slavers? Gee, way to raise my hopes." Joel's face blanched as he realized what he'd said. She turned away, not wanting to see his chagrin. *Thanks for the reminder you're still a jerk.* "It's not slavers. Any idiot with half a brain could see that. Thieves of any kind wouldn't leave a fortune in jewels behind. It kind of defeats the purpose."

"Here's what I think. You're hoping it's this tribe of savages," Fernando exclaimed. "You want to be a kidnapped bride. Carried off by a handsome, half-naked fellow and ravished under the stars."

"Do not," she stammered. Not anymore, not with the reminder and reality of her sister missing. Note or not, Ruth had no proof Carlie was actually safe. Just hope.

"Intrigued by their riches, are you?" Joel snarled it more than he said it, as if annoyed by even the mention of her fantasy.

She glared at him. How dare he think her so shallow? "Not really. I'm not a gold digger."

"Yet your eyes light up when you speak of them. Why else but for their riches?"

"For your information, I've always liked flowers more than shiny rocks. I don't really care what they own or how rich they are. I'm a researcher. They're a legend. How could I not want to meet them?"

If possible, Joel seemed even more unhappy with her. "I would have thought any woman would balk at meeting men who force women to become their brides."

"I should, but it's kind of romantic." She sighed, because it was. Not that it would happen to her. Who would want to steal her wide ass and marry it? They'd need at least two men to accomplish that. Again, only something that happened in romance novels, especially those by Stacey Espino.

"Romantic?" Joel sputtered. With a shove, he heaved Fernando off the log and took his place, his thigh pressing against hers in a most distracting manner. "There is nothing sexy about a stranger kidnapping you and forcing you to go through a strange ritual where he makes you his mate for life and seduces you whether you like it or not."

When put like that, it sounded bad, but she wouldn't let him ruin the fantasy she'd entertained while writing her dissertation. "I could handle it if he treated me nice."

"What about your career? Your life? Family?"

"Where better to study my botany than here in the jungle? As for my life, a cramped apartment filled with second hand stuff is not a selling point. As long as I'm happy, my parents would accept it and besides, my best friend is out here somewhere in the jungle. Possibly a bride already. Or worse." It was the or worse part that made her eyes fill with tears.

"Ah freakn' hell. Don't cry," Joel muttered. "I'm sure your sister is fine."

She knew that. Or hoped the note she'd received didn't lie when it said Carlie was safe and needed her to come. "I'm not crying," she sniffled. "It's just - I'm so worried about her. I hate not knowing if she's okay. It's why I couldn't stay behind."

"I understand." How reluctantly he admitted it. "But understanding doesn't mean I like it because I think it's dangerous out here for you. More dangerous than you realize."

"And if you were me? What would you do?"

A wry smile twisted his lips. "Like I said, I understand. But I still don't like it."

"Thanks. I think." She said the words softly, letting her damp gaze meet his bright blue one. The air between hung heavy with expectation. Sizzled. He reached a hand toward her but it never connected.

"Let's get a move on if we want to hit the edge of the river by nightfall," Kendrick barked, his abrupt interruption shattering the moment. "You can gossip like old ladies later."

This time, Ruth didn't resist the temptation. Dignity be damned. She stuck her tongue out at Kendrick and enjoyed every second of his tight lips and blazing eyes. She should have known he'd make her pay for it. If she'd thought their pace quick before, now it was grueling.

But he'd have to try harder if he thought she'd give up.

*

Would she just give up already? Kendrick had pushed them hard all day, waiting for her to break down. Stumble and not get up. Cry for mercy. Anything.

He'd even readied his speech, the one where he said, 'I told you so!' A speech he never got to use, and which left him without a scenario he liked. Giving her to Joel to bring back to the village meant his friend getting mated without him, because he somehow doubted Joel could resist the temptation. Not acceptable.

Letting someone else in their group take her back his wolf vetoed with a jealous snarl. Having her out of his sight at all also didn't appeal.

The one plan he and his wolf seemed to enjoy best involved him carrying her out of the jungle. Screwing her silly in a hotel, enough she'd stay put until he got back from the mission they still needed to complete. But again, that plan meant leaving her alone. Unprotected. Vulnerable.

He couldn't decide, so he did nothing. Not that it mattered when she ruined all versions of his plan up by refusing to act as expected. Despite the slaps of the branches, the frights she'd endured – that one spider deserved a postal code it was so large – she wouldn't give up. No matter how tough or scary the moment, she just pursed her lips, hiked her backpack higher, muttered curse words under her breath – if fiddlesticks, darn it all, and freakn' stupid bugs counted – and trudged on.

How he wanted to hack a wide path for her to walk through unhindered. Carry her over the slippery rocks. Press her against a tree and suck on her full lower lip.

God, how he wanted her. She was utterly magnificent. Her skin glistening with exertion, hair standing on end, cheeks flushed, beautiful. So beautiful. And his hard cock throbbed for a taste. Forget his earlier qualms at her less than petite size. He could see how well she'd fit against him. Plush and delicious. Oh how nicely he'd sink into her, her fleshy thighs a vise to keep him deep. His gums ached with teeth dying to burst forth and claim her as his.

There existed just one teensy tiny problem with that plan.

She was still a freakn' human. Not a wolf or a shape-shifter. Not even someone who knew their secret. And to top it all off, his buddy had a thing for her too.

What was wrong with him? She couldn't be his mate. There were too many things wrong with her for it to work. Although, his initial impression that she could stand to lose a few pounds? Yeah, that went away quick considering every time he peeked her way, or caught her scent, his cock got hard enough to pound nails. How he wished he could stop imagining her sweet backside bent over, a perfect cushion for the pushing.

Tall with curves that went on and on, he could see himself worshipping every inch of her creamy skin. He just couldn't picture doing it alongside his buddy. Nor could he imagine a forever after with a human. Shifters were a rough bunch, and secretive to boot. He couldn't just tell her what they were, not without being one hundred percent sure of her reaction. What if she freaked? Left?

Destroyed him like Joel's mom killed the spirit of Joel's father?

Why couldn't Ruth have gone back to the village when he first demanded it? He could have handled her from a distance. Forgotten her perhaps?

He needed to get his head in the game. He'd come here looking to rescue some women, not mate with the sister of one. Add in the fact someone manipulated them into bringing a civilian and he really had to wonder what they'd find once they reached the coordinates on the map. Something didn't seem right. Actually, it stank to holy heaven. But, he couldn't turn around. Somewhere in this humid jungle, three girls needed his help. Despite his tingling wolf scent, he had to go on if only to get answers for their families.

A growl left his lips as Liam helped Ruth up from her latest fall. *Ours,* snarled his wolf. No she wasn't, he rebutted. Try telling that to the irrational jealousy pounding through him, demanding he challenge Liam. Try explaining to his chivalrous side, raised to help those weaker that demanded he scoop her into his arms and carry her so she'd stop injuring herself. Try shutting up a wolf that whined, a wolf that demanded he mark her now before it was too late.

Joel was right. This mission was the worst idea ever.

*

Best idea ever.

Sure, Joel trudged through a jungle — sweaty, confused, horny, very horny, but he couldn't say he was depressed. Didn't give a damn what his father was up to. Wasn't worried about proving himself better than everyone thought. However, he did have to wonder at his sanity as he mulled over the question of mating with a human.

Humans plus wolves equaled extremely bad idea. Or did it? Others mated with humans just fine. Not all of those pairings ended up with a shifter going crazy when their human left. Heck, Kendrick's aunt married a human and they were still going strong forty years later.

Could it work for me? The blame for his newfound interest in the question rested squarely on Ruth. Tougher than he'd have credited, she didn't once complain about Kendrick's forced pace. She bore everything with grace — and killer looks. Literally. If she could have made Kendrick explode with her eyes, they'd be picking up pieces.

It shouldn't have made him snicker. But it did. He'd not missed the heat behind Kendrick's glare. Nor could anyone miss the bulge a little lower, a hard discomfort Joel also wore since meeting her. He just hid his better with a shirt.

Of course, Joel could hide it in a better spot. Say between her legs while she screamed his name, but once he did that, the game was over. He'd end up mated to a human. Freaking and wondering if she'd accept him, wolf and all.

Also of concern was Kendrick's interest. Was he just reacting as a normal male to the only female in the group, or did his best friend battle the same dilemma? Did Kendrick feel the mating urge too?

God, he hoped not. He loved Kendrick like a brother, but sharing a woman? For life? That was not his idea of a happily ever after. However, what could he do, either of them do, if Fate had decreed Ruth was theirs? The mating fever might only end up one-sided, but if they claimed her and she left, that meant twice the men crushed.

He'd still not come up with an answer to his dilemma when they found their next camp. Poor Ruth, she huffed as she slumped to the ground on her back, arms and legs spread like a starfish, her heavy pack still on her back, and probably not too comfortable.

Help? Joel vetoed his wolf's query. Touch her? Not a good idea. He turned away, out of sight, but unfortunately not out of mind as her scent carried through the moist air. A grunt. Two grunts. He couldn't stop himself peeking over to see her trying to sit up and not succeeding as gravity clung to the pack on her back, her muscles giving her a hell of a *screw you* message.

No matter which way he looked at it, it was kind of funny. Especially when she thrashed her legs and let out an annoyed yell. He snickered, and thought he'd kept it discreet until he looked over again and found her glaring at him.

Oops.

Easing her arms from the straps, she rolled off her baggage and got to her feet, trying to appear nonchalant, but failing due to the pink spots in her cheeks.

A slap against the back of his head distracted him. "Hey!"

"Stop watching her." Kendrick kept his words low.

"I wasn't."

"You were."

"Okay, maybe a little. Seriously, though, dude. She was like a turtle stuck on her back. Can you blame me?"

"Try harder. Remember our purpose is rescue, not getting hitched or banging group members."

"Only until the mission is done, though. Then maybe as a goodbye to the jungle I could tap a piece?"

"Would you stop thinking of her like that?"

"I can't help it. Every time I look at her, I want to do such bad things." His tone turned wistful as his gaze veered once again in her direction.

Snapping fingers drew him back. "Focus, Joel. Or I'll be forced to do something for your own good."

"Forced to do what?"

"Can I trust you not to touch or kiss the human?"

Could he? There went his wandering eyes again, this time catching her swatting at a butterfly determined to land in her messy mop of golden hair. She batted it, her raised arms lifting her t-shirt high enough to show the top of her rounded belly – and milky, white skin. Skin that would feel so –

The punch hit him out of nowhere along with Kendrick's growled, "You can thank me later."

How about right now? Joel threw the second punch and their version of a tension reliever was on. Or as it was known in Kendrick's house, family time.

Chapter Five

"Why are they fighting?" Ruth asked as she paused rummaging through her bag in favor of watching Kendrick and Joel duke it out.

Peter shook his head as he walked past her with an armload of fronds. "Because they're guys."

"You're a guy and I don't see you fighting."

"Yet." His grin made her lips curve.

"And they say women are hard to understand." She shook her head with a smile. "Hey, while I've got your attention, how important is sleeping in a tent, do you think?"

"How do you feel about waking up covered in bug bites and looking like a lumpy troll?"

"That bad?" Her shoulders slumped. "But I saw Kendrick sleeping under the stars last night and he seemed fine this morning."

"Because he's got tough skin. Your soft skin doesn't stand a chance. I'm going to guess your question has to do with the fact you're still having a hard time with your tent."

"No comment."

"Here, let me help you put it up while they're busy."

"Would you?" Exhausted, she didn't think she could handle trying to figure out the contraption.

"No problem." In mere moments, Peter had it up and ready for the stakes, which she hammered in just as Joel and Kendrick separated, chuckling and slapping each other's backs. Men. She'd never understand them.

Exhausted, she barely managed to wash herself and eat before she passed out in her tent.

The following morning, she woke early enough to get ready and packed without interference from one of the guys on her behalf. The second day of marching proved no easier than the first, not with her sore feet, an aching back, and a less than pristine smell. *So much for taking the stairs everywhere I go to try and keep in shape.* Muscles she never knew existed protested their abuse and threatened to go on strike if she didn't give them a break.

However, she forgot all about the woes of her body when Kendrick announced, "This is where they took them."

"This is it?" Ruth asked, catching up to him and peering around the nondescript area with its hacked vegetation. "Are you sure?"

He snorted as if he couldn't believe she'd question him and moved away to examine some of the more crumpled areas. Jerk.

Ignoring him, Ruth walked the perimeter of the area and tried to picture the scene, recreate it, just like one of those crime scene shows she liked to watch with a big bowl of buttery popcorn. Now that she knew what to look for, she could see the indents of where the tents must have sat, the bent grass and leaves already springing back, except for the parts too squashed to recover. Peering more closely at the ground, she almost held her breath as she examined it for clues – and hopefully, no signs of blood.

She wasn't alone in her circular search. While Joel, Fernando, and Liam wandered off in different directions outside of the camping area, Kendrick and

Peter paid close attention to the site itself, crouching low to run fingers over the ground, even leaning forward to sniff the very earth. How odd. Did the tracking skills they learned teach them how to differentiate smells? She'd never heard of that.

Eventually, the whole group rejoined and exchanged observations.

"More than one abductor," Joel announced.

"Six or seven by my count," Liam confirmed.

"They kept mostly to the trees," Fernando said, his hair rumpled and his shirt off. Did he detect better with fewer clothes? A shame the others didn't use the same methods.

"No signs of violence," Kendrick added. "But I did notice a powdery residue, heavier around the tents of those left behind."

"Sleeping agent?" Joel queried.

"Seems likely, given the girls were taken without waking anyone."

Ruth blinked as they kept spitting out clues. "How do you know all this?" They exchanged a conspiratorial glance.

"Trade secret," Peter finally answered with a wide smile.

She didn't understand the chuckles at his reply, nor did she grasp a lot of their cryptic comments about other things they'd observed. Leaving them to talk, she wandered away and stared at the dead ashes of the fire pit. To think, only days ago, her sister was here. Alive. Not a victim of kidnapping or God knew what torture.

Tears pricked her eyes.

"Why is she crying?" she heard Kendrick ask in a not so quiet whisper.

"Because her sister is missing, dumbass."

"Stop it."

Lost in her momentary lapse of self-pity, Ruth didn't realize Kendrick spoke to her until he came to stand directly in front and tilted her chin up with a calloused finger. "I said no more tears."

She sniffled. Loudly.

"I said enough."

"I will c-cry if I w-want to," she retorted.

"I don't need you getting hysterical on me."

"I'm not hysterical," she muttered.

"Says the girl who is crying. If it's any consolation, we didn't see any sign the girls were hurt."

"B-b-but you don't know for sure wh-what happened to them," she hiccupped.

"What happened to believing that note about them not being harmed?"

She'd lost that optimism with the reality of the jungle. "What if you're right? What if I'm being stupid? What if Carlie's hurt? Or dead? Or—"

"Enough of that," he rebuked. "You're tougher than this."

"No, I'm not." Her shoulders rounded in as she slumped.

His brows arched in surprise. "Since when?"

"If you knew me in real life, you'd know I'm a wuss without a brave bone in my body."

"Says the girl who won't listen to anything I say, in the middle of a jungle, surviving just fine."

"Only because I have to."

"Necessity doesn't make you strong. The courage was always there, you just chose not to exercise it before."

"Carlie's the brave one."

"If you say so. I say, stop feeling sorry for yourself, have a shot from that flask Fernando keeps hidden in his pack, and get ready to move out. I want to make the next set of coordinates on my list before nightfall, not play Dr. Phil while you deal with your abandonment issues."

"I do not have abandonment issues," she said to his already retreating back. "In case you hadn't noticed, my sister was kidnapped."

"And we'll never find her if you insist on having a pity party, so move it."

Despite his brusque treatment, Ruth couldn't deny she no longer felt as depressed. She couldn't say she was ready to try cartwheels of optimism either, but at least he reminded her of why she'd come on this trip. One, because she wanted answers, firsthand ones, and two, because in her heart of hearts, she knew Carlie was alive. And dammit all, for once she would play the sister who came to the rescue, minus the ice cream. But hey, at least she'd arrive with several flavors of men – something her sister would surely appreciate.

With Kendrick insisting they not waste the several hours of daylight left to them, they only had time for a drink and a quick bite before resuming their mission.

Great. More walking. But at least the view was nice, she could admit, watching the flex of Kendrick's buttocks in his cargo pants slung low on his hips, his muscled back glistening with a sheen of sweat, his shirt removed as he forged ahead through the brush. And when she lagged, she had only to glance behind her, at a grim-countenanced Joel, also shirtless and yummy, to find an extra spurt of energy to go on.

Why she felt it important they not view her as weak despite it being her natural state, she couldn't have said, but she did her damnedest.

*

Kendrick didn't want to feel sorry for Ruth, he really didn't, but dammit all, did she have to look so disappointed, and worse, cry when they didn't find any decent clues as to her sister's whereabouts? It annoyed him that his first urge was to hug and console her. He restrained himself, and meant to ignore her, but he wasn't a complete ass. He could understand how Ruth missed her sister and worried for her safety. If it were his family, he'd have lost his mind. But understanding didn't mean he could let her bow to her sorrow, especially since he didn't see any reason for it yet.

While he couldn't explain how he knew, Kendrick read the signs enough to know the kidnapped girls didn't suffer any abuse during their capture. As to after, only time would tell. The council didn't seem to think the girls came to harm, though. Needed help getting out of the jungle, yes, but on their two feet and not in body bags – a certainty they wouldn't explain when they set him up to go on this mission. Damned secretive bunch.

In spite of himself, he goaded Ruth until her bothersome tears dried up and her fighting spirit came back. A part of him argued it wasn't up to him to reassure Ruth, but raised as a decent person, he did so anyway. Hell, he had to admire her spirit. Despite her brave face and attempts to keep up, any idiot could see she wasn't cut out for this kind of exertion. He'd even slowed his pace for her, his only concession to her comfort, but it still proved a struggle. If only she'd cry uncle and ask to turn around, he'd have gladly escorted her just to get her out of here, especially once he smelled the campsite of her missing sister.

He'd only managed to speak briefly to the team members in private, not wanting any more awkward questions from the only human in their group. They'd each smelled the same thing. That was to say, nothing. Not entirely true. They smelled what they expected from a camp of humans, the usual sweat and musk, food odors. What was lacking, though, was that of their captors. Liam thought he got a faint impression of something feline, but he lost it, and despite them searching the ground – while Fernando scouted from the treetops when Ruth wasn't looking – they never caught another glimpse. It was as if, like the ghosts they were named for, the mysterious kidnappers vanished into thin air, and took the three women with them.

Kendrick didn't like it. Not one bit, however, it wasn't because he worried about his own safety. His eyes veered to Ruth just as she tripped over an exposed root, barely catching herself from falling face first. Human and vulnerable, did he have to worry about the ghost warriors coming for her next?

Over my dead body.

Turning his back, lest he forget his own decree and offer a helping hand, Kendrick jogged ahead and beckoned Joel over. He waited to speak until he knew they were out of earshot, of human ears at any rate. "I was thinking we should double up the watch."

"Expecting trouble?"

"Usually welcoming it, but …"

Kendrick didn't need to say anything further for Joel to grasp his drift. "Surely they wouldn't be so brazen as to try and take her given who she travels with?"

"Have you forgotten she is with us at their behest, or so the note would have us believe?"

"Good point. I'll speak to the others."

"We should also make sure she sleeps closest to the fire so they have to go through us first."

"You're acting awfully protective," Joel stated.

"Cautious, you mean. We've already got three women to rescue, let's not make it four."

Why he continued to lie to his best friend, he couldn't have said. The more he traveled with Ruth, the more his certainty grew she was his mate. However, now was not the time or place to deal with that particular problem. Once they completed their mission, maybe then he'd examine how he could make mating with a human work – a claiming that would also involve his best friend – and deal with a fear that it would all prove too much and she'd run.

Damn, things were a lot easier when all he had to deal with was missing luggage and ornery guides. But he'd asked for an adventure. He just wished it didn't come with so much emotional baggage – and complications.

*

Funny how their mission had changed, at least for Joel. What started as a rescue operation was now widening to encompass safety for the lone human in their group. *If they try and take her, they'll have to go through me.* He almost wanted to dare them to try. Despite himself, Joel couldn't help the protective instinct. Human or not, and whether he liked the fact his wolf kept trying to claim her as mate, he wouldn't let anyone harm her. He'd die first.

But who will protect me from her?

That was the biggest worry of all. The more they traveled, the more he got to know of their fragile female companion, the more he craved Ruth. And not just her body, but her laughter. Her smile. The sweet color that rose in her cheeks when she got flustered. The way she studied things around her with such evident pleasure. How she handled her fear, with a shriek, but bravery too, as she squashed bugs that should never see the light of day.

Forget the mating fever, he feared he'd gone past that straight into obsession, and it scared him, especially since he feared she didn't feel anything close to the same. How could she? She was, after all, only human, and that scared him most of all.

Beside a creek tumbling over rocks, clean and fresh, they stopped for the night – and not a moment too soon for one person in their group.

Panting, and appearing much too heated, Ruth tossed her pack to the ground and sank on it. "Oh, thank God," she moaned.

"You should go for a swim," Peter advised her as he stripped off his shirt. Displaying lean, tanned muscle, Joel clenched his fists lest he ask his teammate what he thought he was doing.

Jealousy. Uncontrollable. Annoying. And all her fault. Why couldn't she have been a wolf?

"Is it safe?" Ruth asked, peering at the water with such longing.

Why did she have to look so delectable? Joel wanted to kiss her. Kiss her and make her hunger for him until she gazed at him the same way.

"I'll protect you from the killer fishies," Peter claimed as he offered her a hand up.

That's my job, Joel almost snapped. Except it wasn't. Distance. Didn't his plan with Ruth involve keeping his distance and ignoring her?

"We should set up camp first," snapped Kendrick, solving his dilemma. Or not.

"She's going to faint if she doesn't cool down," Peter replied without batting an eye. "She can do it after."

"I say now."

When Ruth bit her lip, Joel saw the moment she came to a decision, and of course, the blame resided entirely on Kendrick's order. Her spine straightened. She didn't acknowledge the words telling her no and she walked to the stream bed, boots, pants, and all.

Peter stopped her before the edge and sat down on a rock to pull off his footwear. She followed suit, but she hesitated when Peter dropped his pants and left himself clad only in tight Hanes shorts.

Yeah, forget controlling the green-eyed monster. A soft growl rolled off his lips. Peter was going to die any minute now. Ready to rearrange the infringing wolf's face, he managed to rein himself in as Kendrick placed himself in front of Peter.

"You're right, we should all bathe." His friend stripped down with a challenging stare in her direction, resulting in her turning her back, but still removing her bottoms and top, leaving her clad only in a light pink bra and white bottoms.

Kendrick waded in the water before she was done, with Joel right behind him. It wasn't hard to guess the reason. Watching her splash water over her creamy body, her bra getting more and more translucent, displaying nipples, erect and evident even through the fabric, Joel wondered if anyone would notice him jerking one off.

"We have a problem," Kendrick muttered, his gaze fixed on their very own water nymph.

"Do we have to talk about it right now?" Joel asked, fascinated by the image of Ruth rising from the water, her wet hair streaming down her back.

"Considering we're drooling here with ridiculous hard-ons in waist-high water over the same chubby human, yeah, we need to talk."

That got Joel's attention. "She's not chubby."

"No, she's perfect," Kendrick sighed. "Which is the problem. You're not the only one who thinks she's his mate."

The confirmation of his suspicion. Joel almost punched his friend at his confession. "You too?"

His friend nodded.

"Damn. So what are you going to do about it?"

"I don't know. She's human." Kendrick sounded so mournful.

"Very."

"Fragile."

"And not in on the secret."

"She's stubborn."

"Strong."

"Sexy."

"We're screwed." More heartfelt words, he'd never uttered. If they both tried to claim her, would they frighten her off? Could one claim her and hope the other walked away? Would jealousy over a woman finally tear their friendship apart? Or could they both have her? Sharing. One woman, one life, with his best friend as his rival for his mate's heart.

Freakn' hell. An already messed up situation just got uglier. But the view got better as Ruth stepped from the water, her back to them, and probably unaware that the back of her white underpants were see-through.

With matching groans, he and Kendrick sank deeper in the water. It seemed they'd need a moment before stepping out. Maybe two.

Chapter Six

Maybe I should have stayed home, Ruth thought, not for the first time as she struggled with the stupid tent. Up in just a few easy steps, her rather large ass! She knew she messed up somewhere along the way, probably when Kendrick walked by carrying a large load of wood like it weighed nothing, his shirt stripped off to show a body that didn't spend a lot of time indoors in front of a television. The man could have modeled those washboard abs in a fitness magazine. Worse, he caught her ogling.

Flustered, she ducked her head, but caught in the throes of an arousal she couldn't stop, she kept lifting her eyes to take a peek. Her inattention bore fruit as her hands did something to the unfolding tent, which now mocked her in all its lopsided glory.

"Need a hand?" Wandering over, Liam cocked his head at the contraption and she could see he fought to hide a smile.

"Am I that obviously inept?"

"There's a trick to these things. Don't worry. I didn't do much better my first time round." Somehow, she doubted that. All these men seemed much too capable. Did they all go to some super-duper outdoorsman school? It was uncanny how at home they seemed. Look at Liam – he seemed like the type to spend hours in the bathroom gelling his hair. Heck, he still looked picture perfect in the midst of the jungle as he knelt in the dirt and wrenched the poles apart, snapping them back to their starting position.

"Do it like this," he said, and with a twist and a little manipulation, the tent unfolded into something she could actually sleep in. It didn't stay that way as he folded it back. "Now you try."

Tent teaser. Ruth tried to replicate his actions, but didn't quite succeed. His hands covered hers – with none of the electrical awareness she felt with Joel or Kendrick – and he guided her into the motions to twist the poles.

"What the hell are you doing?" The harsh query startled her and she let go of a piece only to have another snap off and whack her in the face.

"Ow!" She slapped her hand to her cheek and glared at Kendrick, who scowled back, just as angry.

"Chill, dude. I was just showing her how to set up the tent."

"Ms. Anderson doesn't need any help. She's an experienced adventurer. Aren't you, honey?"

"Yes, I am," she muttered through clenched teeth.

"See?" Kendrick said with a smile, displaying too many teeth and no mirth in his eyes. "She doesn't need your help. Any man's help. Do I make myself clear?"

"I didn't realize things had gone that far," Liam replied.

"They haven't. My orders still stand."

"You do know how irrational that sounds."

"Very."

Liam smirked. "I'll let the others know."

Know what? That Kendrick was a jerk who wanted her to fail? Well, she'd show him. Ignoring him, harder to do than it sounded with him looming over her, slowly and much more awkwardly, she managed to get the tent to pop up.

"Ha! I did it."

"Give the girl a prize," he mocked, clapping his hands.

Not realizing she still had company, she jumped. "Oh stuff it, you grumpy bear," she exclaimed, tired of his attitude toward her and even more tired that despite it, she still thought him hotter than the Cajun sauce at her favorite restaurant.

"Wolf."

"Excuse me?"

"Never mind. From now on, if you want to prove you belong on this expedition, you look out for yourself. Or else."

"Or else what?"

"Or you'll regret it."

"Ooh, threats." After the day she had, what worse could he do? She sneered. "Going to hit me?"

"Spank," he corrected. "Bare bottomed."

There went her brave streak. Flustered by his threat, once again heat rose in her cheeks, and she ducked her head. His soft chuckle didn't help.

"So brave in some things, yet so innocent in others. Who are you *really*, honey?"

I'm confused is what I am. One minute he barked at her, the next he seemed ... Seemed what, she pondered as she met his ardent gaze? "I'm not your *honey*."

"I think that's where we're both mistaken. Sleep tight. Don't let the wolves bite."

"Isn't that supposed to be bed bugs?"

"You're in the jungle now, honey. You need to worry about bigger predators."

With those words, Kendrick strutted off. Damn him for his confusing attitude. It was easy to hate him when he acted the domineering jerk. But when he spoke to her so softly, gruffly, while staring at her with a gleam that heated her all over? Stupid wet panties. She only had so many clean pairs.

Crawling into her tent, she zipped it tight, then turned on her flashlight to check the nooks and crannies for critters. Satisfied she slept alone – even if she'd prefer a hard body at her back – she crawled into her sleeping bag. Slumber found her right away, and she would have slept like the dead until dawn if an urge to pee hadn't woken her.

Stumbling outside with her little flashlight, she didn't go too far to squat. Wiping, she disposed of the biodegradable tissue and headed to the water's edge to wash her hands. Crouching down, her flashlight at her side, she rinsed her hands, half asleep on her feet.

Only idiots didn't pay attention in the jungle. Apparently, she'd lost some IQ points since she came on this trip because she could now claim she belonged, not only to the dumbass group, but the stupid blonde one as well because she never saw the danger coming.

*

During his turn to watch the camp, Joel didn't announce his presence when he saw Ruth stumble from her tent to relieve herself. He shadowed her movements, noting her tired mien. As a human, the journey hit her harder than the rest of the group, and she didn't recover as quickly. Damn Kendrick.

It wasn't right they shun her when she so obviously needed them. *Needs me.* As his mate, didn't she merit all the care and attention he could provide?

He shouldn't let her human status sway him from the path fate chose. He wasn't his father. Or so he damn well hoped.

Why did he assume he'd fail? Or that Ruth would leave him like his mother had? If he treated her right, made her happy, she'd have no reason to leave him. Screw Kendrick and his attitude. Joel spent a miserable day and evening avoiding her, avoiding what he wanted.

No more. Starting now, he'd do what he had to in order for Ruth to choose him. He'd do what his wolf and body demanded. He'd do what was right in spite of his fear.

As she paused by the water to rinse her hands, he kept close, knowing all too well the dangers the dark murk could hide, thus he saw the shadowy motion before Ruth did. He dove in her direction and hit the scaled body rising from the water, threatening his woman.

With hands stronger than a human, he clamped the jaw of the croc shut, but in doing so, left himself at the mercy of the big thrashing body. Ruth's shrieks woke the camp.

"Quick. Something in the water is trying to eat him," she yelled.

Joel wanted to die of embarrassment.

"Need a hand, Joel?" Kendrick shouted, amusement in his tone.

"Are you trying to insult me?" he replied back, releasing the snout with one hand so he could pummel the reptile.

"He's fine," Kendrick said in response to Ruth's hiccups of fear.

"He's wrestling a crocodile!" she snapped, pointing the flashlight beam in his direction.

Momentarily blinded, Joel lost his grip and the croc snapped its head free from his grip. Crap.

Blinking out spots as she kept bobbing the light his way, he stood, drenched head to toe in the water, searching the crests and shadows for his opponent.

He felt the change in the current behind him and sprang to the side just as big jaws clamped shut where he'd stood.

"Oh. My God. What is wrong with you guys?" she shrieked. "Someone get me a gun."

"Don't give her a gun," Kendrick sighed.

Please don't, Joel seconded as he wrapped his arms around the croc, this time from behind, a little jungle style full nelson to put the big lizard in submission. In other words, choke it out. However, the big bastard wouldn't go down, and Ruth continued to freak.

Time to end this charade. Not being a truly huge croc, only a five-footer, if that, Joel twisted hard and held on as the beast thrashed for air and freedom. Joel remained steady as the frantic motion abated. Even better, he was finally light free as Kendrick swiped Ruth's waving weapon.

When the last ounce of life left the crocodile's body, he trudged to shore and dropped his prize. "It's dead. You can stop freaking now."

Gaping, Ruth peeked at him, then the crocodile, then him, then the lizard. She burst into tears and threw herself at his chest, but not for comfort.

"You idiot," she hollered, pounding at him. She owned a pretty good swing too, not that Joel flinched. Noticeably, at any rate. "What possessed you to attack that thing? You could have been killed!"

"But I wasn't."

"By some fluke."

No, because wolves rated higher on the predator list. *I probably shouldn't mention that, though.* "I was never in real danger. One of the others would have done something if I got in trouble."

"When? Before or after it bit off your head?"

It occurred to him where her anger came from. "Were you scared for me?"

"Of course I was."

Well, hot damn. The admission warmed him through and through, despite her grudging tone. "You know, most girls would say thank you for saving their life."

"Thank you for being an idiot?"

"An idiot hero who saved your life."

"You did, didn't you?" He would have done more than wrestle a little lizard just to get that wondrous moment where her eyes lit up. "Thank you."

"That's it? I hug a croc to death and all I get is *thank you*?"

Amusement lit her gaze. "I thought you said you weren't in any danger?"

"I wasn't, but I still expect a prize." And with the others returned to their tents, probably not sleeping, not that he cared, he intended to claim a gift. One kiss.

How dangerous can one kiss be?

Very, as it turned out.

Cupping her head, he drew her to him. Felt her hand brace against his chest, not pushing him away, but hesitant. Unsure. Her heart fluttered erratically. The lids of her eyes shuttered a gaze that wouldn't meet his, but instead, stared at his lips.

The jungle, the sounds, smells, everything seemed to hush in that single moment as he finally touched his mouth to hers. Kissed her, laid his scent upon her, understood in that moment, that she was already his, human or not, even if the mark didn't scar her skin. *My mate.*

No more fighting it. No more denying it. Ruth belonged to him. The sweetness of her kiss branding him as surely as a set of teeth. In that one sweet moment, he gave up. Or gave in. Whatever, it didn't matter. He tasted her lips, felt the passion she hid simmering under the surface, and decided in that moment that human or not, he'd take a chance. And pray she never broke his heart.

*

Kendrick watched from the shadows, a silent witness to the kiss. A passenger in the crazy jealous train careening through his body.

He envied Joel the first taste of those lips. Wished he could have been the one to come to Ruth's rescue, to have the right to claim such a glorious prize. A prize he didn't want. A woman he should walk away from. A woman whose only flaw lay in her humanity.

Should he or shouldn't he? Give into the burning of his body, or keep torturing himself? Fight with his best friend over a woman? Because he didn't doubt from the way Joel hugged Ruth tight, devoured her with the hunger of a man denied too long, he'd chosen his path. But did the road to Ruth's heart have room for one or two? If she could handle a pair, did Kendrick have it in him to share?

A week ago, he would have said *hell no*. Even just yesterday, he would have punched someone for suggesting it. But that was before he finally understood what it meant to meet his mate. To meet a woman who made his entire being yearn for her touch, smile, soul.

How frightening for a man who'd not thought of commitment as part of his future yet. Who still had so many adventures he wanted to embark on. Places to see. Things to do.

Dammit. Could he just stay away and let Joel claim her in the hopes the muddle in his brain would disappear?

Ours, snarled his wolf, angry at the suggestion of giving up. Despite the chaos, it sounded like his other half didn't intend to give Ruth up without a fight. And honestly, Kendrick wasn't the type to back down from a challenge. Human or not, he wanted her.

Oh my God. I want her. Tenacious nature and all. An Amazon goddess who appeared more beautiful each time he saw her. However, that wasn't the only thing he liked about Ruth. He eavesdropped as she talked to the others – dead men once the mission was done. He heard the intelligence in her remarks, the kind nature, with others at least, but then again, what had he done to earn her good grace?

Acted like the biggest asshat around, that's what. And what did that gain him? Nothing. Not even peace of mind. He did have a list of other ailments, though. Misery. Horniness. Jealousy. Horniness. A major case of like. And horny – had he mentioned that?

Would analyzing and fighting his feelings change anything in the end?

God, the situation was messed up, but he needed to get his head in the game. The crocodile was a reminder the jungle held many dangerous surprises.

But none so dangerous as the human who made him want her. The woman Joel would claim if Kendrick didn't do something, right now given the heavy panting and groping.

"You can go to bed now," he called out. *Alone*, he silently added. "We've got a long march ahead of us in a few hours."

As intended, his words broke the embracing couple apart, Joel, with a growl of annoyance, Ruth, with a gasp and a hand flying to cover her lips. Kendrick could just imagine the embarrassment in her cheeks. When Ruth fled to the imagined safety of her tent, Joel didn't follow, but he did peer Kendrick's way and flicked him a hard salute before stalking off, back to the tree limb he'd chosen to watch from.

Kendrick smiled in grim satisfaction. He loved Joel like a brother, but in the game of mating, all was fair. Even cock-blocking. And starting tomorrow, the race would start to win Ruth's heart before the mating fever took everyone's choice away.

Chapter Seven

When she awoke the next morning, alone in her tent, Ruth wondered if she'd dreamed the crocodile attack and ensuing kiss. Wondered if a simple embrace of lips, a soft, sensuous slide with a hint of tongue, could really feel so darned good. As if a kiss could almost make her come in her panties.

Impossible. There went her overactive imagination again. Apparently, she harbored delusions. No way would Joel kiss her when he'd shown her almost the same level of disdain as Kendrick. The man who let her deal with the snake that decided to give her boot a hug when they stopped for a drink could not have devoured her mouth with such passion.

He did not kiss me. None of that happened.

Convinced of it, she emerged from her shelter ready for another grueling day and a breakfast no Denny's would ever serve. Hold on a second. What was that smell? She inhaled the delicious aroma. Roasted chicken? She swiveled her head until she saw some meat spitted over a low burning fire, and not just any meat, judging by the chunks and the damning leather skin splayed over a rock. She stumbled on her way to the little girl's jungle room as she realized she didn't imagine the crocodile, which meant the kiss really happened.

Stunned, of course she immediately searched him out. Joel met her gaze, without flinching or looking away. Met her gaze, held it, and somehow, with one scalding look, managed to make her feel as if he touched her again, especially when half his mouth curled into a sensual grin.

Sweet heavens. She needed a cold shower, and fast. Cheeks burning, she whirled away, intent on finding some water to splash herself with when she hit an ice wall in the grim countenance of Kendrick. The man appeared to have reverted to his natural state – a.k.a. jerk. What fun. Not.

"Good morning." A low greeting, rumbled in a voice that tickled across her skin. The mighty man deigned to acknowledge her.

"G-good morning." Smoothly said. Ruth couldn't have explained why the way Kendrick spoke set her knees to trembling, or sent tingles to her lower parts. Whatever the reason, it didn't bode well.

"Coffee?"

The offer took her by surprise. Was Kendrick actually acting decently toward her? Could one dare say friendly?

Oh my God, am I dying? Had something bitten her and injected a deadly poison? Was the world about to end? What happened to make him show her kindness? She eyed him dubiously. "Did you spit in it?"

"No. But I did add powdered creamer and sugar."

Just the way she liked it. But how did he know? And more disturbing, why did he bother? "Why are you being so nice? What happened to 'Keep up if you can,' and, 'Don't help her, she's Satan'?"

His lips twitched. "I never called you Satan."

"You might as well have," Ruth grumbled. It seemed awakening her distrust in his motives gave her a spurt of courage, enough to confront him.

"Could you just maybe accept that I'm doing this because I'm sorry?"

"No. You're not the type to apologize. And I doubt you've changed your mind."

"I haven't. I still think it's too dangerous."

"Aha! I knew it," she crowed.

"I wasn't done talking."

"Does it matter? You haven't changed your view on my presence."

"Not completely, but ..." He held up a finger. "But I can acknowledge you're worried about your sister. It also occurred to me that it might not be entirely safe to leave you alone in the village given the guide's defection."

"You think he might come back to harm us?" Way to reassure her.

"He's welcome to try."

Why did his vicious grin make her insides melt? "So now you're keeping me with you because it's safer?"

"In a sense."

"Oh, that's priceless. What happened to 'You won't be able to keep up' and 'Every man for himself'?"

"You're tougher than you look."

Well, at least he didn't say, 'for a fat girl.' His reasoning still resembled a caveman's misogynistic outlook. Yet, she couldn't help a curl of pleasure at his almost praise and his roundabout declaration she needed his protection. Say what you would, there was something hot about a man who wanted to take on the role of protector. *Him, Tarzan, me, Jane.* Something she could totally picture, given his shirt hung from his back pocket. How did a man legally manage to attain his level of physique? Toned, hard and thick all over,

Kendrick sported a lush mat of hair on his chest, soft, springy curls the same color as those on his head.

Did it mean she forgave him if she fantasized about running her fingers down his pecs? Oh boy. She needed to get away from him. First she made out with Joel. Then she fantasized about getting naughty with his friend. Time for some water, maybe some food, and see if she could get rid of her obviously jungle-induced horny state. It wasn't natural.

Lusting after two guys. And badly. *The heat's turned me into a slut.* But how to escape him and the cup of coffee he offered. On second thought, she grabbed the coffee, but to forestall any further conversation, she blurted, "I need to pee." Yay for her brilliant exit strategy. The only thing worse she could have said would have probably involved another word that rhymed with *moo*.

Fleeing to the woods, her entire body prickled, convinced he watched. She almost turned to look. Almost gave into paranoia to see if Kendrick stared longingly at her backside while Joel shot him venomous looks.

Ahhh. If only. And then, in a perfect world, they'd fight, bare-chested of course. Sinewy bodies flexing and moving and … She almost welcomed the branch that slapped her. She needed the wakeup call. Fantasizing about two hunks fighting over her, indeed.

Talk about crazy. As crazy as having them decide to put their imaginary jealousy aside and pursue her together. It took two branches that time to snap her out of it, but the general idea didn't stray far.

Screw it, if I'm going to fantasize about the impossible then it might as well be times two.

*

Kendrick didn't laugh when Ruth fled his presence, cheeks flaming. He'd flustered her with his new attitude. Excited her too, it seemed. The subtle musk of her arousal, a perfume like no other, had him salivating for a taste. No freakn' way he'd deny it any longer. The woman was his.

"What are you doing with my woman?" Joel asked, his tone low and angry.

His and Joel's woman. Crap. The reminder irked. "Your woman? I didn't think you'd gotten that far last night," Kendrick replied, a little coolly, still insanely jealous his friend got to kiss her first.

"Yeah, well, only because we were so rudely interrupted. I'm done trying to fight it. She's my mate, human or not. One taste and *bam*. It's like lightning hit, dude. Yummy lightning, all sugary, sweet, and soft." Joel taunted him with his knowledge.

"With a steel core. She's got more spunk than you think."

"She'll need it to deal with my dad." Joel's moue of distaste had Kendrick forgetting their rivalry for a moment to pat him on the back.

"A dad we'll protect her from."

"We?"

"I can't pretend anymore either. She's also my mate. We're in this together, old friend."

"You don't know that for sure."

"You're in denial if you don't realize it yet," Kendrick said wryly. Not the ideal situation, but honestly, it wouldn't be the first time Joel and Kendrick tagged-teamed in the bedroom. There would just be one girl less, and for a lot longer. Say, a lifetime longer. It didn't horrify him like he expected.

"I love you like a brother, man, but we're talking about one woman. One. For both of us. I don't know if I can handle it. Especially with her being human. She's delicate."

"So we play gentle." Kendrick rolled his eyes. "Holy crap, Joel. Talk about a lame excuse. She's a hell of a lot sturdier than the human girls we banged in college."

"Sturdy? Nice way of putting it. What are you going to call her next? Big-boned? A moose?"

A gasp from behind made Joel wince. He whirled. "Hey, *querida*. I didn't sense you sneaking up."

"I wasn't sneaking, but you're both standing in front of my tent, and I need to pack it up and get ready to go.

"I, um, that is, I wasn't talking about you."

"I'm not sure I follow." Her closed expression and hurt eyes said otherwise.

"The moose comment. I didn't mean it applied to you."

"Of course it didn't." Her cool tone clearly said she didn't believe him. "Now do you mind moving so I can pack my things?"

Kendrick kind of enjoyed watching his friend sink because it left him in the open, but friends didn't let friends drown.

"He's telling the truth. He was talking about the crocodile he killed for you last night. It was moose sturdy."

"It was?"

"Yup."

Her demeanor relaxed. A shy smile tilted her lips and Kendrick's groin tightened. "Thank you again. That was a brave, if stupid, thing you did."

"Wanna thank me the same way you did last night?" Joel arched a brow suggestively, and Ruth's cheeks, so damned expressive of her feelings, flared.

"Um. No. Thanks for the offer, but I—um—that is—" She stammered as she ducked to the ground, hands fiddling uselessly with her shelter.

"We need to get ready to go. I'll give you a hand." Kendrick squatted beside her and caught her hands before she did something to hurt herself. A shock, electrical and yet somehow carnal, shot through him, and his wolf rumbled in pleasure.

Mine.

Kendrick could understand Joel's jealousy and need to claim this woman. He also knew what his friend wouldn't yet admit, that fate had decreed Ruth have two mates. Not the ideal situation, but given who he had to share her with, one he could handle. And in time, Joel would come to grips with it too.

However, sharing didn't mean he couldn't claim her first, which meant he needed to catch up to Joel when it came to the charming department. Time to adjust his attitude. Turn over a new leaf – in other words, treat Ruth like he'd usually treat someone he cared for. But better, because he did, after all, want to get her naked. Mmm. Naked.

Oops. Almost drooled. He caught himself in time, but his momentary lapse didn't go unnoticed. Joel watched him. Eyes narrowed, Joel tilted his head. Kendrick replied with a tight smile and a head bob of his own.

If Kendrick hoped to win Ruth over, he had his work cut out for him. In his quest to get her to quit the expedition, he'd acted like a class A jerk. He had a lot of ass kissing to do if he wanted to get her to like him. A lot. However, he had faith in himself. One way or another, he'd get Ruth to forgive and forget the stress he'd put her through. Get her to realize he wasn't a bad guy usually. Get her to stop glaring daggers at him.

God, where's a box of chocolate when you need some? Sweet bribes or not, it was time to do what he should have done day one. Use the manners his ma taught him. Show her the real Kendrick. Woo his woman.

Let the courtship begin. And may the best wolf nibble first.

*

What is going on?

Judging by the staring contest happening on either side of her, a prettier girl would have assumed Kendrick and Joel fought over her. Ruth, though, didn't have that kind of confidence in her feminine wiles. More than likely, the two guys were horny, and with no prospects other than each other, wagered who could get in the fat girl's pants.

She'd welcome them both to try. Seriously. What woman didn't secretly fantasize about a pair of hunky guys fighting over her?

A less pleasant thought occurred. What if this sudden turn about was a ploy to get her to turn back? Soften her up with kisses and flattery. Convince her they had her best interest at heart so they could send her back to the village. She couldn't stop her journey now. She'd come so far. Learned so much, like how tough she actually was. She'd never have dreamed in a million years that she would have the fortitude and strength to undertake an adventure this grueling. But she was doing it, darn it! She'd kept up with the big boys. Earned their respect, or so she thought, given she no longer needed their help, not even to kill eight-legged freaks with hair. Freakn' bushy hair. Spiders like that were just wrong. So very, very wrong. But on the upside, she'd never have to buy a can of Raid for her apartment again. She'd gotten quite adept at insect genocide.

As both Joel and Kendrick began to move in her direction, she got annoyed. Days of their almost ignoring her to suddenly acting all weird and nice. Screw their plan, whatever it was. She was here to stay.

"It's not going to work," she blurted. Then immediately clamped her lips shut as too many eyes swung her way. She ducked her head and pretended to eat.

"What's not going to work?" Joel asked.

"Your plan to be nice to me so I'll agree when you tell me to stay somewhere safe."

"Can't a man be nice to a girl because he wants to?"

"Not you two. You have a plan," she accused.

"A plan? Yes, but it doesn't involve leaving you behind," Kendrick promised with an odd heat in his gaze. She swallowed hard and looked away to see Joel only a few paces away.

"This is our way of apologizing for our behavior. It was rude of us. From now on, we treat you like one of the gang."

But do you look at the gang like you want to lick them in places that don't usually see the light of day? Or was it just her fanciful imagination? Yes, Joel had kissed her like a man in thrall after he fought the croc, but it was dark, and his adrenaline was pumping. She just didn't inspire that kind of passion.

"From now on, we're going to treat you like family," Kendrick added.

"Oh God, don't tell her that," Joel groaned. "That's just cruel. Your family would kill her."

"Good point. She'll need equipment."

"Or a body shield."

"Um, what the heck are you two talking about?" she asked, her mind still ping-ponging back and forth as she tried to follow their conversation.

"I've got four brothers, and a sister tougher than them all," Kendrick explained. "Plus a whole shitload of aunts, uncles, cousins, second cousins. It gets kind of crowded at holiday times."

"That sounds like a lot of people." Her family consisted of her sister, parents, and one set of grandparents. "Why are you telling me this and what does it have to do with me?"

Kendrick smiled, a boyish grin that almost melted her. Almost, then she recalled the fact he didn't think she could keep up. "As Joel so kindly pointed out, treating you like family might be a little more than you can handle. We're a little rough sometimes."

"A little?" Joel choked.

Intrigued, she had to ask. "How rough?"

"Rough as in we have paneling now instead of drywall 'cause it's easier to replace."

"Oh. I'm going to ask a stupid question, I fear. But why does it need replacing?"

Kendrick's brows rose. "Because of the fights, of course."

"Your family physically attacks each other?"

"Well, not the whole family. Mostly me and my brothers. My sister used to as well until she got hitched. Now she thinks she's some fragile lady or something. As if."

She must have looked appalled because Joel jumped in. "The fights don't usually last too long. His mom usually breaks them up after a few minutes."

And how big was his mother to have the strength to separate them? "Sounds delightful."

"It is. Totally. You'll see after we get out of here and go back home."

She didn't point out she didn't live in the same city. Offered on the same polite lines as, 'I'll call you', and 'Hey, we should get together sometime.' People uttered those types of platitudes all the time, but never followed through. She didn't put any stock in his casual invitation. Out of curiosity now more than politeness, she turned her attention to Joel. "And what about you? Do you also have a boxing ring at your house?"

A sad expression crossed his face. "No. But I wish I did. It's just me and my dad."

"Oh. Your mother passed?"

"Not exactly. She left when I was a boy. My dad didn't handle it too well." His bitter chuckle and shoulder shrug didn't hide the pain of the admission. Even sheltered as she was, she knew enough to see he'd not enjoyed a happy home life. It made her heart ache for him.

"Oh, don't let his puppy dog eyes fool you," Kendrick interrupted. "My family adopted him at an early age, and with that face, he made out like a bandit at every family gathering. He was the only one of us to usually get two helpings of dessert."

Joel's grin was completely unabashed. "Can I help it if the truth will give me candy?"

"You guys are nuts," she said with a shake of her head, but a smile. She couldn't say she disliked this new version of Kendrick and Joel. On the contrary, her crush on them deepened. She just couldn't tell which one she liked more.

"But we come by it honestly. You'll like my family."

"If you say so. But that won't be until *after* the mission."

"It is going to get more dangerous now," Joel cautioned. "You'll have to be more vigilant. Kendrick and I will watch over you, but in case we're occupied, you need to look out for yourself. Keep yourself safe."

"I have been so far. I'm not giving up."

"I wouldn't expect it any other way," muttered Kendrick.

Well, at least that sounded more like she expected. "I'm on to you," she warned, briefly meeting their eyes – hot, smoldering eyes with an odd gleam. She ducked back. "I won't let you talk me out of coming."

"We wouldn't dream of it," Joel said, almost purring.

"Nope. You're much better off where we can keep an eye on you," Kendrick added. "A close eye."

And boy, did he mean that.

From one extreme to another, Ruth thought. She'd gone from wishing Joel and Kendrick would give her a little hand, to them getting underfoot, and worse, acting as if they vied for her attention. Like family indeed. She didn't know any families that would have fought constantly over who got to help her. Kendrick and Joel raced, laughing and joking over who would get to her first. Coffee? Joel won that round. Reheated croc meat sprinkled with salt he had stashed in his gear? Kendrick. Oh, the look he'd given her after her first groan of enjoyment at the smoky taste. And on it went, making her more and more suspicious.

Was she the object of a bet? *Who is going to screw the chubby girl first?* She'd read a book about that not long ago. But, in the end, the fat girl did find love.

However, Ruth also saw some movies where the jilted girl, betrayed and angry, got a knife, or chainsaw, and killed everyone. Or something violent like that anyway, not that she had a fetish for really low-grade horror movies or anything.

Whatever the reason for their ridiculous turnabout, she didn't trust it – even if she perversely enjoyed it. Joel and Kendrick hovered, each tackling one of her chores and showing her the proper way of doing things. Odd how their method involved them placing their hands over hers, guiding her, or so they said, their breath and lips warm against the shell of her ear.

It wasn't just the jungle feeling humid that morning.

By the time they'd finished packing to leave, she was ready to tear off her clothes and beg one of them to take her. Either would do. She didn't of course. It wasn't exactly the time or place. Nor did she entirely trust their motives.

She decided the best plan of action involved ignoring her new stalkers. Now if only they'd cooperate. As they began their trek, Kendrick took point, and Joel took her rear. Exactly how they'd begun the previous day's march.

And then it got weird.

Kendrick hacked a wide path and held back branches for her. Joel, at her heels the whole way, always seemed to steady her a moment before her foot would snag a root or trip over a rock. Not a single bug landed on her head. No snakes asked for hugs. She didn't get the mother of all stitches in her side. It was a nice, if long, hike.

Stopping to camp that night, she went to splash water on her face before tackling her shelter. Minutes, only minutes, she spent refreshing herself, and yet, when she turned around, there were Kendrick and Joel putting the finishing touches on her bedroom for the night, their own bedrolls flanking it on either side.

Hands planted on her hips, she stalked over. "What the heck are you doing?"

Kneeling on the ground, tying down a stake, Kendrick peered up. "Putting up a tent?"

"I can see that. I want to know why."

"To help, of course." Joel's shrug seemed to imply she should know that.

"I don't need any help. You've shown me how to do it. Now let me do it."

"But it's already done."

"This time. I mean next time."

"Fine. We'll let you do it next time."

Kendrick gave in too easily, and she frowned. "What are you up to?"

"Does a man have to have an ulterior motive to help a woman?"

"Yes. And it usually means he expects a *favor*." She knew her inflection left no doubt as to her meaning, but it was his reaction that intrigued her. Kendrick's lids went heavy, brooding almost, as he eyed her, and undressed her. Then, somehow, that same gaze touched her, or at least her mind imagined he did, and hardened her nipples into points she couldn't hide through her flimsy shirt and sturdy bra. She crossed her arms.

"I'll take a favor if you're handing them out," he murmured, stepping closer.

She took a pace back. "I don't think so." She went to take another step, but a hard body stood in her way. She whirled to find Joel, his stare just as intense. "You too?"

"I'd have to be dead not to want to kiss you again."

"It's my turn," Kendrick growled from too close behind her. Hemmed in on both sides, heat radiated from their bodies, heated her already feverish skin. Flustered, she raised her hands and placed one on each chest.

"I am not a toy, or a prize, or a slut. So if you'll excuse me, I'm going to pretend we didn't have this conversation. And from now on, I'll take care of my own things, thank you very much." She stalked away with her head high, panties wet, and shaking inside.

God how she wanted to just melt against them and see how far they were willing to go. Sanity prevailed, how unfortunate. But facts were facts.

First of all, there were three other men in their party, probably watching and laughing as the chunky girl made a fool of herself. Second, this was a rescue mission, not a singles trip. This was about rescuing her sister, not getting laid. And third, what good girl thought that letting two guys seduce her – at once! – was a good idea?

This one does. And that's the problem.

Chapter Eight

Despite her sore muscles, Ruth found the next day's march easier, and it wasn't just because of Kendrick's revised stance on giving her a helping hand. Muscles she'd just recently declared cruel and useless were toned already from the enforced walking so different from the city treks they were used to.

She barely flinched anymore when something with too many legs crossed her path. And she knew how to dismantle her tent. *Look at me, turning into a true adventurer.* Maybe when she got back to civilization she'd look into joining some of the more exotic expeditions her university offered. If she could handle this untamed jungle, she could handle anything. She only wished she had more time to study the various flora they passed. The botanist in her drooled at all the vivid greenery and blooms. She'd managed to snag small samples here and there, which she pressed between the pages of her waterproof journal. Her father gave it to her as a last minute parting gift, telling her to track her adventure. As if her poor, tired body would let her stay up for something like that. Despite its blank pages, the book did give her a great storage spot for the flattened leaves and petals.

When they called camp early for the day, Kendrick not keen on them traversing a wider stretch of marshy land in the encroaching twilight, Ruth decided to take some of her remaining energy and rectify her lack of green exploration. After taking care of pressing business, she detoured away from camp and deeper into the jungle. Not too far, though. She wasn't completely oblivious to the fact she wasn't in a local plant nursery. Wild things roamed, not all of them on two legs. Not to mention, whoever kidnapped her sister and the others could lurk and she'd never know it.

It still didn't stop her from exploring the little patch of lush flowers she found. Stepping in for a closer look, she noted how the muddy soil sucked at her feet. This was as far as she'd go in that direction. Most people thought of quicksand as smooth clearings of harmless seeming dirt. However, Ruth knew from her studies that sometimes the most dangerous type was the marshy kind with cloying mud and tangling vegetation. Get caught in that and a person could end up in major trouble. Or so she'd read, and seen in a documentary taped by the grad students in some other tropical forest the year before.

Spotting a speck of color amidst the whiter blooms – *ooh, a cross-pollinated specimen* – she ducked, and just in time too, as something soared over her head. A big, furry body, which hit a fallen tree bough with a skittering as it extended its claws to grip the rough bark.

Covered in a spotted, sleek pelt, Ruth forgot to breathe as a set of golden eyes turned to peer at her. The tail, long and sinuous, snapped and writhed, an almost separate living entity as the cat pivoted. Facing her, its body bigger than any jaguar she'd seen in a zoo, was a living, breathing predator. Uh-oh.

"Nice kitty?" she asked.

A soft growl rolled forth.

"I hope that wasn't your reply for hungry kitty," she muttered, still in her crouch as she cast her eyes to the side to look for a weapon of some kind because, of course, she'd come armed with a pencil and notepad, not an actual weapon.

"Stay down," Kendrick barked from somewhere behind her a moment before another furry animal soared over her kneeling body. The new arrival landed on the log, which the feline had already vacated, and tumbled past it. The wolf hit the ground beyond and stumbled. Shaking its shaggy, dark head, it tossed her a quick look then took off in the direction of some trembling foliage.

"Holy shit," she breathed, the rare invective making it past her lips.

She didn't get a chance to see much more as Kendrick, his voice tight with anger, lashed her, drawing her attention as he yanked her to her feet. "What on earth were you thinking?"

Thinking? Well, that was easy. "That I was probably going to die rather painfully."

"And why was that going to happen?" he asked, still holding her by her upper arms, giving her a little shake.

"Um, because of the jaguar with big freakn' teeth. I'd say that was obvious."

"Wrong answer. It was going to happen because you wandered off without an escort."

"I went to pee. I don't need someone to wipe my bottom or hand me tissue, thank you very much."

"I didn't say you did. But, once you were done, you didn't come back to camp."

"How did you know? Are you watching me when I, like," she dropped her voice, "you know, pee?"

"No. Of course not. However, as team leader, I do keep an eye on everybody in our group and if one goes missing for more than a few minutes then I start looking."

Why did his reply deflate her? "So, you do that for everyone?"

"No. Just you. But I can lie and pretend otherwise if you'd like."

"It's because you think I'm weaker." And there was that bravado again, rising to the rescue and standing up to Kendrick and his bullying.

"Not weaker. More like, less able to handle things," he countered.

"That's sexist." She planted her hands on her hips and glared at him.

"Realist."

"Semantics."

"Is this a game like Scrabble, because if so, I demand the right to use a dictionary."

"Sinkhole."

"Is that a polite term for asshole?"

"No, I think you're on a sinkhole, or quick sand, or something along those lines, or hadn't you noticed you're getting shorter?"

Kendrick peered down at his disappearing calves. "Well that explains why I'm now looking up at you. How short do you think I'll get?"

"Why would you care? Get out of there."

"Aren't you curious? I wonder if there's a bottom. What if it only comes to my knees?"

"And what if it doesn't stop at your knees and you keep sinking? Even better, why are we debating this? Who cares how deep it is? Get out of it."

"Make me."

She eyed the muck. "And get dirty? No thanks."

"Says the girl who smells like a locker room after a rugby match."

She scowled at him. "You say the nicest things."

"I didn't say I minded it. I like a woman who's not afraid to get down and dirty." He winked.

"I draw the line at mud, though, which means you're on your own."

"So, you'll let me die, suffocate in the icky, sticky mud?"

"Hey, I told you to get out. Not my fault you don't listen." She quite enjoyed the smirk she gave him.

"Oh that's priceless coming from you Miss I-can-handle-the-jungle. Hear me roar."

"I've handled it."

"Yes, you have. And quite nicely too."

"I wish you'd stop doing that."

"Doing what?"

"Complimenting me. I prefer if when you're mean." Because when he was nice, she just didn't know what to think anymore. Kendrick acting like an asshat proved easy to ignore. Kendrick the flirtatious hunk made her want to throw her arms around his neck and plaster him with kisses.

"But I'm not a mean guy at heart. Just a chauvinist," he admitted with a wide smile -- as he continued to sink past his knees.

"Would you get out?" she pleaded, now getting worried as it grew darker, twilight losing the battle to nightfall. Soon, she'd barely see the hand in front of her face, and there was Kendrick sinking in the mud, indulging in some obviously testosterone based game that she couldn't understand.

What if the jaguar came back? Or the freakn' wolf that didn't belong in the rain forest? What the heck was that about? An anomaly or something the researchers missed in their study of the area? No matter how it got here, two large predators roamed the area and she'd not worn her tranquilizer gun since the first day when she almost darted her foot. The quivering tufted capsule was a reminder of why left hand klutzes should never play with guns, even sedative based ones.

"Uh-oh, I think I'm going to need your help." He sighed in resignation as the mud reached his waist. "Reach for me."

"And risk falling in? No, thanks. Let me find a branch." She turned to squint, looking for something long and sturdy enough for them both to grip.

"Ruth, quick. Give me your hand. I think I hit a really soft spot."

She turned and saw his chest was partially submerged. Panicked, she held her hands out and grasped his strong fingers.

"Pull."

She heaved and leaned back. He didn't move. She strained. Not even an inch did he budge.

"It's no use. I'm not strong enough," she panted. "Let me go so I can get some help."

"Don't leave me."

"I won't, but I'm going to yell for help."

"What? No. Don't do that."

Before she could squeak, he'd yanked her toward him, and she flopped into the mud on her knees, her lips at just the right height for him to plant one on her. Oh, the electric tingle as his mouth massaged hers.

However, she was all too conscious of him sinking, and of joining him she feared as her knees pressed deeper into the soft muck. "Are you nuts?" she gasped, pulling away from his tantalizing lips. "We'll both die."

"No we won't."

"Look at you, up to your chest."

"Oh, did I forget to tell you? I hit bottom a while ago. See, we're safe." He stood up, dragging her with him, their muddy bodies glued together.

It took her a moment to register what he did. "You lied to me?"

"I prefer to think of it as *pranked*."

"I thought you were going to die."

"Aren't you glad to know I'm not?"

"Not particularly at the moment." Annoyed or not, though, she didn't pull away even though her mouth hovered just inches from his.

"I know how to make you forgive me."

And he did, or at least how to silence her. Either way, his second kiss, now that she knew they weren't in mortal peril, was even yummier than the first, if inappropriate given she'd already made out with his friend. Dangerous, given their location and the predators roaming about, but with his hands cupping her buttocks and his tongue firmly in charge of her mouth, she couldn't find the will to protest. But, she had no problem enjoying.

Until a low snarl rumbled.

*

Kendrick wanted to groan in frustration as Joel returned the cock-blocking favor of the other night, arriving in time to break up the most wonderful kiss.

Poor Ruth. Not realizing the wolf would never harm a hair on their heads, she trembled in his arms as her wide eyes peered in the darkness, unable to make out Joel's furry shape. Worse, he couldn't reassure her because sane people knew wolves were wild.

"Run. Go back to camp," he whispered.

"I won't leave you alone," she bravely replied, her courage belied by her shaking frame.

"I'll be fine. Don't you worry about me. Now go. I'll be right behind you." Giving her a little push in the direction of camp, he added a sharp slap on her ass to get her moving. Okay, that was more for his enjoyment, but it had the desired effect as she scooted.

"What the hell was that?" Joel demanded, hands on his hips, unconcerned about his nudity as he confronted his friend.

"Not much, given someone came back too soon. You couldn't have chased the cat for a few more minutes?"

"I would have if the damned thing didn't take to the trees and disappear." As they both headed back to camp, eyes and ears peeled for a return, they could hear Ruth's chaotic flight ahead of them.

"Real or other?"

"I'd say the feline wasn't of the tribe we're looking for, but then again, having never met one of the ghost warriors, I could be wrong. The scent, however, was strong, unlike the smells from the campsite the girls were taken from."

"A relief, I guess. Now, how do we explain a wolf in the jungle to Ruth?"

"I'd think you'd be more worried about explaining why you're returning to camp with a naked guy," Liam said, striding from the darkness, a bundle of fabric in hand. He tossed it in Joel's direction.

"Thanks, dude. How did you know I needed something?"

"Ruth's practically hyperventilating in camp about the wolf that's about to eat Kendrick."

"As if I'd let this mangy cur harm a hair on my head," Kendrick joked.

"Cur? Ha. You wish. We both know who's the more handsome wolf," Joel joked as he pulled on the track pants.

"In your dreams."

"Oh my God, you're okay!" Ruth's shriek hit him a moment before she did. One thing about her height, a man needed to brace himself when she got enthusiastic. Good thing for him, Joel caught Kendrick before he could tumble back. Even luckier, Kendrick got an armful of woman intent on hugging the life out of him.

"Are you hurt?" she asked, leaning back to check him for damage. He wished she'd go back to the hugging.

"I'm fine. Not a scratch."

"Joel rescued you?" That quickly, she moved, transferring her embrace to his best friend, not noticing, it seemed, that he was shirtless and barefoot. "That was so brave." She squeezed him tight before releasing him to plant her hands on her hips.

"Uh-oh," Kendrick muttered. "Here it comes."

And so it did, a harangue about them both being idiots for confronting the wolf without a weapon. However, Kendrick allowed it because for one, he knew she did it to relieve the fear she'd recently experienced, and two, because it showed him something really important. *She likes me.* Enough at least to not want to see him mauled by a wolf. Even better, she liked his kisses, which created a problem.

One taste and Kendrick was addicted, but no closer to getting her in his bed. Or sleeping bag. Or against a tree.

Wherever they would finally end up doing it, he wasn't any closer. And neither was Joel, a fact they both lamented as they washed up.

"Dude, at the rate we're going, we'll either die of blue balls or go mad with the mating fever," Joel complained as he watched Ruth talking animatedly with the others in their group. Dead men, all of them, or so his wolf insisted.

"Maybe we should tell her we're interested."

"Both of us? Yeah, I can see that going well. She'll probably call us perverts and go running in the other direction."

"Then what do you suggest?"

Kendrick shrugged. "I've got nothing. And I'm tired of waiting."

And so was Joel, it seemed, because he strode over to Ruth and declared, "From now on, you don't go anywhere without me. It's too dangerous for you to roam alone."

Son of a bitch. "Or me," Kendrick added, joining them. "We can't take any chances with your safety."

"My safety? You're the idiot who pretended to sink into a bog so he could steal a kiss, then stayed behind to confront a wolf. It's a good thing Joel came along to save you."

"Yeah. Nothing messes with these pipes," his best friend boasted with a grin and flex of said muscles.

She didn't seem too impressed, facially at any rate. Her body, though? It smelled quite interested.

"Muscles won't protect you from teeth," she pointed out.

"And neither will your stubborn speeches. Or have you forgotten that we got into this mess in the first place because you wandered off, by yourself?"

"I was hoping you'd forgotten." She tried an innocent look, and Kendrick fisted his hands at his side lest he grab her and kiss her for looking so damned cute.

"Sorry, honey, but from now on, either Joel or I, or both of us, will be glued to your side."

"What happened to pull your own weight?" she grumbled.

"We're men. We can change our minds."

"I thought that was a woman's prerogative."

"Women's lib put an end to that one, honey."

"So who's sleeping with you first?" Joel asked with a nonchalance Kendrick knew was false.

Ruth gasped, then choked, her face flushing. "Excuse me?" she stammered.

A half smile on his face, Joel repeated. "I said, who's sleeping with you first? For safety reasons, of course."

"No one."

"How can we properly protect you then?" Joel countered.

"I am not sharing my tent or sleeping bag with you."

"Ha. I knew she liked me more," Kendrick crowed.

"Or you."

His smile wilted. "Why not?"

"Because."

"Because why?"

"Because you're both driving me nuts and I don't like it. Good night." Her flounce would have worked a lot better if they didn't stand in front of her tent. She took only a few steps before realizing that. Whirling, she refused to meet their eyes as she shoved them apart and dove into her tent, leaving behind only the scent of her arousal.

Whatever her claim, she wasn't indifferent to them. She just needed a few more gentle nudges to calm her human morals before they got her right where they needed her. Naked and in their arms.

Chapter Nine

After their declaration the night before, things went from insane to psychotic. It began right after she returned from her morning commune with nature – a.k.a., things best done in bathrooms where bugs didn't bite tender cheeks. Despite their promise to not leave her unattended, Ruth didn't catch sight of them peeking while she peed, but it didn't reassure her.

Finishing quickly, she returned to camp to find her tent packed, bag zipped without the unsightly bulges, and a cup of coffee handed to her by Joel, a plate of meat by Kendrick, while the rest of the gang looked on with smirks. If she didn't know better, she'd have sworn the pair engaged in a silent rivalry for her attention.

She sat down on a log to eat and drink. Her new best friends took up a spot on either side, and although the log had room, stuck close enough they branded her hips and thighs with their own bodies. She ignored them to sip her coffee.

"How'd you sleep?" Joel asked, chewing on a piece of dried fruit.

"Fine."

"Did you *dream* of anybody?" Kendrick brushed an invisible piece of lint from the top of her leg. Innocent, yet her tummy fluttered.

"Nope. Dead to the world. Like a rock. You?" Query a tad too bright, she tried to concentrate on eating without dropping anything on herself.

"Oh, I had a *hard* time," Joel admitted.

"Worried about the wolf coming back?" she answered, discerning his unease right away.

"Um, no. Not exactly."

"I was, though," Kendrick rushed in to say. "Especially for your safety. I really wish you'd reconsider letting one of us share your tent, just in case."

"Two would be better," Joel argued.

"But wouldn't fit," she exclaimed. "Wait a second. Why am I even entering this debate? I don't need anyone to sleep with me." Although, their inadvertent offer of two did make her blood run hotter than it should.

"We'd make it fit," she thought she heard Kendrick murmur.

"Who says we'd sleep?" Joel added.

Fatigue must have addled her wits more than expected because they sounded like suitors, lovers, men intent on making her body sing, together. No way. She was imagining things again.

"Are you sure I'm not dying?" she mumbled.

Joel, eyes crinkled in mirth, answered. "Maybe of unrequited lust. But, I can fix that anytime you need."

She groaned. Forget embarrassment, at the rate she fielded innuendos and touches, she'd gone past blushing straight into disbelief. "Oh please. Don't tell me that line ever works?"

At least Joel possessed the grace to look abashed. "Will you hit me if I said it did?"

She snorted. "I won't hit you. You might tell me that's a turn on too."

"Nope. Not into the whole whips and chains bit. But I am not a stranger to violence, given I'm used to Kendrick's sister. Naomi was a vicious little thing growing up. Still is. Her not so delicate nature explains the size and strength of her two husbands, though."

"Two?" She choked on her coffee. "Oh my God, Kendrick's sister is a Mormon?"

Startled, Joel's eyes widened. "No. Um. Yeah. Mormon, eh? Kind of. I wasn't supposed to mention that. I think. Although, I guess you would have found out eventually." Joel teetered sideways as Kendrick reached around her to smack his friend.

She lifted wide eyes to Kendrick who shook his head. "Don't listen to him. He's an idiot."

"For what? Telling me about your sister? Don't worry. I won't tell anyone and get them in trouble with the law. I do have to admit to finding it fascinating, though, that she chose two husbands. Isn't it usually the other way around?"

Having recovered himself, Joel rejoined the conversation with a snicker. "Explain that. You're going to have to, eventually."

"Explain what? You guys really aren't making sense. Did you eat anything strange this morning? Did you boil your water?"

"We're not sick."

"Are you sure? You might not even realize it if you were." Pressing the back of her hand against Kendrick's forehead, Ruth's breath caught, yet again, at the skin-to-skin touch. Why she kept having the oddest reaction to Kendrick and Joel, she'd not yet figured out. But, given the way she almost came when each of them kissed her, she really had to wonder how explosive sex with them would be, and at this point, given the heightened state of her libido, either of them would do.

"Well, now that you mention it, I've got a twinge in my chest."

"A twinge? Are you having a heart attack? Is your side tingling?" Instantly, she pressed her palm against Kendrick's ribcage. The steady beat of his heart, maybe a little faster than she liked, met her.

"Lower."

"Wrong spot?" She slid her hand down, and despite her concern, couldn't help but note the hard ridges of Kendrick's abs. She paused over his belly button. "Here?"

"Almost." He placed his hand over hers and slid it further to the waist band of his pants and—

She found her hand caught and her chin tilted away from Kendrick to Joel. "He's fine. I, on the other hand, am obviously delusional. Maybe I should rest, but not alone, in case I get worse."

Glancing from his hopeful grin to Kendrick's scowl, she finally caught on. The competition again. With a sigh of exasperation, she pushed away and went to find a place where she could cool down and forget them. "You are both impossible." And confusing. And arousing. And everything she didn't need – but wanted.

*

Me, impossible? Joel wanted to respond with something along the lines of, 'No, I'm most definitely doable.' Given her confused and annoyed expression, very annoyed, he decided against it.

"This is not working," he sighed to Kendrick as Ruth stomped off yet again, her damned humanity in no way affected by the fever consuming him alive.

"You mean your corny bar pick-up lines aren't."

"Corny? I'll have you know, my lines work great, usually."

"On drunk girls." Kendrick snickered.

And therein lay the problem. Unused to relationships because he'd spurned long-term human ones, and unmated shape-shifters tended to more transient affairs, he didn't know how to woo Ruth.

"I'm going to die of blue balls," he moaned.

"You just need to change your method of operation."

"But cheesy come-on lines are my thing. If I can't use that, what can I do?"

"Do what your instinct says."

"I've been doing that for days and I don't think I'm any closer to claiming her." His only consolation? Kendrick wasn't either.

Kendrick sighed. "Well duh. She's human. You didn't just expect our girl to drop her panties at the first *hello*, did you?"

"I can smell her desire."

"And? So can I, but she's not a slut. This is the good girl mothers warn about."

"You mean *your* mother. I thought it was a myth. None of the single girls I ever met teased me so bad."

"She's not teasing. She's in denial, I think."

"Denial about what?"

"Us. Think about it. The way she was probably raised was to date a boy first before letting him round the bases."

"Date? Kind of impossible at the moment, don't you think? Not to mention, I don't know if I have the willpower to stop at each base." Joel sighed.

"The problems don't end there, buddy. Since she belongs to us both, we need to somehow let her know she doesn't need to choose. That she can have us both, and do it in a way that doesn't send her screaming into the jungle."

"So what, we let her think we're Mormons like Naomi?" Joel grinned.

"Dude, why on earth would you have encouraged her to think that?"

He shrugged. "Did you see the look on her face when I slipped about your sister and her two mates? I had to tell her something."

"Fair enough. Actually, maybe it's a good thing. If she thinks we're Mormons, maybe she won't think it's so strange we both wanted her. Hell, it might make claiming her easier."

"Do you think that will actually ever happen?" Because right now, given how she kept fleeing their every move, he had to wonder.

"Of course it will. Eventually. She's fighting it right now, but at some point, she'll cave, and then we'll just have to make sure she enjoys it enough that she doesn't think it's weird when we ask it to be permanent."

"How long is it going to take?"

Kendrick shrugged. "No idea. But in the meantime, we should stay close to her, and not just so we can help her."

"Why? Do you think she's in danger? We haven't seen or smelled anything out of the ordinary other than the cat, and I'm pretty sure it wasn't a shape-shifter."

"As if we'd recognize it," Kendrick replied dryly. "For all we know, half the scents around us don't belong. I'd prefer not to just trust my nose with her safety."

Good point. Joel's eyes flitted to the trees towering around their camp. "What do you think the note writer really wants from her?"

"Honestly? Her. Maybe the Moon Ghosts liked the sister so much they wanted another."

"What I still don't get is how some savages in the jungle managed something like getting a note, a map, and bus tickets out to her so that she arrived in time to meet the group. We've been walking for days without seeing a damned thing."

"And yet, still keeping in touch," Kendrick replied, wagging his phone. "We have only assumptions the Moon Ghosts are throwback primitives."

"Have you asked your council contact about them?"

"Seth doesn't say squat other than we have all the info required to complete our mission."

"Figures. Even our secret shape-shifter government is out to hide things from us."

"Back to Ruth, though. We'll just keep chipping away at her. Showing her she can trust us."

"Coming up with new corny pick-up lines."

"Until we finally get her to sleep with us."

"And we mark her. Then what?"

"Yeah, I'll let you know when I figure it out." For once in his life, Kendrick wished he had his sister here. She would have told him straight up what he needed to do. Or slapped him for being an idiot. Anything other than confusion would have worked at this point.

On second thought, why couldn't he speak to someone from home? Hadn't he just pointed out his link to the outside world via his satellite device?

He dialed his sister's number, trying not cringe at how much his need for advice would cost the guys footing the bill for his phone. But hey, this counted as an emergency. At least, in his mind.

"Hello."

"Ma?"

"If it's not my good-for-nothing son, calling his sister instead of his mother to let her know how he's faring."

"Um, hi. Sorry I haven't called. I've been kind of preoccupied."

"Apparently." Her dry reply made him wince.

"Try not to hit me, but I kind of was hoping to talk to Naomi about a problem Joel and I have."

"Don't tell me you and Joel got some local girls pregnant?"

"Ma! Of course not."

"You did find the condoms I packed you?"

Unfortunately, yes, along with the note from his mom every boy wanted to read before sex, *Keep your head covered at all times.* "Yes, we found them. Thanks. I think."

"Are you going to tell me what's wrong now?"

"Can't we talk about why you're there instead of Naomi?"

"Babysitting my grandbabies, of course. Must be bad if you're changing the subject."

"Not bad. Just unexpected." He clamped his lips tight. How did mothers always draw more out of their kids than they wanted to tell? She didn't reply. "Ma? You still there."

"Yeah. Just trying to wrap my mind around the fact you and Joel finally admitted your love for each other."

"What? No? Ew. Why would you think that? As if we would ever—"

"Then why on earth would you need your sister's advice over mine?"

Uh oh. He'd hurt his mother's feelings. He sighed. Only one way to fix that. "JoelandImetourmateandshe'sthesamegirl." It emerged in a single word he said it so fast.

"Was that so hard?" his mother said in a smug tone. "So you've met your mate and it's the same female. I don't see the big deal. It's not like you're not used to the whole ménage thing. If you ask me, it's working out quite well for your sister and Francine."

"And if our mate wasn't human, it would probably work out quite well, too."

"Human?"

Kendrick almost grinned at his mother's shocked squeak. "Yes. Very, and unknowing of our kind."

"I'll be damned. How's Joel handling it?"

"Better than expected, now that he's come to grips with it."

"So, what is her name?"

"Ruth Anderson."

"Doesn't sound very local."

"It's not. She joined our expedition at the last minute because her sister is one of the girls missing."

"I'm surprised you haven't claimed her yet."

"That's the problem, we want to. Bad. But, she isn't taking our overtures seriously."

Silence greeted him.

"Ma? You still there, Ma?"

"I am. I'm just picking up my jaw from the floor because I thought you said she hadn't dropped her pants for you yet."

"Not exactly what I said, but in a nutshell, yes. Joel and I have tried everything to get her to, you know, *be with us*, but either we're interrupted or she stomps off muttering about her luck."

A choking sound, followed by a giggle, then a full out snort and laughter met his announcement.

"This is not funny."

"Yes it is. I always wished you'd both meet a nice girl who wouldn't give into your smiles and ridiculous pick-up lines. And now that it's happened, it's even better than I expected. I like her already."

"But you'll never get to meet her if this keeps up," he growled.

"So take a more direct approach. Stop pussyfooting around and seduce her."

"Both of us at once?"

"Are you insane? Of course not. She's human. One at a time. Mark her. Then, after she's done hitting you for both getting into her pants, make her understand you're not averse to sharing. Use your sister and brother Mitchell as an example of how it can work."

"She already thinks we're Mormons."

"She what? *Oh*." His mother couldn't speak for the laughter.

"Nice help you are," he grumbled, but affectionately. "Miss you, Ma."

"Miss you too, baby boy. Tell Joel I've got some canned peaches waiting to get baked in a pie when he gets back."

"I will. Love you. Bye." Throat tight with the most unmanly of sensations, he hung up, homesick for his mother, and drooling for a taste of her damned peach pie.

Chapter Ten

Stay away. Stay away. Ruth kept telling herself that, especially after the way the guys previously cornered her into a manwich. But dammit, like a stupid moth, she wanted to get burned, or so she assumed when she took the spot between them on a log – at their behest and despite their matching grins – the lure of the crackling fire they'd built to ward off an unusual chill too much for her to resist.

Thighs pressing against hers, making her much too aware of them on either side, she held her hands out to the dancing flames.

"If only we had some marshmallows," she joked.

"Mmm, something soft and sweet to bite into. Sounds *yummy*." Sounding so innocent on the surface, she couldn't help a curl of heat from forming at the implied innuendo. Or was she imagining the sexual overtone? By now, she surely wasn't the only one craving real food.

The others in the group, with feeble excuses, wandered off, Peter to sleep, Liam and Fernando for a stroll – which, given they walked all day, made no sense to her or her sore glutes.

Silence set in as her tongue stuck to the roof of her mouth, a sudden shyness overtaking her. It was one thing to converse with the guys, or go toe-to-toe with them when Kendrick pulled his macho routine, another to come up with small talk when she was all too aware of them alongside her. Not for the first time, she wished she understood what game they played. What they wanted of her. What she wanted of them. Actually, that answer came easily. Sex. But with which one?

Uncomfortable at the direction of her thoughts – naughty ones she just couldn't seem to prevent, especially once Kendrick's fingers claimed possession of her knee in a casual manner – she blurted, "How many more days until we reach the X on the map?"

"Hard to tell. It depends on the terrain. I figure we'll come across the ruins on your map tomorrow; that is, *if* what you received is accurate. Then, at least another two, maybe three days to the mark where the X is, depending on how quickly we travel and any obstacles in our path."

"And then what happens?"

"If your note is telling the truth, then fingers crossed, we'll find the girls and turn right around," Joel replied.

"More walking?" She groaned. "Can't we call a helicopter for a pickup? Speaking of which, how come we didn't just have one drop us right on the spot?"

"Distance is an issue. As is missing clues only seen on the ground from the air."

"Well, that sucks."

"Tired?" Kendrick squeezed her knee when he asked.

"Nope." She lied, not wanting to appear weak in front of them.

"I guess I won't offer a massage then."

Keep her distance – which she'd already failed to do – or succumb to the temptation of a rub? "Now let's not be hasty."

Joel chuckled. "Let's loosen those muscles." Standing, he moved behind her and dug in with his digits. She groaned. His fingers spread and danced along her tight shoulders, to her head-lolling delight. To her shock, Kendrick slid to his knees in front of her and grabbed a foot. She jerked it away.

"What are you doing?"

"What's it look like I'm doing?"

"Catching your butt on fire?"

"Am not." He said it, but Kendrick also peered behind him to make sure.

She grinned.

"Wench." His tilted lips matched the mirth in his eyes.

"That's for the spider comment this afternoon."

"But I swear I saw it."

"Sure you did," she said, nodding her head, not believing him for one moment – now, at any rate. Earlier, when Kendrick claimed he saw a poisonous arachnid, she couldn't move into his arms fast enough. Only Joel's growl that nothing was there made her realize Kendrick did it to cop a feel. She found it hard to stay mad at him for his prank, given the girly part of her appreciated the reason for it. And yet, that was all he attempted. She still didn't know if she liked him for not pushing her for something extra, or was annoyed that like Joel, he kept teasing without attempting to take that next step.

If only one of them would act, take charge and make the decision for her. At this point, her body craved some kind of relief, and so long as it was Joel or Kendrick offering, she didn't care which.

Still kneeling, Kendrick grabbed her boot and removed it.

"Don't you dare. I'm ticklish." At least she was clean from the river bath she enjoyed earlier, a bath she was pretty sure had an audience of one, maybe two. Thankfully, the water flowed deep enough for her to kneel down and avoid giving too much of a show. She could have confronted her peepers and demanded they leave, but with every step that got them closer to the X on the map, the more her nerves coiled, especially as she noted the group's watchfulness. There were worse things to worry about than a pair of hunks with a penchant for voyeurism.

"I am trying to relax you, so would you shut up and enjoy it?" Kendrick growled.

Ruth bit her lip, not to stem any more arguments from her, but because she almost moaned in a way that might have proven embarrassing as their strong fingers dug into her tense muscles. A moment later, her head lolled and she groaned blissfully, not caring who heard. "Oh my God. Yes. Mmm. Right there."

Fully clothed, in plain sight, and not having anything sexual done to her; nevertheless, Ruth's sounds of pleasure could have rivaled those heard in a bordello, and her panties bore moist witness to her enjoyment of their touch. If this was how they wanted to fight over her, then fight away.

Though relaxed, her body humming happily – it didn't mean she didn't sit bolt upright when a pair of lips began to caress her neck while a set of hands roamed up her thighs, closer and closer to the origin of the ache in her body. What were they doing?

Who cared? Wasn't this what she wanted? Her breathing hitched as Joel found the sensitive spot at the back of her neck. He nibbled and a soft sigh parted her lips, followed by a squeak as Kendrick rubbed his jaw along her thigh. Sure, the material of her cargo pants was in the way, but it didn't stop the tingles from racing through her. From her hoping he'd move a little higher. A little more to the middle. A …

What am I doing? And in plain sight? Had she completely lost her mind, allowing two men to stroke her so intimately? What would they think of her if she allowed it to go any further? What of the rest of the group? No. This had to stop now. Stop before she did something she'd regret the next day.

With a squeaked, "Thanks for the massage. I'll see you in the morning," she fled, her heart pounding and her clit throbbing for their touch. And she did mean *their* touch.

What am I going to do?

Both of them, was the easy answer. The wrong answer, obviously, but tell that to her aroused state. In the war to get in her pants, she couldn't declare a victor. Couldn't choose. Didn't want to. Worried she misread their intentions. Fretted she didn't, and missed out.

A braver girl would confront them and ask if they were trying to both bed her at once – then strip so they could. But that required a little more courage – no matter how much Kendrick claimed she owned – to do.

And what would she do if she did confront them and they stated their intention was to seduce her, the both of them at once? It both excited and shocked her. Good girls did not sleep with two guys. Good girls didn't even think of it. Then again, good girls didn't come on jungle adventures with a group of men in the first place.

Or was it a competition of sorts to see which of them she'd choose?

Of worry as well, what if they only toyed with her? Did the fact she'd not succumbed to their advances make them more determined to see her fall? Did they just wait to taunt her? The men she'd gotten to know wouldn't, but she'd seen her judgment fail her before. How she wished Carlie were here to give her advice. How she wished she could get a few moments to herself to evaluate things, but everywhere she turned, there they were. Sleeping alongside her tent. Shadowing her every move. Touching her at every turn.

How could a girl think when she got no respite from their attention? No relief from her dilemma. True to their new mission in life, they stuck to her like glue from the moment she woke until she fled to her tent, knowing they slept only inches away, a thin canvas the only barrier. The nightmarish trek of the first few days faded as they cleared the way for her with brisk whacks of the machete, helped her over tricky spots, their hands holding hers for too long each time. Flustered and only too aware of them every time they did, she yanked away, cheeks burning, her body constantly on fire as it reacted to their virile closeness.

Over the next few days, when they camped for the night, Joel and Kendrick took turns setting up and taking down her shelter and placing their sleeping bags alongside hers, only because she refused to let them into hers. Heck, she still didn't understand why they needed to get so close. When asked why, they sputtered some crap about protection. Yet, it didn't explain the dirty looks they gave the rest of the group if they came anywhere near her. If she didn't know better, she'd think they'd laid some kind of claim to her. The others, Liam, Peter, and even flirty Fernando, once so friendly, didn't come too close or offer her aid anymore. All backed off as Joel and Kendrick, in an abrupt about face, strove to make her journey a more pleasant one.

More like extra torturous. She'd heard the term blue balled in reference to men, but what did you call a woman who thought she would die if she didn't get sexual relief soon? Stupid? Here she had two men that seemed intent on bedding her, and yet, she did nothing about it. *Because what if I'm wrong?* That thought more than anything plagued her and kept her distracted from the true mission. Maybe once she located her sister, she'd have an answer, or at least a second opinion. *More like competition because once they get a load of the other girls, I doubt I'm going to look so appealing.*

Now there was a depressing thought, which in turn, raised a question, which she blurted out loud as Joel hammered in the stakes for her tent while she handed them to him one by one. She'd given up arguing about her ability to do it herself – why bother when they seemed so determined?

"Do you have a girlfriend back home?"

Whack.

Ooh, that had to hurt, she thought with a wince as his hammer missed the peg. To Joel's credit, he didn't even flinch. "No." He sounded peeved for some reason.

"Oh. That's good."

"Good? Glad you think so, considering I find it kind of offensive you'd think I'd act this way with you while involved with someone else."

Appalled as she viewed it from his angle, she blanched. "I'm sorry. That never occurred to me. I guess with me not really knowing you, I don't know if you flirt like this in the real world or not. I've known a lot of guys who act like they're single and make advances only to go home to girlfriends and families."

His expression softened. "Fair enough. But just so we're clear, I am not the type of guy to cheat or betray someone he cares about. So you needn't worry on that score."

"Worry? Why would I worry?" Her query emerged a touch high-pitched and breathy. No denying it, he was claiming an interest in her.

"Are you truly as innocent as you appear?" he mused. "At times, I find it hard to believe, and yet, your own body betrays you. I never thought I'd find a blush so sexy. And I don't think I've ever heard the word *no* so many times in a row. You're the only woman I've ever encountered who's fought so hard against her desire."

"Who says I want you?" Oh God, she couldn't believe they'd guessed it. So much for thinking them oblivious to her less than pristine thoughts.

A soft chuckle made her shiver. "Oh, I can tell when you're feeling frisky. One might even say I have a built-in radar for it."

"Next you'll tell me you can smell it." And she bit her tongue. Too late. What was it about Joel and Kendrick that she found it so easy to reply to them? Whenever they engaged her, she kept replying aloud with the thoughts running through her head. Things she would usually keep secret. She spoke to them comfortably and honestly like she would a true friend. Except she didn't know many friends she'd have this odd a conversation with.

His fingers brushed hers, long, tanned, and so easy to imagine on other parts of her body. A shiver went through her and she wanted to suddenly flee as she wondered if he could sense her interest at this moment, as he claimed he could. As if sensing her imminent flight, his fingers curled around her wrist and held her in place. "Why don't you let us give you what you need? Why do you run away?"

Why couldn't the earth swallow her up now? She didn't know how to answer him. So she denied his claims. "I don't know what you're talking about. I don't need anything from you."

"Liar." He chided her softly, the word tickling across her senses. "I think you're afraid of yourself and what we make you feel."

Very afraid, which was why she stayed away as much as she could. If only they'd do the same thing. "What do you want from me?"

"Would you run if I said, *forever*?"

"I'd say that's the corniest line yet."

Surely she didn't spot a flash of hurt in his eyes? As if she'd believe he looked for a happily ever after with her. Good-looking guys like Joel and Kendrick might play with a girl like her, but they settled down with little-miss-size-five when the time came. A woman who would probably drive them crazy, but keep a perfect house, and pop out the prerequisite two-point-one kids and drive the kids to soccer. All things Ruth wanted too, she just doubted she'd get it with the current lot.

Once they left the jungle, reality would intrude, common sense would prevail, and they'd go their separate ways. Them, to settle down with nice hometown girls; her, back to her university life as an intern and student. She'd eventually meet someone nerdy like her, settle down, and live out some boring years. Just like her mother. And grandmother, and everyone else she knew.

Funny how that didn't muster the slightest enthusiasm. Imagining one night, though, just one in either Kendrick's or Joel's arms? Worth the heartbreak, or not?

As she crawled into her tent that night – alone, and still in a state of arousal from Kendrick, who caught her when she stumbled – cradling her body a touch longer than needed against him – she wondered why she let herself suffer.

If Joel could be believed, he wanted her, maybe only for the moment, but still, why did she hesitate on taking it to the next step? Her emotions were already invested. Remove that excuse and what was she left with? *Maybe because I'd like him to seduce me first.* He kept talking, but not acting, as if he waited for something from her. She couldn't take that step. But if he did … She'd never have to wonder if she threw herself at him like a hussy if he made the next move. Not worry he'd reject her. However, at the rate things progressed, she might have to wait a long time for seduction.

If she discounted the massage disaster, Joel hadn't smooched her since the crocodile incident, even if he kept asking for a kiss. Why didn't he just take? It wasn't as if he didn't torture her daily. Touching her, innocent brushes of skin that caught her breath. Subtle rubs of his body on hers when he helped her climb or cross slippery stones. It was enough to drive her mad with longing. Smoldering looks, or so she interpreted, but he'd yet to drag her off in the bushes to plant one on her. Why?

Add in Kendrick's almost identical attention – along with the memory of his kiss she'd by now replayed a thousand times – and she wanted to scream in frustration.

Is something wrong with me? Or is there something else?

Any wonder her emotions seesawed wildly? One moment she wanted them away from her because she didn't trust their motives, the next she wanted either or both to take away the decision, and then there was her almost constant state of arousal. Thank goodness for their daily walks. She looked forward to them as her only respite from the dilemma they presented. But once they got to camp, it started all over again.

Would it kill one of them to make up his mind and drag her into the woods for a quickie?

No. Wait. She didn't want that. Yes, she did. No. Darn it all. Why couldn't she figure out what she wanted? And who?

In close confines, with no privacy, and her sister's life on the line – or not, depending on if she believed the note – she had no right to think about her pleasure. She needed to concentrate on her sister and what the X on the map meant.

Damn them for distracting her from her mission. *Teases.*

On the next day of nature walk, well into the jungle, they came across a landmark that corresponded to her mysterious map. Ancient Mayan ruins. Overgrown, tumbled, and worn by time, nevertheless, their remnants excited the explorer in her, especially when she noted the unique spire with its donut hole, just like the one on her hand-drawn missive.

Her excitement must have shown because Kendrick declared it their campsite for the night, despite the fact twilight remained a few hours away.

Delighted she'd get a chance to explore, Ruth struggled to put up her tent herself, waving Joel away when he would have stepped in to help. It took her a little longer, but in the end, with only one snapped body part, she got the stupid shelter up. Grabbing a camera, a notebook, and a pen, she tossed the rest of her stuff inside, but then hesitated. Joel and Kendrick didn't want her exploring alone. But busy with other things, she didn't want to disturb them and have them tag along as unwilling babysitters. *I won't technically leave the camp, though.* Or so she consoled her conscience as she went to ogle the remains, the unexcavated, untouched ruins. Oh my, did that excite the explorer – and Indian Jones lover – in her.

Many theories abounded about the Mayans and their disappearance. Famine. Disease. A mass exodus. Extermination by another group. Even theories as farfetched as alien extraction existed. Fascinated by their evolved culture, Ruth devoured texts on archeological finds, but reserved her own opinion, the evidence contradicting itself in many respects. No people, yet no bodies. No signs of violence – the kind you'd see with a raid for slaves, yet no evidence of a gentle departure given the belongings left behind.

A mystery. She loved the excitement of it. While the men scouted for firewood, a task they banned her from days before when her constant shrieks at scattering bugs kept bringing them running, she didn't worry about giving them a hand. Or as Kendrick dryly called her aide, "More hindrance than help." Her skills lay in a different direction. Botany.

She loved plants. All kinds of plants. Here in the jungle, the researcher in her was giddy at all the flora. But the lure of her green friends, though, couldn't compete with the Lara Croft persona hidden inside. What girl didn't dream of exploring some ruins? Discovering treasure? Solving the Mayan mystery?

Flashlight clipped to her belt, Ruth approached the overgrown looming presence of the stone block building. Its height and tiered levels intact, even after all this time.

She circled the temple-like structure, noting the denseness of the vines and foliage creeping all over its pitted stone surface, reclaiming the building and land. She almost missed the darker shadow of an opening in the bramble. A trampling of little critter footprints led into the stone-crafted tomb. Crouching down, she shone her flashlight at the hole. She couldn't see far. Grasping some of the crisscrossing vines, she tugged, clearing and widening the opening, her excitement mounting. When it proved big enough for her to enter if she ducked, she scooted in, the bobbing light in her hand dancing upon the stone walls covered in cobwebs and dust. Another step and the cooler air dissipated the humid heat of the jungle – a welcomed relief.

How marvelous. She must have appeared like a slack-jawed idiot as she gaped around at the stone, still fitted together after all this time, so obviously manmade and old. Really freakn' old.

And I'm exploring it! As she walked, her feet scuffed the dirt and silt of time lining the floor. It wasn't hard to note the passage of four-legged denizens. Branches, leaves, even the scattering of small bones lined the passage.

Treading carefully, her flashlight beam darting ahead for signs of danger – hole in the floor, vicious animal, Indiana Jones style trap – she almost held her breath in the silent, tomblike tunnel. She forgot to count her paces as she walked, ignoring the side passages for the moment, still retaining enough wits to know how easily she could get lost in the mazelike structure. Eventually, though, she did hit an intersection that forced her to choose – left or right?

She gnawed her lip as she peered back behind her, the small square of daylight so far away. It finally penetrated her thick skull that she'd not told the others where she went. What if she fell down a hole? Or injured herself?

And what if I turn back and can't return? Will I forever regret not taking a chance?

Spine straightening, she made her decision. She would go on, but take precautions. However, leaving to tell someone where she roamed would probably result in her getting grounded. They should figure it out, though, her conscience argued, given the hole she'd created in the vines, but once inside, it could get confusing, especially once she chose a direction. They'd need a sign to know which way to follow.

Holding the flashlight between her teeth, she penned a quick note, one word really, right with an arrow – just in case. She tore it free and tucked it in the seam of the rock wall. There. Now they could follow her trail.

Then she went exploring.

*

Kendrick noted Ruth wandering around the ruins, and while he kept her within sight for the most part, he also gave her space. More for his peace of mind as he tried to figure out how to deal with her. He couldn't just do as his mother suggested. This was his mate. A delicate human girl who gently rebuffed his advances even as her body betrayed her interest. While his wolf seemed to think he should swoop in and claim her, knowing the bond didn't affect her, he feared frightening her off, especially since he wasn't the only one working to gain her affection.

Snapping off a bough, Ruth a speck of motion at the corner of his eye, Kendrick had to turn his back on her a moment as he hefted the pieces he'd harvested and brought them back to the center of camp. Joel, his own arms laden, followed him.

"I think she really doesn't get it," Joel admitted as he dumped his load with a noisy number of thumps.

"Get what?" Kendrick asked, tossing a quick glance at Ruth to see her bending over to pluck something. Reassured, he knelt and cleared an area, surprised at the lack of signs of previous campfires given the location appeared perfect. A result of a jungle determined to keep what was hers pristine, or had they inadvertently stumbled somewhere they shouldn't? Ancient burial ground? Fire ant nest? Unsuspecting ambush site? Sniffing the air, Kendrick still noted nothing out of place. All the odors he'd expect appeared – lush foliage, spore, pollen, the decay of fallen plant life. There was no special hush, or urge to stay quiet. The birds sang. Bugs whirred. In the near distance, animals conversed.

"What do you think? I've done every nice thing I can think of short of asking her outright—"

"Or bending her over a log," Kendrick muttered, his favorite fantasy slipping out before he could stop it.

"And she acts … I don't know what to call it. One minute she's blushing. The next, I can smell her desire. Then she's getting annoyed with me and when she realizes it, she's back to the blushing. What the hell am I doing wrong?"

"Maybe we're being too subtle."

"Me, subtle? I've tried every pick-up line I know plus some new ones and she's still not biting? Do you know she asked me if I had a girlfriend?"

"She did? She didn't ask me that."

"As if I'd disrespect any woman of mine that way."

"Should have given her a sound tongue lashing."

"I wish." Joel sighed. "Maybe this whole human thing is just doomed before it starts. If I wasn't worried about leaving the camp undermanned, I'd go for a run."

"You and me both. But my gut says we're close, so no taking off. We stick together."

"This totally blows."

"Then it's time we put an end to it," Kendrick announced.

"What are you suggesting?"

"Bend her over and take her."

"This is my mate we're talking about."

"Our mate. And I'm beginning to think she won't cave until we show her the way. Or the light. The big O."

Joel bristled. "She's not some one-night-stand whore. I can't just seduce her. Although, I'd really, *really* like to. Why did she have to be a human? A normal shifter girl would have jumped us by now."

"You guys are pathetic," Peter tossed their way. "Why are you sneaking around the issue? She's your mate. Man up and claim her sweet ass."

"Don't talk about her like that." Joel's gruff threat saw him nose to nose with the tanned wolf.

Peter backed away, hands raised. "Whoa. No disrespect meant. We know she's already claimed, bite or not. Just saying, why are you treating her so different? She's your mate. Fuck her and bite her. Simple."

"That's what my mother said, more or less," Kendrick grumbled.

"She's human, though," Joel argued. "Which means we can't be like we usually would."

"She's a woman who is shy, self-conscious, and worried about her sister."

"Shy? Have you seen her go toe-to-toe with me?" Kendrick couldn't mask his incredulity.

"That's because you purposely get her mad. I don't blame you, it's a hot look."

Before he knew it, Kendrick rubbed his knuckles and Peter sat on his ass on the ground, a look of surprise on his face.

"Bloody freakn' hell," he yelled. "Would you just fuck her already? This is getting ridiculous."

"She hasn't chosen one of us yet. Once she does, we'll take turns claiming her."

Fernando chuckled. "One at a time? Chickens."

"As if you'd share your woman with another guy." Kendrick sneered at their suave group member. He'd not forgotten how the Latino hovered around his woman, constantly propositioning her.

"A man, he comes once. A woman can come so many times she'll literally pass out from pleasure. There is something immensely exciting about watching as someone you trust fucks a sweet and wet pussy. Maybe sucking on her tits while you finger her, her whole body tense and shivering as she takes a cock deep. But there's nothing wilder than sandwiching her, seesawing your dick up her ass while another takes her pie. It's like the never-ending orgasm for everyone."

"So you've done this?"

"In my college days I did a lot of things. And I can tell you, watching another guy do a girl? It's intense. Even before you get into the mix, you get excited as you imagine doing stuff to her while she's getting her sweet pussy filled. Or watching her give some excellent head. Then, when you join in, her cries, her scent, her excitement is overwhelming. With the mate bond, I'd imagine it will be even more intense than usual, lucky bastards." Fernando sounded truly wistful of their luck.

Eyes flicking to Joel, Kendrick wondered. What would he think if he saw Joel between her thighs? Would he want to tear him off? Or would it excite him enough to join in? Tag-teaming meant one at a time, something he could handle and did while drunk a time or two, usually with more girls, though. But with one woman, they'd truly end up close, too close for his comfort? Or would it excite him? Two shafts buried inside her, moving in alternate strokes, connected on such an intimate level. Kendrick couldn't quite imagine it.

Neither could his buddy. "I don't think so," Joel muttered. "That's taking trust and friendship a little too far. Besides, if you think I put you to shame now, you'll want to hide in a corner for sure since I'm long enough to touch her tonsils."

Kendrick snorted. Then outright laughed. "Whatever. As I recall, mine's almost as long, but thicker. And we all know what the ladies really prefer.

"Long."

"Fat."

"Long."

"Fat."

Fernando stepped between their glaring countenances. "While I would love to hear the outcome of this debate, it occurs to me that the reason for this discussion has been out of sight for a while. Given we're looking for women, abducted out of the blue, it might make sense for at least one of us to be with her if she's going exploring."

"You'd better not be trying to volunteer yourself," Kendrick growled. Jealousy saw a threat in every overture concerning Ruth.

"You know what? I'm done reasoning with you idiots. Peter is right. Just fuck her already. Both of you. Then maybe you'll get some blood back to your brains and start thinking with them again."

"Where is she?" Joel asked, a frown between his brows. "He is right. She's been gone a while."

Kendrick took a step in the direction he'd last seen her in, not worried yet, given her penchant to wander, that and the fact the sun still shone, but he didn't like her absence either. "I don't smell anything."

"Yeah, because your sense of smell is so foolproof against a tribe of jaguars that's managed to exist undiscovered for centuries." Joel rolled his eyes.

"Not so undiscovered if we know about them."

"We'll argue the theories later. I'm going to look for her."

Like hell. "Nope. I will. As my second, I place you in charge of the camp and its setup until I get back."

"Dick."

"That's *thick dick* to you." Kendrick grabbed his crotch and leered while dodging a jab from his friend.

"Oh, game on, dude. Don't be so sure you've won yet."

But this wasn't a game. *This is my life. My future. My woman.*

Best friend or not, Kendrick wouldn't necessarily play by the rules. And he was done being Mr. Patient. It was time he made a few things clear to Ruth. Forget subtle. Time he took her by storm, passionate storm.

Now, if only he could find her. It didn't take him long to pick up her trail, and while he didn't sense any danger, her disappearance into the ruins didn't reassure. Once inside, he moved faster, not liking how the stone seemed to press in all around him.

He did pause to smile at her little note tucked in the stone. How considerate of her to think to give him a hand. As if he needed it. He could follow her scent anywhere.

A good thing too, given the twists and turns, not all paths still having a paper trail, some rodent-sized denizens having already stolen the notes for their nests.

When he came across her, he slowed and shook his head. She didn't even look his way so engrossed was she with the wall. Face smudged with dirt, her hands trailing over the rock, he almost laughed at her. Enraptured, she never noticed him sneaking up behind her. Inhaling her scent. Getting hard. Hungering. Wanting.

Slow down. He needed to take it carefully so as to not frighten her with his more animalistic side. But he couldn't resist making her jump.

*

"You shouldn't wander off alone. It's dangerous."

Kendrick's words startled her from her contemplation of the grooves on the wall. Whirling, Ruth clasped a hand to her chest.

"Must you sneak?" Lost in the marvel of her discovery, she never heard him arrive. But she should have expected it, given his new goal in life involved sticking to her like glue.

"I don't sneak. I skulk. I am a professional skulker, best in my family." A wild boast that made her smile and giggle. It was then he hit her with it. His first genuine smile. Not just any smile, but an intimate grin, just for her.

Hear that? The silence. It was the sound of her heart stopping in shock. God, she'd thought him cute before, but a truly happy Kendrick, wearing a sexy, teasing grin, was enough to make her knees weak. It took all of her control not to throw herself at him.

"Skulking is for animals."

"Yeah. That sounds about right." He inched closer, his lips still curved so sexily.

Flustered, she gave him her back and returned to examining the markings on the wall. "I found some neat carvings."

"Oh really?" His query came from right behind her.

"They're fascinating."

"Tell me more." His low rumble sent a shiver down her spine. She spent less time concentrating on the faded images and more time noticing how close he stood. Closer. Touching. He pressed against her back, one arm curling possessively around her waist, his hand splaying as his groin molded itself to her backside. No mistaking the hard bulge there.

She swallowed. "More? More what?"

"What's so interesting, honey?" he murmured against the back of her neck.

Interesting? His lips. Him. The way his hand slowly slid lower. His mouth and its soft nibbles. None were answers she could utter. "Um. Eh." Words completely fled her mind as his breath feathered over her skin. Tingling, her blood heating, she froze, unsure what to do. What did he intend? Was she ready? What about Joel?

Was she ready to make a choice? Ready to possibly deal with the fact not all was as it seemed? That perhaps she was just the finish line to a competition?

Alone for the first time in days, with a man who made her panties soak and her heart stutter, did she care?

This is what I was waiting for. One of them to make a move.

Kendrick pressed closer, every inch of him molding to her back, his lips brushing the skin of her nape. Shivers ran through her, and then a small moan as he kissed a sensitive spot, then licked it.

"Wh-what are you doing?" she managed to whisper.

"What I've been dying to do for days," he admitted before spinning her around and plastering his mouth to hers. About freakn' time.

Oh, the pleasurable shock of it. Hard, yet somehow tender, he slanted his lips over hers, kissing her with a hunger she matched. How oddly delightful to have to tilt her face up to reach his lips. To have her body stand straight and tall, leaning into his, all the parts lining up perfectly.

He nipped her lower lip and she gasped, pulling back a bit. His eyes, flashing orbs in the shadowy room, appeared wild and unnatural.

She pulled out of his embrace and took a step back. "Your eyes? What's wrong with them?"

He blinked and the strange reflection of light disappeared. "What do you mean?"

"Nothing. I—" She leaned back against the wall behind her, the cool stone inviting to her feverish skin. However, she did find it perturbing the rock moved with an ominous grinding sound.

Before she could scream, she hit the floor, a big body atop hers. Even protected behind her shield of flesh, she heard and felt the impact of rocks caving in, perhaps not directly on them, but definitely not far.

It took too long in her mind for the chaos to stop. Then, even longer for Kendrick to react.

"Kendrick." She wiggled under him. "Kendrick? Are you all right? Speak to me." She bucked, trying to dislodge him. *Oh God, please don't tell me he's dead.*

He got heavier, and his rough jaw rubbed against her cheek as she thrashed under his weight. "Do that again, honey."

"What?"

Something hard pressed against the vee of her thighs as he made his meaning clear. A pity she didn't own cheeks like Rudolph's nose, she'd have lit that tunnel right up.

"What happened?" she asked. Dumb question perhaps, but she needed to say something other than, 'rub me again.'

"Nature took back the passageway behind us." He didn't seem too bothered.

"Isn't that bad?"

"The guys will get us out."

"Without machinery?"

"There's probably more than one way into this place."

"So shouldn't we probably start looking?"

A heavy sigh left him. "I guess we can't stay like this." Off he rolled, the pitter patter of rocks and dirt raining off him. Blinking in the darkness, blind without her flashlight, she blamed dumb luck for his hand locating hers and pulling her to her feet. She wobbled, but instead of reaching for a wall – given how well that turned out before – she reached for him. Her fingers encountered the fabric of his shirt, and she clung to it, terrified of losing him in the dark.

As if sensing her fear, he murmured, "Don't worry, honey. I'd never leave you. Hold onto me and we'll go somewhere a little less dusty."

Ah yes, the dust, what a nice reminder to her lungs that took that moment to suddenly protest the debris she kept inhaling.

Coughing and gagging in a most delicate fashion – *blerg, erk, spit* – Kendrick nonetheless kept a hold of her hand and guided her away from the scene of disaster. How he could move in the dark with such surety she couldn't figure out, but thanked his uncanny skill as they encountered no walls, pits, or other things that would have hurt. He also kept her spirits up, keeping at bay her fear they were trapped.

"So tell me about yourself. I'm assuming you don't have a boyfriend."

She immediately bristled. "Why, because I'm fat?"

"You're not fat."

"Then why do you assume I'm single?"

"Because no man in his right mind would let his woman go gallivanting off to the jungle by herself with a group of strangers."

"Maybe you wouldn't, but not all men are threatened by a strong woman."

"There's threatened and there's the fact a true lover would have joined his girlfriend to keep her safe, not just physically, but emotionally."

A beautiful sentiment, but Ruth didn't know men like that. Most thought only of themselves first. "Would you have taken time off to go on a harebrained chase, as I believed you called it at one point?"

"I'd move heaven and earth if that's what my mate needed for her happiness."

She snickered. "Mate? Nice term."

"Well, you have to admit, girlfriend sounds kind of high schoolish, and wife requires a whole lot of pomp and ritual. And now that you've skirted the original question, back to it. Are you single?"

"Yes. I find between my internship and classes, not to mention my family, I don't have much time to meet guys. Well, I do, at school that is, but none that interest me. I'll be finished in a year, though, and then maybe I'll get to travel and meet someone." But she couldn't imagine meeting anyone who fired her libido like Kendrick or Joel.

"In case you hadn't noticed, you're already traveling."

"To save my sister."

"Yes, it is a rescue mission, and I'm the first to admit, I never expected to meet such a temptation."

"Oh please. Now you sound just as bad as Joel with one of his cheesy pick-up lines."

A yank of her hand, laced in his, placed her palm against his chest and his rapidly beating heart. "Oh, now you've wounded me. Comparing my heartfelt admission to his lines of crap."

"Well you asked for it when you lied," she retorted, pulling at her hand, annoyed he'd try to pretend his words were the truth. Temptation indeed.

"Do you really think so little of yourself?"

"I own a mirror and a scale. Back home, that is. I know what they show. I'm not the kind of girl to make men fall over themselves."

"Maybe because you hadn't met the right men. Do you know what I see when I look at you?"

Yes, she wanted to know, even if he skewed the truth.

He didn't wait for her reply. "I see your curves. Voluptuous and absolutely delicious-looking – all your creamy skin, tempting me to taste." She swallowed. "I see the strength you keep hidden, that inner stubborn core that doesn't let you give up." She had that? "I see you fighting your body, refusing to succumb to pleasure because you're not the type to do things lightly or by halves. I see you denying your heart."

"I think you're seeing more to me than actually exists," she said softly.

"I think you don't see enough."

As Kendrick slowed their steps to a stop, she realized she could see grey shadows.

"Hey, there's light," she managed to sputter in a rough voice.

"Light. Air. And a good place for you to sit awhile and catch your breath. Here, have a drink of water."

She saw the dark blur of the canteen he held to her lips and drank, gulping the tepid liquid and letting it soothe her throat. Why she'd not thought to grab hers before wandering in here was just another mark to chalk up on her list of blonde moments.

Refreshed, she peered around with more interest. Her eyes adjusted somewhat to the gloom, and what she saw awed. In a domed-shaped room, the ceiling high overhead, light filtered through the cracks in the stone, slits put in place by time and infiltrated by foliage.

She peeked down to see she sat on some type of stone table, a little dusty, but otherwise fairly free of debris except for one fist-sized chunk of rock, which she hefted. She cast a dubious glance upward.

"Is it safe in here?"

"For the moment. But we might not want to yell too loud."

"Why would we yell?"

Fingers tickled up her side and she squeaked.

"Shhh," he admonished. "What did I say about the noise?" He pushed her knees apart and inserted his body between them.

"What are you doing?" she whispered.

"Keeping you distracted. Is it working?" he asked as his fingers dug into her waist and drew her close.

"Yes. No. Can't you think of something else to do?"

"Else? Like what?"

"Showtunes?"

"I don't sing."

"We could talk."

"Too noisy. And besides, we just did that and you more or less called me a liar."

"I did not."

"Do you believe me when I say you're beautiful?"

"No."

"Then I shall have to show you."

"How?" Was it wrong to hope he kissed her again?

"I think it's time I took what I want."

Her heart pattered. "What would that be?"

She couldn't miss the white gleam of his teeth as he replied, "You know."

A sigh left her. "Actually, I don't. You're very confusing."

"Isn't it obvious I want to kiss you again?"

Yeah, but she couldn't figure out why. She didn't believe his claim he found her beautiful. "Haven't you already won your bet?"

"You think I kissed you because of a wager?" His laughter rang out and she winced as she peered at the ceiling. He quieted, but only to press his lips against the lobe of her ear. "I kissed you because you're driving me absolutely insane, Ruth."

"Insane good or bad?"

"Oh, bad. Definitely bad. I mean, I barely know you, but the things you make me think. They're so freakn' naughty. Would you like me to show you, honey?"

Yes. Now, if only she could talk. Impossible when all she could concentrate on was his warm breathing teasing across her earlobe. His hands tracing circles on her lower back and occasionally cupping her cheeks. His groin pressed against the front of her, hard, insistent, and so unavoidably aroused.

"No answer? Then I'll take that as a yes." He kissed her, and this time, she kept her eyes shut tight, allowing herself to focus only on the intimate joining of their lips. The sweet, moist mesh of their breath.

We should be looking for a way out, not making out. A part of her rational mind tried to get her attention. Her carnal side shoved it in a closet and locked the door. Then it urged her to open her mouth and let Kendrick's tongue in.

Best advice ever.

Sensual, not slobbery. Exciting. He kissed her a la French. Caressed her like a pro. Had her panting and aching. Needing.

When his mouth left hers, she whimpered.

"Hush, little honey. We're not done." His soft endearment went well with his new destination as his lips led the way and traveled the column of her neck, nipping and sucking. Tasting her skin, teeth worrying the flesh, possibly leaving a mark, his mark. For some reason, the thought excited her.

He didn't let her t-shirt stand in the way of his exploration. Up it came, and over her head, leaving her in only a bra. Nope. There went the pink, cottony affair and her nipples puckered as air flowed across them. In the almost dark, Ruth didn't feel the self-consciousness she usually suffered. Didn't worry about her size. Or shape. She just reveled in the exploratory worship of his hands as he cupped and kneaded her small handfuls. He rolled her nipples, each tug and squeeze shooting pleasure down to her pussy.

She let out a small cry when he lowered her back on the table. Her shirt, and somehow his, shed at one point, a thin barrier against the hardness of the dusty stone top. But who cared if she lay in the patina of centuries? With Kendrick's heavy body atop hers, his mouth busy sucking at her nipples, drawing tortured gasps and moans from her, she could have lain on a bed of nails for all she noticed.

Just don't let him stop. Because if he kept lavishing attention on her nipples and rubbing his hand against her crotch, she was going to come.

No. He stopped. *Come back.* Or not. His mouth left a sinuous trail down her rounded tummy, halting only at the barrier of her pants. One quick snap and he'd undone them.

Hot and sweaty wasn't how she wanted him encountering her girl parts orally for the first time. *Am I planning a second already?* She dragged him back up to her mouth, her rapid grab netting her two fistfuls of hair.

"I was about to do something," he growled.

Unable to voice her issue, she mashed her mouth to his, and he forewent further argument, kissing her back just as passionately. But he'd not completely given up on his quest. His hand entered the opening he'd created in her pants, sliding into her panties and then over her slick flesh.

She almost took his tongue off she bucked so hard.

"Oh my sweet, sweet honey. I've been waiting forever it seems to touch you like this."

Her fingers dug into his scalp as her body quivered, so taut with erotic tension, her whole being sitting on the verge of ecstasy. He didn't seem to mind her rough handling, a strength she'd previously tempered with old boyfriends. Not so with Kendrick. Judging by the moan that came out of him, he liked her rough passion. He sucked at her lower lip as he slid a finger into her. She went still, whimpering as she tried to spread her thighs further for him, but failing as her pants prevented her. She pumped her hips as he pressed into her. Her flesh sucked at him eagerly. All of her met his touches with an ardent pleasure. Even her orgasm.

It hit her with the force of a meteor, slamming into her body, shocking the air from her, and sending her consciousness soaring.

To heaven.

*

What had been a near disaster when the tunnel collapsed turned into utter glory. Or so Kendrick thought as Ruth's channel convulsed around his fingers, her climax strong, lusty, and sweet, just like her.

Oh good God, he wanted inside her so bad. He pumped her with his fingers, torturing himself with the sweetness of her release, watching her face as pleasure took her. His free hand went to the buckle of his pants, his cock dying for its turn. But it seemed he wasn't going to get his wish.

"There you are," Joel exclaimed in a patently false, cheerful tone. "So glad to see you're all right. We were so worried when we felt the earth shaking."

Kendrick knew his best friend saw his middle finger extended, which is why the prick flashed him a pair. But Kendrick still won the round when a rudely interrupted Ruth squeaked as she scrambled to cover up. He wanted to tell her not to bother, however, he didn't sense that would go over well.

Human females, especially shy ones, didn't like to gallivant in the nude. Or at the very least, topless. Which he totally didn't get. What was the point of having an Ontario provincial law that allowed women to go boobs bared if no one ever took advantage of it?

Then again, he revised that stance as he saw Joel's hungry eyes watching her perfect little tits jiggle as she shimmied into her shirt, braless. He could see the benefit in covering her from head to toe and hiding her from anyone's view but his own. God, it sucked he had to share.

"We were just taking a break. Poor Ruth got a touch overcome by the dust when the tunnel collapsed."

"Ah, that would explain the mouth to mouth," was Joel's sardonic reply.

"Can we stop talking about this? I'm embarrassed enough as it is," she hissed as she dressed, looking caught between annoyance and embarrassment. Best of all, though, she smelled of desire. Unseen by her, Kendrick raised the fingers he used to pleasure his woman and sucked them, watching how his friend's nostrils flared in jealousy.

Despite not achieving his goal of claiming her, Kendrick knew it was just a matter of time, and not a long time, before he placed his mark. Perhaps even as soon as tonight. How he'd dearly love to end up between her thighs, nothing between them, his cock pounding her hard and fast. *As I bite into her flesh, making her my mate.*

The question was, would Joel be there too?

*

At the first ominous rumble, Joel dropped everything and ran for the ruins. He didn't need to see the cloud of dust puffing out to know part of it collapsed. *With Ruth inside!*

Darting into the tunnel, blinking furiously at the cloud silting in the air, he tried not to panic.

Kendrick's with her. He'll keep her safe. Unless they got flattened by a rock.

Not impossible given the size of some of the chunks he found obliterating their passage. What eased his mind somewhat was he didn't scent blood or hear any cries for help or of pain.

He took this to mean they managed to escape the architectural disaster and took refuge or searched for an exit in an intact portion. Joel loped along the debris-strewn corridors, sniffing for a sign, ignoring those that didn't pertain.

In the end, he heard them before he saw them. Heard her cries and moans of pleasure as Kendrick touched Ruth. *My woman.* His wolf growled. Demanded they stop their pack mate from claiming what was theirs.

Still, Joel didn't go rushing in like a rabid dog when he got close enough to smell her arousal. He crept along like a wraith, and peeked into the dimly lit chamber. For some reason, Fernando's words of earlier came back to haunt him. How would it feel to watch another touch his woman? Pleasure her as he looked on? Ready or not, he was about to find out.

He eased his head around the corner and froze at the tableaux they presented. Kendrick bent shirtless over her, his mouth latched to her breasts, sucking her straining peaks while he kneaded her white skin as she thrashed in bliss.

Joel grabbed himself through his pants, stroking when Kendrick moved down the pale skin of her torso, aiming for the honey between her legs. She halted him and Joel almost groaned aloud in symphony with his friend at being diverted from the prize. But he quickly panted as they kissed and Kendrick slid a hand into her pants, stroking her. His ministrations brought her hips up and increased the pace of her cries.

How Joel wished it was him fingering her, bring her the ecstasy, touching her as she came with a glorious cry that made him shudder all over. God, how he wanted to be a part of that. Then reality hit. Kendrick would claim her if Joel didn't do something. And who knew what would happen then?

Would Joel forever lament the woman he almost had? Would the fever and need for this woman suddenly disappear? Maybe he should let Kendrick claim her and hope the human lost her appeal. *No.* Never. He didn't want that. Not anymore.

Ruth called to him. Entranced him. Beautiful and courageous, a part of him knew that even without the mating fever, she would have drawn him, seduced him. Wolf or not, she seemed to entail everything he imagined a woman should be. And more.

Did he feel any guilt in interrupting? Not one bit.

So when Kendrick mocked him, licking his fingers, taunting him with the knowledge he tasted her honey first, Joel snapped.

He dove on his best friend, his lighter body still managing to take Kendrick's down with sheer momentum and annoyance. He ignored Ruth's surprised shriek for the pleasure of hitting Kendrick. "Mine," he growled, more wolf than man at the moment.

"Mine too," rumbled his best friend.

The answer, share, didn't really penetrate, not when he finally had something to ease his frustration. Smack. Punch. They tussled, careful, though, in their fracas, to avoid rolling into the object of their affection, who didn't try and step in the way. If not busy defending himself, Joel might have laughed at her huffed, "Idiot men."

She got that right. Idiot men in love and still coming to grips with the fact it was with one woman. However, they forgot their differences awful quick when she cried out.

Separating, Joel sprinted in the direction of her scent, Kendrick at his heels. They soon found Ruth, sprawled on the ground rubbing her ankle. Joel dropped to his knees and lifted her foot. "Did you twist it?"

"Yes, but not too hard. Just enough to fall. You know me – two left feet."

"You shouldn't have wandered off," Kendrick chastised.

"I was afraid of getting in the way of your male bonding moment."

"I'm sorry," Joel said, his thumbs rubbing circles on the skin of her ankle.

"Me too."

"I guess I should add me three since I'm beginning to think the fight was about me. Or am I being blonde again?"

"Yes, it's about you, but not your fault." Joel could see his answer confused her more than anything else.

"What's going on with you two? It's like you're both ..." She trailed off and bit her lower lip.

"What?" Kendrick asked. "Like we're what?"

"Nothing."

Joel took a deep breath and said it aloud. "Like we're both trying to seduce you."

"Are you?"

"Yes." Their echoed reply resulted in her breath stopping.

"Ruth? You okay?" Should he give her some first aid, the mouth-to-mouth kind?

"Are you going to say something?" Kendrick stroked her cheek with the pad of his thumb and her lashes fluttered.

"Why?" She said it so softly they almost missed it.

"Because we need you," Kendrick admitted.

"Want you."

"But why?" She truly sounded confused. "Why me? And why both of you? Isn't that—I mean, it's wrong, isn't it?"

"Wrong to who?"

"Everyone. Society. My mother." Ruth made a face.

"Love comes in different shapes, honey."

"Love?" She said the word in a startled voice. "You mean sex."

Kendrick looked like he'd argue, but Joel shook his head. "It's only wrong if you don't want it. Do you? Not want this, that is?"

"I—I don't know. I shouldn't, and yet a part of me does." She seemed embarrassed by her admission. "Maybe it's the dark. Or this jungle."

"Or the fact this is fate?" Kendrick whispered against her temple.

"Fate I sleep with the two of you? That's the corniest line yet." She tittered, yet managed to make it sound wistful.

"Or the truth," Joel murmured, dragging her onto his lap. He threaded his fingers through her hair and brought his mouth down on hers.

At first, her lips moved hesitantly against his, but then Kendrick's face bent close to take the skin at her nape, and oddly enough, the addition relaxed her.

Her mouth softened and Joel took full advantage, plundering her sweet depths, sending his tongue into slide along hers until she clung to him, panting.

"This is crazy," she murmured. "I shouldn't be doing this."

"On the contrary," Kendrick replied. "We should have done this long ago."

"On that I agree," Joel added before diving back in for another taste. Oh, and taste her he did. Her passion, so recently assuaged by his friend, roared back, the scent of her desire surrounding him. Teasing him. The shirt she'd so hastily donned went flying as Kendrick got rid of it. Joel took care of her pants, pushing them down until they went the way of her top and boots. When she would protest, he'd kiss her while Kendrick tweaked something on her body. They made her forget all she'd learned about good girls and morality, and drowned her in sensation.

Worried about chafing her delicate skin, Joel lay on his back and dragged her atop him, his pants the only barrier between them, his shirt left behind in his mad dash to find her. His hands roamed the skin of her back and buttocks, cupping, caressing, occasionally encountering Kendrick also touching. It didn't bother him as he expected. How could it with her excitement driving him mad?

"God, she's so wet," Kendrick murmured in a voice thick with need.

"Let me feel." Joel slid his hand between them, his fingers sliding through her curls to her moist cleft. Mmm, so slick, and despite the fact Kendrick already seesawed a digit, he added his own finger, stretching her tight channel to include one more. So taboo, and yet so right.

"Oh. Oh." Her cries of pleasure grew in pitch.

"Help me roll her," Kendrick growled. Quickly grasping his plan, they flipped her to her back, her head nestled in the hollow of his shoulder, her bottom half denuded and perfect against him. His hands roamed her body, learning every ones of her curves, the spots that made her gasp. When Kendrick bent his head to suck at her breasts, Joel slid his hand to the prize between her thighs. Wet, so wet, he circled her clit with a slick finger, his cock a throbbing presence against her lower back.

"I can't take it anymore," he gasped as her channel pressed on his digits, the flesh quivering, needing something more to fill her.

"That makes two of us. Make that three," Kendrick chuckled as he drew her up against him to kiss, a perfect diversion while Joel quickly unbuckled his pants, letting his cock, so hard for her, spring forth.

Breaking off his kiss, Kendrick rolled Ruth back to face Joel. Her hands flattened against his chest, but she didn't quite kneel – Kendrick held her suspended just over him, probably to spare her knees from the harsh stone floor. Joel was beginning to see the benefits of a partner more and more. In her suspended position over him, he could easily rub his swollen head against her slick clit while his lips captured hers. The sweet moan she emitted was caught by his mouth and the one after as he continued to slide himself against her.

"Fuck it, Joel. I can't keep watching. Ready?"

"Hell yeah." Lifting her just enough to position her over his cock, Kendrick pushed her down on Joel's length. He felt her stretching and enveloping him in her decadent heat, felt her, just about died, and gasped for air.

"Oh God," she moaned.

"That's it, take it honey," Kendrick encouraged.

Poor Joel was beyond speech. The molten heat of her stole all rational thought. Thankfully, Kendrick was there to help him out. With his hands on her hips, he moved her atop Joel, rocked her body so that it took him deep, so deep, Joel wanted to howl. So deep he never wanted it to stop. Back and forth, Ruth slid, a willing passenger of her passion.

And then she was gone.

About to protest, Joel opened his eyes and saw the most erotic sight. Kendrick held her around the hips and thrust into her, but it was Joel's chest she dug her nails into. And then Joel's mouth she kissed as his best friend slammed into her from behind.

The smell of sex and passion permeated the air. Tinged everything in a hazy, erotic rush that made him cheer his friend on silently, his cock heaving and thrusting in time to their strokes.

Then it was his turn again for her to ride his cock, bouncing and gasping as Kendrick twisted her nipples. Up Joel thrust, burying himself to the hilt and grinding, swirling into her as she practically sobbed in pleasure.

Airborne she went again, bent over and crying out as once again Kendrick took possession of her sweet pussy, pounding her soft flesh while Joel reached out to grab her perfectly hard peaks, rolling them between his fingers before leaning up to bite them. She yelped.

"Oh God, I'm right there," Kendrick gasped.

"Fuck her." Joel couldn't believe he said it. But he did, and said it again. "Fuck her hard. I want to hear her scream."

And yell she did as Kendrick bucked wildly into her. Joel would never forget the sight of her climaxing; she was beauty personified. And then that perfection was sliding back onto his cock, her channel quivering with the aftershocks of her orgasm. His dick went wild in the wet heat of her quivering flesh.

With Kendrick's hands guiding, she bobbed up and down Joel's length, bounced hard enough her sweet little tits jiggled and Joel's hips arched up, pushing into her deeper, faster.

Joel reached between their bodies, found her clit, so swollen already. He rolled it between his fingers and drew out the most delicious holler of his name from her as she came again. Holy freakn' hell. He'd never imagined a woman's sex could squeeze him so tight. She milked Joel with the force of her orgasm. Drew his cock into her body, pulsed all around it until with a yell to bring down the ruins, Joel came.

And almost forgot himself. His wolf surged to the forefront. Begged him for a bite. He just about gave in. Sanity prevailed by the barest of threads. Biting meant wounding her. In the jungle. Without a first-aid kit amidst all the possible bacteria their wild locale could bring.

Much as it hurt his gums and made his wolf howl, he abstained. But, he didn't know for how long he'd manage that. Judging by the battle waged on Kendrick's face, they didn't have much time before they lost all control.

He just hoped they could make it to civilization – and a bed – first.

Chapter Eleven

Oh my God. What did I do?

Coming down off her orgasmic high, Ruth let the insanity of what she'd done overwhelm her. She'd just slept with two guys. No, that wasn't accurate. *Slept* sounded too tame. She'd fucked two guys, at the same time.

Never mind she'd enjoyed it – had she completely lost her mind? It was one thing to fantasize about getting naughty with two men, another to act on it – and so totally enjoy it. Enjoyment aside, euphoria fading, reality set in, along with a good dose of shame at her behavior. How could she have done it?

Embarrassed and needing some space – and some clothes – she went to move off of Joel only to have him wrap his arms around her and draw her down to his bare chest.

"Let me go." She pushed at his chest to no avail.

"What's wrong?"

"Nothing." Her tight voice gave her away.

"Why are you so upset? Did we hurt you?" Kendrick asked, his hand stroking her back, his voice laced with concern.

"I'm not upset or hurt." She didn't come close to sounding convincing and her throat got tighter as they tried to comfort her, but guilt at her wantonness wouldn't let her relax.

"Shh, *querida*. It's alright."

"No, it's not." Again, she pushed at his chest.

"Why do you say that?" Kendrick queried, his hand still rubbing circles on her back.

"Good girls don't – don't –" Forget saying it aloud. Her tongue wouldn't let her, not with her shame clogging her throat. What would they think of her? So what if they'd teased and insisted? Sleeping with two guys, best friends, while on a mission to save her sister was wrong. Pleasurable. At times frightening with its intensity. Shocking to a girl raised to believe in one man, one woman. So not done where she came from. So taboo.

"Good girls don't have the time of their life?" Bless Joel, he tried to lighten the situation, but embarrassment nevertheless assailed her.

"Yes. No. Don't you think there's something a little wrong with this picture?" A picture she'd love to have a copy of so she could take it out and look at it and remember, alone, her moment of glory.

"Looks perfectly fine to me," Kendrick drawled.

"Most definitely," Joel agreed. "We could do it again if you'd like, just to make sure."

"Again? With both of you?" she squeaked. Did they not grasp that what they'd just done was the problem?

"Well, I'd prefer to wash off first, but if you're impatient, then I could be persuaded." The fingers on her back tickled lower, and lower. Darn it all if she didn't feel an answering spark, despite her embarrassment at her wanton behavior.

"I …" She clamped her lips shut as she realized she didn't know how to answer. In all her wild imaginings, she'd never actually slept with both guys at once. Fantasy was one thing, but reality? So much better. "This doesn't bother you at all?"

"What part?"

"You know. Um, the whole *sharing* thing." Because it sure as hell wigged her out.

"I'll admit, it wasn't my first choice." Joel tempered his reply with a soft kiss.

"Or mine. But hey, a man's got to do what a man's got to do. It's not like we had a choice."

In other words, because she wouldn't choose or they couldn't, they decided to both have a turn with the only girl around. The rest of her climatic euphoria dissipated. How foolish of her to think for even a moment that sex with the two of them meant something more. She'd just helped them scratch an itch.

"Glad I could help," she snapped, pushing off Joel's body and standing. Naked in the gloom, she crossed her arms over her chest as she looked around for her clothes.

"Why does she look angry?" Kendrick whispered.

"I don't know. I thought she enjoyed it."

Her cheeks burned as they spoke. "She's right here. And yes, it was fun. But it won't happen again."

"What? Why not?" Kendrick almost yelled.

"Because it's obvious it only happened because you had no other options available."

"You don't seriously think that, do you?" Joel asked, jumping to his feet, his hands buttoning pants that never even got removed in their haste.

"Oh please, like either of you would have paid me a second glance outside of the jungle. I'm blonde, but not stupid."

"You think we wouldn't have done this if we were anywhere else?" Joel sounded dumbfounded by the idea. Like she'd fall for that.

"You're beautiful." Kendrick sounded so sincere.

"When there's no competition around," she retorted, giving up on her underwear, which were too wet to comfortably put on. She slid on her pants instead, feeling better once they covered her bottom.

"We're attracted to you. And trust me when I say it has nothing to do with you being the only woman. We'll prove it when we leave the jungle."

"Sure you will." Tears blurred her eyes as part of her wanted to believe them, but years of rejection and rude remarks came back to haunt her. "Just like you'd both sleep with the same girl at the same time if you had the choice."

"No, that's something we only did for you."

"Because I wouldn't choose between you. I get it. I do. And it was great, really. Although, I'd appreciate you keeping it to yourselves."

"We don't kiss and tell," Kendrick replied tightly. "But we're also not going to hide the fact you belong to us."

"Belong?" For a moment, her heart pattered in excitement at his dominant claim. "I'm not a possession. I don't *belong* to anyone."

"Of course you don't," Joel soothed. "What he meant to say was, we both have feelings for you, and you can't expect us to hide that fact. The others of our group are going to notice, no matter what, that we've become involved."

"No they won't because this won't happen again. I won't be used."

"We're not using you, dammit!" Kendrick's yell was met with a sifting of dust.

"Shit. We need to get her out of here." Before she could finish hauling her arms through the holes of her shirt, she found herself hustled down dark paths. How they knew the way out when she couldn't see the hand in front of her she couldn't figure out, but eventually, she recognized the square of sunlight when they turned a corner. Breaking free of their hands, she practically ran for the opening, eager to escape not just her gullible shame in letting two men use her body so pleasurably, but her own desperate desire to believe them.

Allowing herself for one moment to trust them when they said they liked her, wanted her, and expected more from her just couldn't happen. Not if she wanted to keep her sanity. Not if she wanted to keep her heart. A heart she feared she'd already lost, to two men.

Stumbling through the hole, Ruth crawled onto the trampled grass only belatedly noticing the bare feet. A pair of very tanned bare feet.

Uh-oh.

*

Ruth's shriek saw Kendrick sprinting the last few yards to the exit. Forget talking to Joel about her rejection and disbelief in their affection. His mate needed him.

With no heed to possible danger, he dove through the opening, Joel right behind him. They sprang to their feet behind Ruth who stood face to face with a tanned male. Immediately, his body bristled and his wolf snarled at the stranger. Sniffing, he took in the aroma of the man eyeing them with a hint of mockery. A cat, or so his wolf claimed with head-tossed disdain.

"Who are you and what do you want?" Kendrick boldly asked.

The golden eyes perusing him didn't even blink, and the stranger did not reply. Did he even speak English?

"I think we've found the Jaguar clan," Joel muttered in a low voice.

"Duh," Kendrick replied, his eyes never leaving those of the warrior before him. But it wasn't the single cat standing benignly with his hands at his side that had his wolf's hackles up. It was the sense of others. Despite the possible danger before him, his eyes moved to peer at the shadows surrounding them, the not so empty dark spaces around the ruins where he could sense others. Felt eyes on him. Not menacing, but not welcoming either.

Ruth, not saying a word – for once – stepped closer to him. Kendrick didn't tuck her under his arm like he wanted, not when he might need both hands free to fight.

From around opposite sides of the building, Liam, Peter, and Fernando came jogging into sight and skidded to a halt. "I see you found our visitor."

"More like he found us," Kendrick muttered, not at all pleased at having gotten caught off guard.

"There are others in the woods," Peter added.

"I thought you were watching," he snapped.

"We were," Liam replied. "One minute nothing, the next minute our camp was surrounded."

Definitely ghosts like their name suggested, especially when out of nowhere the rest of the jaguar clan dropped, a cadre of warriors painted to match the jungle, and more silent than the any predator should be. Having warned his team beforehand, and with strict orders from the council, no one attacked, turned furry, or offered violence. Without a word exchanged, they placed their hands palms open and out to their sides in a gesture of peace. When no one spoke, Kendrick said, "What happened to meeting up at the X on the map?"

A shrug lifted the shoulders of the stranger who'd first confronted him, and in perfect English laced with an accent, he said, "You were taking too long."

So language wouldn't prove a barrier. One small blessing. "We had an unexpected passenger."

"Invited, you mean," the jaguar tribe member replied with an enigmatic smile.

Kendrick didn't like or trust the remark or expression. He tried to shove down his misgivings and stick to the mission. "We've come for the girls as arranged."

"The girls are already spoken for." The tallest of the warriors stepped forward, a beast of a man with long, flowing hair, and striking, mismatched eyes.

"What do you mean spoken for? I was told to retrieve them."

"Plans have changed. You're too late. They stay."

"No one told me of this." Then again, Kendrick hadn't spoken to anyone in days as the thick canopy made their signal intermittent at best.

"Not my problem."

"You can't mean to keep them. They're human."

"If you say so." A hint of mockery curled the cat's lips, his mismatched gaze amused at something.

"I see you've brought us a present. My mate will be overjoyed. She's spoken of her sibling."

"You have news of my sister?" Ruth ignored the safety Joel and Kendrick offered, and stepped forward to confront the large man.

Kendrick would have yanked her back, but a headshake of the first speaker stayed his hand. But only for now. Somehow, he didn't get the impression the warriors meant him harm, a good thing too, considering they were vastly outnumbered – *and I'm no good to Ruth dead.*

The guy with the freaky eyes smiled at Ruth. "I do have news. Good news, I'm sure. She is alive and well. Very well. But anxious to see you."

"Are you the one who sent me the note?"

"All your questions will be answered in due time. Please come with us."

Like hell. Kendrick surged forward to snag Ruth, but a wall of bodies came between them. He pushed at them, snarling. "Get out of my way. Ruth. Get your sweet ass back over here."

His woman, however, didn't reply, and too many hands held him back.

"The female is our concern now, wolf. Thank you for escorting her. You may refresh yourselves and spend the night. But you leave in the morning. We have missives you will take with you to reassure the parents and authorities that the women are quite content with their new husbands and lives."

"Excuse me? Not happening. We're not leaving without seeing them for ourselves," Peter said.

"Kendrick, they're taking Ruth," Joel muttered.

"I see that," he snarled, craning to catch a glimpse of her, but the tall felines stood in his way. "Bring her back."

"She is going to see her sister. It is why she came along with you, correct?"

"Yes."

"Then, fear not, she is getting what she asked for."

Holy shit did Kendrick want to wipe the smirk off the dude's face. "I don't think she meant to do so as a captive."

"Not a captive, but an honored guest. A bride in waiting. She'll be in high demand among our kind."

The claim made his blood run cold. "Over my dead freakn' body. Bring her back now, cat, or else."

"Or else what? You are outnumbered and outclassed, dog. You have no power here."

"Says you. I'm not just going to sit quietly while you kidnap Ruth."

"Why? What is the human to you?" The speaker sounded genuinely curious.

"The human is my mate."

"Our mate," Joel growled.

"And yet bears no mark." The big guy shook his head. "A foolish mistake to bring your unclaimed mate when visiting our lands, a deficit which makes her available. Although, she's not likely to stay that way for long."

"You can't have her. She belongs to us."

"She belongs to whomever claims her," the cat corrected.

"She's not a virgin," Joel blurted. Kendrick almost slapped him until he remembered the legends.

A mocking grin graced the big guy's lips. "Neither was her sister, which I must admit made for a much easier claiming."

"You can't just take her. We're already in the grips of the mating fever. We'll die without her."

"But the question is, would you die for her?"

No hesitation, and emerging in one voice as if synchronized beforehand, he and Joel said, "Yes."

Which was how they eventually found themselves in front of an old dude, straight out of a jungle movie, replete with a feathered headdress, smoking pipe, and dreadlocks.

If I ever get out of this alive, I am sticking to adventures in my own backyard, Kendrick silently swore. Because some shit was too freaky, even for him.

But he came to that conclusion later, much later, after a fight, several concussions, and a strange moment wondering if he'd smoked something better than Gerry Carson's weed in the ninth grade.

Chapter Twelve

Ruth heard mention of her sister by the gorgeous tanned man, and not thinking – yeah, her blondeness overcame her common sense – she stepped into danger. Whisked away from her group – and the safety Joel and Kendrick imparted – she instantly regretted it as bodies, naked but for strips of leather holding minimal scraps of fabric around the hips, herded Ruth much like a dog, not quite touching her, but nonetheless getting her moving in a direction of their choosing.

Disconcerting to say the least, especially given they towered over her, and despite their lack of weaponry, exuded a dangerous air that made her fear not only herself, but also the men she left behind.

What have I done?

On the one hand, she wanted to find her sister and discover what the guy meant when he called Carlie his mate, but on the other hand, hearing Kendrick's annoyed rumble and yell for her to get her ass back made her gnaw her lip in indecision.

She would have liked to reassure him, but when she stopped walking, a nudge in the back, along with a growl more animal than human – despite the origin – got her feet moving again.

Dread mixed with fear formed a ball in her stomach. The further she got from the men she'd come to trust – a trust she should have believed in instead of throwing her insecurities in their faces – the more she questioned the decisions she'd made that brought her to this point. What seemed like a brilliant plan of action a lifetime ago in her apartment now seemed monumentally stupid. *What was I thinking?*

Sure, her intentions were good. Hop on a plane. March for days through a deadly jungle. Find her sister, come home. Naivety, meet stupidity.

The jungle proved harsher than expected. The walk and conditions grueling. She didn't plan on falling for two guys – or more accurately, sleeping with them. And now, to top it off, she'd encountered a strange tribe now taking her God knew where.

I went from a drama and adventure free life to unbelievable peril. It seemed she was determined to continually make bad choices.

They didn't walk for long, thank goodness, but long enough that Ruth had already pictured countless rescues by Kendrick and Joel – swinging in shirtless from a vine, guns blazing, commando style. But she also had time to imagine less pleasant things like the countless ways they died. Her own demise. She'd even imagined her own blurb in the paper – *Young botanist dies in jungle, a victim of her own stupidity.*

Surely, she'd not come this far, experienced so much, though, to have it all end now. She needed to believe everything would turn out right in the end. So she stuck to her favorite fantasy as she walked in silence, the one involving a rescue and subsequent thank you to the heroes – funny how that scenario where she thanked them both on her knees didn't seem wrong despite her earlier freak out. The optimism didn't last. She'd partly written her own eulogy when she stumbled. Something in the air prickling her senses.

A lithe figure dropped from a tree ahead of her party, landing with knees bent in a crouch. Blonde hair whipped back from a familiar face.

Ruth gaped at the lean features she knew as well as her own. "Carlie?"

"Ruth!" The woman who looked like her sister, and yet didn't, flung her arms around Ruth. Despite her appearance, Ruth would recognize that hug anywhere, and she sobbed as she clutched her sibling, shedding tears of relief.

"OhmyGodIthoughtyouweredead," she babbled, the words running together as she clutched Carlie in a death grip.

"Not dead. Far from it. What on earth possessed you to come after me, though?" her sister chided, releasing Ruth to hold her at arm's length.

Sniffling, Ruth took stock of her sister. A vastly changed sister. "What happened to you? You look *different*."

"What do you mean?" Carlie asked with a nervous laugh.

"Well for starters, your hair." Both of them sported wildly wavy blonde locks since birth, Carlie's even more so than Ruth's, or had. Carlie's hair now hung in a sleek wave halfway down her back, the gold of it somehow darker than before, while her eyes – they still shone blue, and yet, something glinted in their depths.

"Do you like it?" Carlie swung her hair in a silken wave.

"I do, but how did you get it to go straight?"

"Nothing. Weird, huh? I guess the jungle didn't like my curls." Carlie made a face. "But who cares, you still haven't told me why you're out here. It's dangerous."

"No kidding. As to why? Hello? Looking at her." A crushing hug had Ruth tearing up again.

"Crazy fool. I am glad to see you, though, even if you're nuts."

"I had to come," Ruth said through her sniffles. "No one knew where you were or what happened. And the local police wouldn't tell me anything."

"Yeah. Sorry about that. With everything that happened, I didn't have a chance to send you a proper message and tell you everything was fine."

"Fine? Fine? How is everything fine? You disappeared without a trace. You and those other girls. We didn't know if you were dead, or a sex slave, or some kind of sacrifice to King Kong." Ruth might have lost control a bit there, but after the anxiety she'd suffered, she couldn't help it given Carlie's almost blasé attitude.

"It's worse than that. I'm married." Carlie smiled brightly, but Ruth, worried for so long, didn't care. She snapped at her sister's flippant reply.

"Married? Married! To who? You were kidnapped from your damned bed, what, two weeks ago?"

"Has it been that long?"

"It has. Two weeks of Mom crying. Me freaking out. Everyone wondering. We've been worried sick about you, and you tell me you're married. What the hell happened?"

Carlie winced. "It's a long story."

"I'm listening." And tapping her foot. And crossing her arms. Somehow, this reunion wasn't following any path Ruth expected.

"Well you see, Acat and Chaob, my, um, husbands, spotted me in the jungle and fell in love with me. Kind of."

"So they kidnapped you?"

"Er. Um. It's complicated."

"I walked for ten days in the Goddamn jungle. I think I can handle an explanation."

"Now, I don't want you to freak out."

"Been there. Done that."

"My mates are special."

"I'll betcha they are. So special they can't just ask a girl out on a date, but steal her and worry her family sick."

"They had their reasons."

"Good ones I hope."

"In their minds they are. It's because of their traditions, you see."

"Whose tradition?" Ruth wanted to shake her sister at her slow and inadequate responses.

"The Moon Ghost Jaguars."

Nothing like having confirmation of something she knew. "Aha. I was right. You were kidnapped by them."

Carlie nodded her head. "Although, at first, I didn't know. I've only really gotten answers to most of my questions recently. Suffice it to say, there's a lot we don't know about them."

"You think?" Ruth couldn't help the sarcastic retort.

"Yeah, and unless you'd like to discover more of it first hand, you should leave right now."

"Excuse me?"

"You heard me. Leave now before you end up accidentally hitched to a pair of men. These guys escorting us are all part of the tribe and the part about them stealing women and making them their brides? Totally true. I'm a prime example. And if we don't get you out of here—"

"Hold on a second and back up. What do you mean accidentally hitched to a pair of men? I am not getting hooked up with one man, let alone two. Well, not again at any rate."

Carlie's eyes went wide. "What did you do?"

"Long story. I'll explain on our trip back, right after you tell me how come you're not freaking out more that some dudes thought they were going to kidnap you and force you to stay married to them."

"I'm not going back quite yet."

Ruth dug her heels in and stopped walking. "What do you mean you're not coming back? Of course you are."

"Eventually. But first there's some stuff I need to do here."

"Stuff. What stuff? Hold on a second. You're not actually taking this whole marriage thing seriously, are you?"

"No. Yes. Like I said, it's complicated."

"Carlie. You can't stay here. You don't belong here."

"I disagree." A tall warrior with one blue eye and one golden stepped forth. Dressed in only a small loincloth, he gave new meaning to the term ripped. But no matter how good-looking, he couldn't hold a candle to Kendrick and Joel.

"Who is that?" Ruth asked.

With a glare to freeze even the most hot-blooded of creatures, Carlie planted her hands on her hips. "Ruth, meet my soon-to-be ex-husband, Acat. And this is my other pain in the ass, Chaob."

"A pleasure to meet the sister of our mate. And soon to be a true sister of the tribe." The tall guy tilted his head in her direction.

"Not happening, Acat," Carlie snarled.

"The choice is not yours to make, *datura*."

"That's what you think," Carlie replied a tad too sweetly. "You will let my sister leave before your warriors start fighting over who gets to keep her."

"Keep me?" Ruth squeaked.

"A challenge has already been issued."

"By who?" Carlie demanded. "She just got here."

"Why not ask your sister? It seems she was busy on her travels here."

Carlie whirled on Ruth. "Who did you come with?"

"A bunch of guys. Why?"

"Did you notice anything strange about them?"

"Strange how? I don't know what you mean. Can you tell me what's going on?"

"She has already said too much," growled the big dude with the mismatched eyes. "Chaob. You know what to do."

Before Ruth could figure out what the hell was going on, her sister jumped in front of her and yelled, "Run, Ruth!"

Run where? Not that it mattered. A sprinkle of dust in the air, the fine particles caught by the beams of moonlight filtering through the treetops, dusted her sister's skin and she slumped into the arms of her husband. Unable to hold her breath in time, Ruth joined her a moment later.

Chapter Thirteen

Regaining consciousness on the ground wasn't one of his most noble moments, especially when Joel recalled how he arrived there. The bloody jaguar tribe, not so much the mighty heroes he'd imagined them, took them on, and won dammit, mostly because one of the golden-eyed cats, through gritted teeth while strangling Joel in a neck hold said, "You idiot, you're going to need your strength if you wish to win back your woman. Just lie still and let me knock you out."

Give up? What madness was that? Since when did he and his best bud calculate odds? Although, noting only he and Kendrick remained standing against the warriors – warriors, he might add, who still outnumbered them three to one – Joel sighed and finally gave in. He wouldn't do Ruth much good dead, and besides, if they wanted him unconscious and not dead then it meant perhaps things could still turn out all right.

Of course, it seemed the sedative the golden-eyed bastard gave him came in more than one dose. Given the lingering throb in his jaw, he had to wonder how long he'd spent passed out. Hours? Somehow, it felt longer than that. Several days? Days of other people in charge of his woman!

The thought didn't sit well with Joel, or his wolf. He sprang to his feet, ready to fight, his furry side wide awake and pacing. Tension oozed from every inch of him. *If they've harmed her, greater numbers or not, I will tear them apart. Feast on their marrow. Kill—*

"At ease, pup. The female is safe." Joel swung his head around to see an odd sight. He shook his head, certain he saw wrong, but no, the old fellow dressed in cutoff jeans, a feathered headdress, sporting an iPod on a leather thong strung with claws and bones, face painted in patterned swirls, still sat smoking a pipe in front of him. No rabbit. No caterpillar. Joel had not turned into some freakn' Alice – Cooper, of course – in a messed up version of Wonderland.

Damn, they must have hit me hard. He shook his head and let his gaze rove the rest of the hut – bare but for some wooden stools, an ash-filled fire pit, and some mats. He returned his attention to the old man, puffing away serenely on his pipe.

"Where is Ruth? I want to see her."

"She is still sleeping off the effects of the slumbering dust. Rest assured she is fine. Her sister wouldn't let anything happen to her. She's feisty, that one. She'll give the tribe strong sons."

Pinching the bridge of his nose, Joel counted to ten, a technique he learned a long time ago when dealing with his father in his less than rational moments – a.k.a. drunker than a skunk on fermented berries they'd forgotten in the woods when he and Kendrick went through their wine making stage. At only fifteen, Joel didn't escape the wrath of Kendrick's mother. She'd not skimped on her informally adopted son. Sigh. He did love that woman. Calmer for the memory, he said, "So let me get this straight. Ruth is safe along with her sister. And the other girls, I assume, as well?"

"Yes. It seems my son and his friends felt the mating call while out hunting and took action. I'll admit it was unusual for so many fated brides to appear at once, and when the spirits told me that the sister needed to journey here too—"

"Wait a second. You sent Ruth the note to come in the jungle with that map."

"Of course. The spirits told me—"

"Your spirits are on crack. You should have never involved Ruth. You could have just sent us the map."

"I did, via the woman. Whom you've delivered. Thank you."

"Thank you?" Forget counting to ten. "You used us! This was never a rescue operation."

The old guy shrugged as he took a long draw from his pipe. He blew out a perfect ring. "Even I cannot fight the will of the gods. Fate chose those women as brides. Unfortunately, it drew too much attention. Rest assured, you didn't come for nothing. All the brides will be sending messages to their families and friends, enough to placate their sensibilities and human authorities."

"You are going to use us as messengers?" Joel didn't bother to curb his disgust. "You do realize we won't be able to just take your word the women are happy."

"I never expected you to. As you slept, your friend spoke with each of the women, enough to reassure him that they are not prisoners and can leave at any time. Given their new status in the tribe, though, they've just elected to stay here as they learn more about the life they've chosen."

"I can't believe those women all just agreed to get mated as you claimed."

"Yes, it is unusual to see so many arrive at once, but a great blessing. In a large bridal raid like that there is always the slim chance one of the girls will reject the mating claim. Rare, but it happens."

"What happens then?" Joel asked, curious despite himself.

"In such a case, we would have returned her."

"Returned her? Dude, you shouldn't be taking women in the first place."

"Tell that to our gods."

Someone save him from religious whack jobs. He counted to three and gave up. "You know how nuts that sounds, right?"

"No crazier than men who can turn into jaguars or wolves. Who are you to say the gods don't exist? Perhaps it is simply you who is not listening or looking in the right places."

What the hell was in buddy's freakn' pipe? "I am not discussing theology with a pot head."

"Ah, cannabis. Such a mellow-flavored pleasure, but so tame. I have better stuff for later if you prefer."

"No thanks. Back to Ruth, if you please. Where is she? And where's the rest of my group?"

"Three of your companions are still at the ruins, guests of the warriors left behind. As for your friend, he is preparing himself as we speak for the upcoming battle."

"What battle?" Joel would dearly love to know what the hell went on. He'd also like to know what the somber drumming meant. In the movies, when the jungle beat began, it meant bad shit was going down.

"Did you not claim the human as yours?"

"Yes. We just haven't marked her yet."

"And you won't until you prove your worthiness."

"Prove my what? We have to fight to get her back?"

"Battle for the honor of becoming her mate. Lucky you, the scent of your wolf is heavy upon her, yours and the other one. But still, there are those challenging your place as suitor for the female."

"She's mine." The claim emerged in a low, possessive growl.

"Then prove it. Fight. If the gods deem you worthy, you and your friend shall win. If not …"

"So if we win, we get Ruth back?"

"Yes. The question is, do you wish to claim her as a human, or take a chance with fate and make her into something more?" The old man's eyes narrowed as he pulled on his pipe then blew the smoke out his nose, the lazy patterns swirling in the air.

Joel resisted an urge to fan himself to avoid the fumes. What was the old dude implying? "What do you mean *more*?"

The old guy smiled, a secretive smile Joel didn't trust at all. He spread his gnarled fingers. "Have you ever heard the true story of our tribe?"

"Of course. All shifters know of you."

"Yes, I heard the version your friend told. Not entirely accurate, and given the lateness of the day, I can't regale you with the entire legend. But suffice it to say, a long time ago, one of the clan did a very bad thing. Two men, lusting after a human girl, caused her death. Beloved of the gods, they cursed us and declared that henceforth, we would no longer birth females to continue our line. Oh no, we would have to pay for them. We would have to work hard to earn riches and show our appreciation for the female. But that wasn't all. Because it was jealousy that killed in the first place, so would all matings be done in pairs, forcing us to share. However, human females are fragile things; many were scared by our savageness. Others were unable to handle the sexual hunger of one, let alone two males in their prime. And there were too few females who called to us. So it was decided only the most worthy could mate. If fate agreed and they were blessed by the gods, they prevailed in a fight for the right to claim a mate. But before they laid their final mark, unto the lucky bride was the gift of the animal bestowed."

Head muddled because of his injuries, or the cloud of smoke, Joel couldn't figure out what buddy intended with his tall tale. "Is this story going somewhere? Because if I'm going to fight, I'd like to get a drink and some food in me first." Not that he felt weak. Odd. Perhaps the smoke chugging from the pipe was better than weed.

"I am almost done, pup. Listen, because here is the part I think you'll find most intriguing. The part you didn't grasp. Unto the lucky bride, via means of a potion blessed by the gods and a pair of bites by true mates, the chosen female can undergo a transformation. She can *become*."

"Are you saying what I think you're saying?"

"Human to jaguar, in our case. Human to wolf, I would assume, in yours."

"Impossible." But tempting. Oh so freakn' tempting. What if Ruth could become a wolf? Then she too would feel the mating urge. She could truly mark him and love him and never let him go.

"Not impossible when you follow the way of the gods and our ancestors. All of our mates undergo the ritual and *become*."

"You mean Ruth could end up like me, a wolf?" The old man nodded. "Sounds too good to be true." And an answer to his dilemma. No longer human, she would, once claimed, belong to him forever. His own thoughts froze him. *Do I have the right to take her humanity from her in order to give her my trust?* He could rationalize changing her would make her better. Better for him. The thought bothered him. Surely his reason for doing it wasn't just about making sure she didn't abandon him. As a shifter, she'd enjoy better health, and healing. And lead a life of secrets and more violence than she was probably used to. He needed to find out more. Why did it sound too easy? There had to be a catch, else why had he never heard of it? "So what's the gimmick? Does it hurt?"

"Very much for the several days it takes to adapt the body for the change."

He didn't like that. He frowned. "And then?"

"If she survives, she changes."

"What do you mean *if she survives*?"

The old guy shrugged. "The gods do not think everyone is worthy just because some warriors choose a girl."

"How many die?"

The old guy puffed his pipe instead of answering.

"So I'm just supposed to take a chance with her life?" Could he dare take the chance he'd poison her because of his insecurities? Some things weren't worth the price. "No thank you."

"Excuse me?"

"No. I don't want you to do it. Not if there's a possibility she could die."

"Fascinating." The old guy leaned back in his seat and puffed.

"What's so interesting about the fact I care enough about her to love her as she is, human and all?"

"Because your friend said the same thing."

"He did?" For some reason, the knowledge warmed Joel. No matter what happened with Ruth, he wouldn't be alone.

"He did, and while I'd love to discuss this more, we've spoken too long. You need to get ready. You slept much longer than your friend."

"I always knew he had a thicker skull."

"If you'll follow Chaob, he'll take you to your friend and explain the rules of the fight. It's been most interesting speaking with you."

"You too, gramps." Joel realized he *did* enjoy the conversation. Odd, at times cryptic, and yet enlightening in the extreme. Not the information about the jaguars, but his own revelation. *I love Ruth. And because I do, I'm going to have to believe in that, and once I get her to admit she loves me back, trust that things will work out. I'll be a good husband, lover, friend, whatever she needs me to be.* He would trust in himself to keep her happy and in his life, not some strange, mystical force.

The golden-eyed warrior arrived from behind a tapestry that hid the way out. "So, dog, are you ready to fight?"

"Anytime, kitty cat. Anytime."

The tanned fellow laughed. "I am Chaob, and it is not me that is challenging you for the female."

"Pity."

"Yes, because my cousin is much bigger. Not quite as big as Acat, but close."

"And Acat is?"

"Carlie's other mate."

"Other, as in two?"

"Did you not listen to our elder?"

"Yeah, but it still takes some getting used to."

"And yet you are destined to share your female with another."

Did everyone have to keep pointing that out? "Yeah. What of it?"

"If you win, then once you claim the female, we shall be related by marriage."

"You're the other fellow Carlie is mated to."

A nod answered him.

"Let me ask you something. The whole changed by a god thing. Did you do that to Carlie? Is Ruth's sister one of you now?"

"Oh, she is most definitely jaguar, and strong."

"Weren't you scared she'd die?"

"Warriors fear nothing."

Joel snorted.

His guide grinned. "Okay, yes, we did worry a little, but she has such a strong spirit we couldn't see her not pleasing the gods."

"I gotta ask, how does a guy, who is obviously well educated, believe in this shit about gods and stuff?"

"Why not? Science cannot explain how we carry the spirit of an animal within us. Doctors cannot tell us why some females can tap into the creature and others can't. And no one can fight the magic or fate that draws certain people together in a bond so close that nothing can sunder it."

"If it can't be sundered, then why do I have to fight for her?"

The white smile grew wider. "Sometimes the jealous need convincing, and because it's fun."

"Fun, he says. Killing other—"

"Not killing, fighting to submission. We're not completely stuck in the Stone Age, you know."

"Says the guy who kidnapped a girl instead of using online dating."

Again, the tanned fellow grinned. "When they come up with a way for us to sniff the prospective ladies, then perhaps we'll change our ways. Until then, why mess with tradition? We're here, by the way," Chaob announced as they arrived at a hut guarded by two warriors. "I wish you luck, wolf. I think I would enjoy having you as a brother."

"You don't seem too bad for a cat," Joel replied, returning the clap to the shoulder. He ducked into the hut and found Kendrick pacing.

"About time you got here."

"Well, hello to you too."

"Did they tell you what we have to do?"

"I can't believe we have to fight to keep our woman. We should have marked her when we had the chance." Joel regretted that lapse. Spotting a jug, he sniffed the fresh, clean scent of water; a small sip and he felt fairly confident it was untainted.

"Yeah, well, you know what they say about hindsight."

"Actually, I don't give a crap, but I can tell you this—as soon as I chase the challenging kitties up a freakn' tree, I am not waiting. I'm grabbing our woman and getting out of here, whether her sister wants to come or not. Right after I put my mark on Ruth. Steal my woman indeed." Joel flexed his fingers and rolled his shoulders.

"Now you sound just like my mother." Kendrick grinned.

"Way to pump me up, man, compare me to a girl."

"Toughest girl I know."

"True. What do you think she'd do if she was here?"

"Bake them all a pie."

"Seriously?"

"Laced with a laxative and while they're all moaning on the floor, lecture them on how it's wrong to steal women."

Joel laughed. "Oh my God. I could so see your mom doing that while Naomi kicks them in the balls and yells something about women's lib."

"Damn. We should have brought them with us."

"These cats would have never stood a chance against the women in your family."

"We'll just have to fight as tough and dirty."

"Dirtier. We need to win her back, Kendrick."

"I know. We will, because losing is not an option."

Truer words were never spoken.

And a more serious battle never fought.

Chapter Fourteen

Lashes fluttering, Ruth tried to make sense of the ceiling above her. She didn't recall ever seeing it before, and given its distinctive appearance, thatched with live branches crisscrossing it, she wondered where she found herself. What was the last thing she remembered?

Hot sex with two guys at once. Oh dear God, how she'd prefer to dwell on that flashback rather than the one that saw her blithely walk away with strangers and end up drugged. *I am that too-stupid-to-live girl in the movies.* Maybe she'd blame her actions on the water. Or her bloody sister and her cryptic conversation. Speaking of whom, where was Carlie?

Ruth screamed as the object of her thoughts silently leaned over her, blocking her line of sight. "I see you're awake finally."

"Uh, yeah. Although, I think I'm having a heart attack."

A playful slap on the arm went well with Carlie's, "Wussy. I woke up to a face full of teeth and didn't even squeak."

"Seriously?"

"Yup." Her sister grinned in the shadowy room. "Of course, I can't vouch for the dryness of my panties."

Ruth couldn't help laughing as she shook her head. "Only you would joke at a time like this. Speaking of which, where are we?"

"The bridal hut."

"The what?"

"It's where they take the unmarried women while the men fight to win her hand in marriage."

"How do you know this?"

Carlie rolled her eyes. "Duh. Because this is where I stayed for a few days while Acat and Chaob proved their *worthiness*." She said it wagging her finger in air quotes.

"Do I even want to know what that means?"

"Probably not. Suffice it to say, you're here because you're a single woman who has stumbled upon a tribe of horny men who believe in love at first sight. You'll stay here as they battle it out to see who is worthy to win you as a bride."

"Great. Guess I'll be here a long time then," Ruth grumbled, sitting up.

Carlie tossed her an odd look. "Why would you say that?"

"Um, hello, who is going to fight to win a chubby, Amazon-sized nerd like me?"

"Six challengers, but it would have been a lot more if you hadn't just had sex with those two men you traveled with."

The pounding on her back didn't stop the choking. "Who told you that?" Ruth sputtered.

Her sister, crouched on haunches in front of her, rolled her eyes. "It was kind of obvious. I'm surprised at you. You're usually so vanilla about your fun."

Did everyone know? Ruth wanted to sink into the ground with embarrassment. "I still am. It was a one-time thing."

"If you say so."

"I do say so. Besides, they only did it because they were horny and there was no one else around."

"Oh, Ruthie. I wish you wouldn't put yourself down like that."

Ruth rolled her shoulders. "Like what? I'm not deaf or blind." She'd endured enough taunting in high school and college to have no illusions. "Face it, I'm not dainty. Or girly."

"So you have curves, you also have the most beautiful smile, great hair, a nicer complexion than me, and you're smart."

Ruth patted her sister's hand. "I love you, Carlie, but I'm not sleeping with you."

Her sister snorted. "And that's another thing I love. Your humor. Seriously, though, as usual, you underestimate yourself. Forget the asshats you dated in the past. Right now, we need to focus on the present. And presently, there are two guys down there determined to fight so they can win you back."

"There are?"

"Very. According to my mates, they lost their minds when you were taken away back at the ruins. One of them even gave Acat a black eye. Which he totally deserved," Carlie vehemently stated.

Ruth couldn't wrap her mind around it. "Are you trying to tell me Kendrick and Joel fought for me?"

Carlie nodded. "Chaob said they only lost because of sheer numbers. So, you'll have nothing to worry about. They'll win the fights hands down. It's the part after you won't like."

"What part after? You're not making any sense."

Carlie grabbed her hands. "See, they don't just make you a bride. They change you first."

"Into what, a new outfit?"

"No, into something not human. Or not completely at any rate."

Ruth narrowed her gaze at her sister, peering into her eyes, wishing she had more light to check on her pupils. "When was the last time you drank some water? Show me your tongue?"

"I'm not dehydrated or nuts. The tribe has found a way to change humans."

"I really wish you'd stop talking in riddles."

"That's just it. I'm not. How much plainer do you want me to make it? These men aren't human."

"Uh, yeah, they are. I think you've eaten one too many jungle fruits, sis."

"I wish. I don't know about your guys, they smell different, but mine are cats, jaguars to be exact, and they've changed me to be like them. And they'll change you, too."

Ruth snickered, then outright laughed. "Good thing I got here when I did. If they've got you believing they're shape-shifting cats, then you've obviously lived in the jungle too long."

"It's the truth."

"Bullcr—" Ruth never finished the swearword as her sister, a sad look in her eyes, let go of her hands and backed away. However, as she retreated, she began to change. A long and low scream rang from her lips, evolving into a screeching yowl as her sister went from woman to …

"Holy freakn' cat!" Ruth scrambled back as the golden jaguar paced in her direction, blue eyes, uncanny, the large teeth frightening. "Oh damn. Oh damn. Don't eat me." She scooted on her butt across the floor. The jaguar stopped stalking her and flopped to the floor, then, chin down, it crossed its forelegs over its head and hid its eyes.

The gesture, so familiar, so Carlie, hit her and sucked the breath from her lungs. *What am I doing?* This overgrown kitty was her damned sister. Not some monster or freak. *My sister.* "Oh, Carlie. I'm so sorry," she murmured, reversing her direction and flinging her arms around the golden furred neck. She rubbed her nose in the soft plush. "Only you would stumble across some ancient tribe and get turned into a giant fur-ball."

A raspy tongue swiped her cheek. Ruth recoiled. "Eew!"

The feline snuffled in apparent amusement.

"I'm glad you think this is funny, because I'm beginning to think I'm the one going nuts." First threesomes, now a shape-shifting sister. What was next? A thought occurred to her and Ruth giggled. "Oh my God, you do realize Mom's going to hate this. You know she's allergic to cats."

With a chuffing sound, Carlie padded off and Ruth moved further as the hairy body contorted. Carlie, naked, pale, and sweating, emerged with a low keening sound, her breaths coming hard and fast. "Fuck that hurts."

"Then why do it?"

"As if you'd have believed anything else."

"True. Damn, sis. Is it permanent?"

"As far as I know."

"Other than the pain, is it hard to do? How many times have you done it?"

"Enough to know it gets easier. It's gone from unbearable to really unpleasant. But at the same time, what a rush. I mean, it's like a whole new world when I change. Everything is so much sharper, more alive.

The cat, its mind and whole perception, is on a completely different, more primitive wavelength. It's kind of liberating."

Ruth didn't see the appeal, just like she didn't understand joggers. How could a sport where a person looked tortured feel good? "So you're happy they did this to you?"

"Yes. No. Maybe. All of the above. None." Carlie sighed. "I'm still figuring that part out. What I do know is you can't tell anyone, and I mean *anyone*, about this. I wasn't supposed to show you, just like I wasn't supposed to tell you about the ritual. But I needed to talk to someone. Someone who wouldn't cry a river or call the government on me for experiments."

"Well, that would depend on the price they'd pay and the credit I'd get," Ruth quipped.

"Evil sister. Figures you'd take this all in stride."

"I don't have much of a choice, but just so you know, I am not keeping any giant-sized litter boxes in my apartment."

Carlie laughed. "Oh, how I've missed you."

"And me, you." Ruth hugged her, trying to ignore the fact her sister lacked clothing. "Never fear. Your secret is safe with me. I'm glad you told me because I don't want to do the ritual. Unlike you, I don't aspire to climb trees or lick cream out of a bowl."

"Don't knock the licking part." Carlie winked. "But seriously, you might not get a choice. Your lovers might make you. It's what happened to me."

"They forced you?"

"Yeah, in a sense, but I'd rather not talk about it right now. We don't have much time."

"So what do we do to avoid this?"

"When the winners come to get you, don't drink anything they give you and make it clear you don't want it. Maybe you'll have better luck than I did."

"Has it occurred to you the doctors back home might be able to reverse it?"

"I won't be going to see a doctor. There is no cure, and I'm not sure I want one. Yes, I'm angry about how Acat and Chaob lied, but at the same time, I don't hate what I've become. I want to explore what it means. See the world with another pair of eyes."

The drums went silent and they both turned their heads to look at the only door leading out of the hut.

"What does that mean?"

"The fight is about to start."

"Joel and Kendrick?"

"Now battle for the right to take you as bride."

A mighty snarl followed by a feline roar split the air. "What the hell was that?"

"Their challengers."

"That didn't sound good. We need to stop this." Because unless Joel and Kendrick hid a shape-shifting secret of their own – which she doubted since she'd pretty much seen and touched most of their bodies, their very human, male bodies – then they were in major trouble.

"How do you suggest we do that?" Carlie asked with an arched blonde brow. "Trust me, I tried to find a way out of this place when I was locked in here. It's impossible."

"But you're like Catwoman now. Surely, you can do something? Like, I don't know, climb the walls. Gnaw through some vines. I can't just sit here waiting to see if my guys win. What if they don't? I won't let some strangers rape me and change me into a pussycat. I just can't." She ended her speech on a hysterical note.

Taking a deep breath, Carlie motioned her back. "Give me some room. I'll see what I can do."

The second transformation wigged Ruth out just as much as the first. Despite her sister's feline grace and beauty, Ruth couldn't imagine becoming an animal. She needed to put a halt to this madness. Needed to find Joel and Kendrick before they got hurt, or changed. And lucky for her, Carlie's new shape provided the means of escape in a hut not built to keep in predators.

As to how she'd extricate herself from this mess? Ruth hoped she'd have a plan by the time they finished climbing down the ridiculously tall tree. If not, she might wish she owned nine lives.

*

"Six guys?" Kendrick remarked, cracking his knuckles as he eyed the dudes lined up across the ring. "Piece of cake."

"You only fight two per round," Chaob volunteered, having designated himself their guide for the event.

"How many rounds?"

"Three per night, until all the challengers are gone. We fought nine groups, Acat and I," Chaob boasted. "Our female was in high demand."

"How many do we have?" Kendrick asked.

"Lucky for you, the scent of your seed clung to the female when she was captured. Only three sets of challengers stepped forth. The first two pairs will not be hard to beat; Bola, however, is a beast."

"Great. So let me get this straight again. We get the challengers to cry uncle and we walk out of here with Ruth."

"After you mark her, then yes. You will be allowed to leave."

"And we don't have to change her into anything?" Kendrick asked.

"So long as she keeps our secrets, the choice is yours."

"Then let's do this."

Stripped down to their boxers – because, as Chaob revealed, they could fight as men or beasts – he and Joel stretched their muscles.

As predicted, despite the fierce roars and chest-thumping, they beat the first two sets of contenders quickly, barely raising a sweat to the crowds' booing annoyance. Funny how the thought of these men lusting after his woman could make him flatten them with pretty much only a single shot. He doubted they'd get away so easily against the last set.

"Whoever wins against their opponent quickest gets to mark Ruth first?" Joel asked with a quirk of his brow.

"I thought we were supposed to fight the cats, not each other," Kendrick quipped. Levity might seem inappropriate given the seriousness of the upcoming brawl, but Kendrick didn't know any other way to greet life. Sometimes you just had to laugh at the hand fate served you and kick its ass.

"What's wrong? You afraid you can't take the big guy and win quickly?"

Kendrick eyed the giant with the faint ring of fat around his middle. "You're on, buddy. First one to subdue their opponent gets first choice of where to bite. I've been dreaming of placing my mark on one of her sweet tits."

Joel groaned. "Damn. I was eyeing those babies. I guess one on each would probably push it."

"She is human."

"Ass or thigh?" Joel mused aloud while Kendrick couldn't help picturing said body part.

Ours? his wolf queried. Soon. Very soon. He just had to do one teensy thing first. He nudged his wolf to pay attention. He fixed his gaze on the obstacles in his way to pleasure. Those two guys standing over there, cracking knuckles, wanted to take Ruth from him. Steal from his wolf. *Grrr.* As if Kendrick would ever let a stranger lay hands on his woman. *Never.* Her heart and body belonged to him. *Yes.* Belonged to Joel. *Grrr.* Better to share with Joel than watch her be claimed by cats. *Double grrr.*

Ready to chase some pussies for some tail? Kendrick asked his inner furry friend. The eager howl in his mind split his lips into a feral grin. A wild smile that momentarily wiped some of the brashness from his opponents' faces. Tilting his head, he caught sight of a three-quarter moon, its belly rounded as the full one approached. The howl which swept forth from him began low and eerie, gaining in tenor, and possessed of an echo as Joel joined him.

Game on.

There was no official bell or signal, no real warning other than their opponents snarling at the crowd before rushing across the cleared area in the jungle.

Basic brawling, one-oh-one – never take the brunt of a tackle head on. Kendrick sidestepped at the last moment and swept a foot out. One cat went tumbling, but the other knew to leap and thus kept his feet.

A swipe by Bola, the one still standing, showed fingers tipped in claws. Partial shifts. Nice. Hard to maintain for any length of time and really dependent on inner strength, of which Kendrick doubted the dumb pair owned much. He ducked, then blocked Bola's hopeful attempt at evisceration. Kendrick wound up and threw a fist into the cat's gut.

Fat on the outside, maybe, but covering thick muscle, the guy barely *oomphed*. Awesome. He did so love a challenge.

Pummeling with his fists, Kendrick put the guy through a flurry of punches as Joel sparred with the other cat. Very few of his landed blows staggered the big dude, but Kendrick could see him getting pissed as the crowd hooted at him, their derision clear.

Giving into his rage, Kendrick's opponent swept a leg while shoving, a move Kendrick would have avoided had Joel's fellow not bumped into him. Down he went, and up he came, however, in that minor lapse, tired of getting his human ass handed to him, the guy changed. What fun. Kendrick now faced a very large, sharp-toothed jaguar.

Yeah, control or not, he wasn't standing in the way of his wolf. Out it came bounding from the confines of his mind, taking over his body, his transformation rapid and smooth from years of practice.

Landing on four feet, he took rapid stock of the situation. Big-ass cat with annoyed glint and slavering jaw coming at him. Human-skinned Joel dancing with a catman, and laughing.

"Come on, you hairy bastard. Do I have to tie an arm behind my back for you to feel brave enough?"

The cat stepped forward, right into Joel's fist. Hard skull or not, it had to hurt and left the fellow dazed. Joel backed up and twitched some fingers at the guy in a come-and-get-me gesture.

Kendrick grinned. Joel always knew how to get the most out of a fight. He turned his attention back to his own opponent, who'd dropped into a crouch and sprang just as Kendrick paid him mind.

Did the felines not have more than one trick? Kendrick learned how to avoid this one when he was just a pup and played with the neighbor's cat, to his mother's annoyance.

Attack sidestepped, Kendrick whirled and pounced, his teeth snapping at the jaguar who managed a lucky score of claws along his side. But he'd gotten much worse from the family scuffles back home, so he ignored it in favor of clamping the skin of the cat's neck and squeezing.

The heavy body went rigid and squirmed away, breaking his hold. He yipped at the twitching tail and the crowd laughed. Blazing gold eyes whipped around to glare.

Kendrick flipped around, scratched his hind paws, kicking up dirt, tail high. With a screech of rage, the jaguar came after him. And now they fought in earnest.

Savagely, teeth flashing, claws digging, fur and blood flew as they each strove to gain the upper hand. What the cat owned in extra weight and pin-sharp claws, Kendrick overcame with cunning and determination.

But even when he held the bloody guy to the ground, his teeth around his throat, the bastard wouldn't yield. He growled and shook. A set of hands grabbed his jaw, trying to pry them off. Seriously. He tightened his teeth, the sharp tips tearing into skin, blood flowed.

"Enough. The wolf has won. The gods deem him worthy of the bride," the old shaman shouted. The crowd went wild.

Muzzle now wet with blood, Kendrick, more beast than man at the moment, lifted his head and howled a victorious yell. He'd won. Won the right to claim his woman. He changed back to his man shape, his wolf, sated and happy at their win over the enemy.

Joel clapped him on the shoulder, grinning from ear to ear. "Good fight, eh? Almost as good as the brawl from that Thanksgiving a few years back."

"Shh. Don't talk about it," Kendrick joked. "Ma still hasn't let us forget about the mashed potatoes on the ceiling. Twelve coats of paint it took to hide the stain. Holy –" As he turned to wave at the stomping crowd, Joel froze at his side. A moment later, Kendrick joined him.

Ah shit.

Eyes open wide in appalled disbelief, her hand held before her lips, Ruth stared at them. An icy chill went down his spine. Uh-oh. Not good. How much had she seen?

Judging by the way she took a step back for every one he took forward, too much.

"Ruth, honey, we can explain."

But, her human mind in overload, his mate didn't stop to listen. She pivoted around and took off running.

Sigh. Maybe he should have said yes to the potion.

Then again, watching her heart-shaped buttocks flex as she ran, he wasn't ready to give in. Sure, she'd received a scare and a shock; however, he knew she was made of tougher stuff than that. It was one of the things he loved about her. While initially cautious or timid, once Ruth conquered a fear, it didn't come back to haunt her.

Knowing that, with the right words – or sensual persuasion – maybe he, with the help of Joel, could make this right. Turn the moment into a positive one. Give her the truth and never live with the worry about their secret getting out. And pray they never made her mad enough she'd sell their story to a tabloid.

But that wasn't the only reason he took off after her at a leisurely lope. Blood running high, in full grips of the mating fever, and victorious in front of a crowd, Kendrick wanted to claim his prize. Wanted to sink his cock into her along with his teeth and make her his in all the ways that counted.

That and he just couldn't resist a chase. *Awoooo!*

Chapter Fifteen

Exactly how did I end up running blind through the jungle with wolves chasing after me?

Brilliant idea to come and save Joel and Kendrick, who it turned out didn't need her help after all.

And here she was so proud of their escape.

The shutters of the prison hut busted open when Carlie took a running leap at them while in her jaguar form. Surprisingly enough, no one flung the barred door open to see what the noise meant. Probably because they were all elsewhere. At least, according to her sister. At the time, Ruth still didn't quite believe Kendrick and Joel foolishly volunteered themselves to fight to win her freedom. But in case they did, Ruth needed to make it to them and stop that madness. As an American, and sister to one of the tribe – planned divorce or not – Ruth could rescue herself. Eventually. She hoped. The alternative, though, possible harm to a pair of men who didn't know what they were up against, was just not acceptable. If their opponents were jaguars like Carlie, Kendrick and Joel, with their all too human and fragile state, wouldn't stand a chance.

Of course, to rescue them first, she needed to make it out the window, onto a narrow ledge, and in the barely lit darkness of the treetop, make her way to a vine and branch twisted bridge. She just thanked her stars that for once her height and weight wouldn't screw her. The tribe members she'd seen so far exceeded her plump waist and thighs, which meant the ropes would hold her. She just needed to remember not to look down.

The climb started out easy enough, even if Carlie declared their escape suspicious.

"We broke out. What's suspicious about that?" Ruth asked in a hushed voice in an attempt to ignore how far the ground still stretched below.

"No way would they leave us unguarded."

"Maybe they didn't and had to go pee."

They both looked up at the same time, Ruth squinting and almost giggling as she imagined getting suddenly wet.

"We need to hurry."

"Hurry where?" Ruth inquired. "You do realize we're days away from civilization. I don't know about you, but I doubt I could survive on my own in the jungle *and* find my way back. I needed a lot of help to get here." But, she'd gotten better. Not quite Jane of the jungle, however, she'd definitely lost her city slicker naivety.

"No, we can't escape. They'd find us before we got far. Maybe, though, we can talk some sense into someone. Or you can claim the guys you came with or something. I don't know. I just know that you don't want to leave something like an unexpected jungle marriage up to chance. I got lucky, but—"

"So lucky," an accented voice purred from the darkness, "that you won't get the punishment you deserve for interfering in the bride choice."

Startled, Carlie dropped from the ladder while Ruth latched on tight. Her sister landed on her feet, knees slightly bent. She tossed her head back. "Aha. I knew it was too easy. I should have known you skulked somewhere. And I am not apologizing for telling. She's my sister. What did you expect me to do?"

A chuckle preceded Acat stepping into the light cast by the single torch thrust into the ground. "You did exactly what I thought you would. But, it's too late. The fight has already begun." As if to highlight his claim, a dual howl, wolves if Ruth wasn't mistaken – strange as it seemed – filled the night air.

"You need to stop this," Ruth demanded as she clambered down the rest of the way.

Acat shook his head, long, dark hair swirling. "Sorry, sister of my mate, but the will of the gods is being done. Fear not, I believe your true mates shall emerge victorious."

Mates, lovers, idiots with a hero complex. Ruth wasn't about to let them get hurt because of some crazy tradition dating back God knew how long.

Taking off in the direction of the chanting crowd, she realized after a moment, her sister didn't follow. Carlie, one hand held in the iron grip of Acat, argued vehemently with her warrior husband. And lost apparently because with a final shake of his head, he slung her kicking sister over his shoulder and stalked off. However, Carlie didn't seem too upset because she stopped her harangue long enough to lift her head and shout, "Don't drink anything. I'll see you in the morning, after I teach my *husband* what equality means."

Great. Finding herself on her own, Ruth kept to her nonexistent plan of somehow breaking up a fight with what sounded like dogs and cats going at it to the cheering of a crowd.

The path, lined only sporadically with torches, wound through tall trees, each twist bringing her closer to the noise, each running step tightening the ball in her stomach. When she finally burst into a well-lit area, it was to confront a sea of backs, mostly naked male ones. She also got a firsthand glimpse of what hid behind the loin cloths, leather thongs tucked between tight cheeks. Mostly tight, at any rate. A few older ones really needed to discover the joy of boxers.

Ruth craned on her tiptoes, trying to see, but for the first time in a long time, Ruth didn't tower over the crowd. Damn, she felt almost freakn' tiny faced with so many giant men. A shame she was only interested in the wellbeing of two.

With hopefully nothing to lose, she forged ahead, hands pushing at and spreading bodies with a softly muttered, "Excuse me. Pardon me. Coming through."

To her amazement, they gave her passage, smirks of amusement aimed her way along with some pinches, enough to make her bottom throb. Not that she cared about the playful slaps when she finally stumbled out into an open area with a clear view.

An unbelievable sight met her eyes. Across from her, on a raised wooden dais, sat a huge man wearing some kind of animal head and cape. While he pounded at the carved wooden arm of his throne, a shriveled older man sat beside him in a smaller chair, smoking a pipe, wearing – oddly enough – faded cutoff jeans. On either side of the platform, and ringing it all around, were men. Lots and lots of men, their skin tanned, their hair long and dark, their bodies nude above the waist. She'd never seen so many abs in one place outside the movie *300*. Forget the chiseled chests, though, they only got a cursory glance once her gaze zeroed in on the action within the ring of hunks.

Shirtless and down to their boxers, Joel and Kendrick fought.

Heat curled inside her at the sight of their partially nude bodies, their muscles seeming more pronounced in the flickering shadows. She almost yelled at them to stop, almost stepped into the ring, as a matter of fact, but a hand held her back.

"Shh. Don't distract them if you value their lives."

Despite the warning, she opened her mouth, but nothing came out as she noted their tanned opponents seemed to have abnormally sharp fingers. Claws. Oh crap. Stunned, she could only watch and bite her lip almost bloody as they dodged and traded blows. She winced and shut her eyes at a particularly nasty shot, barely a few seconds, yet when she looked again, jaguars had taken the place of the warrior men. Great big wild cats – with fangs! – fighting her lovers. Except her lovers weren't men, not anymore. Ruth's eyes just about popped out of her head.

Kendrick's skin changed first and she strangled a scream – more because all the air got sucked out of her lungs – as his body contorted.

"No. No." She moaned in denial as skin she'd touched and tasted morphed into shaggy fur. Not men. Not human. Impossible.

Just like Carlie, Joel and Kendrick shape-shifted into something else, something feral and frightening. Werewolves.

Unlike her sister, who inspired no fear, the wolves and jaguars fighting in the cleared ring did. And with good reason. They attacked each other like wild animals, tearing and clawing at each other. Blood flowing, yet being ignored in favor of more of the biting and wounding.

The horror that Joel and Kendrick weren't what they seemed paled, though, to the realization they fought and were injured because of her. A sick part of Ruth, savage, and obviously demented, cheered them on, mightily turned on by the idea. Another part of her hated she'd brought them to this – caused this kind of trouble.

However, she could breathe a sigh of relief as they did win, and changed back, a shiver-inducing experience as fur slid back into flesh and their animal shape took on the form she liked best. Her heart pounded as if she'd exerted herself alongside them. Blood coursed through her, heightening her senses. But all that froze when they caught sight of her. Eyes blazing in triumph, sweat slick on their blood-streaked skin, a powerful fear gripped her, the terror every mouse, or prey felt when a predator – in this case, times two – set eyes on them.

Rational or not, her body reacted and her feet moved. Despite the stupidity, and knowledge she could never outrun them, she fled. Fled the wolves. The decisions. The pleasure. The future.

OhmyGod, they're wolves.! OhmyGod, they're wolves. OhmyGod ... Ruth couldn't stop that one phrase from ringing in her head. She stumbled and panted, in better shape than ever before in her life, yet knowing it would never be enough. It didn't stop her from trying. Her legs pumped, her arms chugged along, and she wondered how she would escape. How –

A body hit her from behind, and she felt herself tumbling, then she was turning, twisting in midair so that she hit a body instead of the hard ground. It still *oomphed* the breath right out of her.

Recovering quickly, she thrashed only to halt her movement as Joel's, "*Querida*, stop, it's me," penetrated her panic.

Stilling, she let herself meet his gaze, the same blue gaze as before, but now she understood what lay in the depths, the wild thing she'd spotted before. A wolf. She whispered, "You're not human."

"No, he's not," Kendrick replied from behind her. "And neither am I. It doesn't change much."

"Doesn't change much?" The laughter barked from her, sharp and short. "I just watched you turn into the giant wolves from *Twilight*, and you're saying *it's no big deal?*"

"For the record, I hate that movie. And no, it's not a big deal. So what if Joel and I get furry? We don't wear our wolves in the house so you don't have to worry about us shedding hair all over the place."

"I never come in smelling like wet dog when it rains."

"I can walk myself."

"We don't leave the seat up."

"Or chase the neighbor's cat up the tree."

"Often."

"And you're both killing machines," she added. "Don't deny it. I saw you both out there. It was pretty darned savage, so excuse me if I find this all a little nerve-wracking." Piss her pants nerve-wracking, but they didn't seem to care.

"Fine, get a little hysterical, but keep in mind we did what we had to in order to keep you safe. This is not how we are usually," Joel stated, his arms wrapped around her and not letting her budge. "Violence of this level is not a daily part of our lives."

"Most of the time. But don't worry, my mom's usually around to keep things from going too far." Kendrick knelt beside them in the dirt.

"Your mom ... Does she know?" Ruth saw Joel exchange a glance over her shoulder. "Oh my God, she's one too. How many wolves are there?"

"In my family or the city? 'Cause my family also includes a few bears and cats too."

"I think I'm going to close my eyes now and pretend I'm asleep. No. Wait. I know I'm asleep," she muttered. "Have to be. Because this is too insane. Carlie's a cat. Her husbands are cats. I slept with some wolves. This is just a crazy nightmare brought on by too many romance novels and a frog."

"A frog?" Joel queried.

"They must have drugged me when I was sleeping. Made me lick one of those poisonous frogs or something."

Joel snickered. "This isn't a dream, *querida*, or a frog-induced hallucination."

She squished her eyes shut against the sensual tone of his voice.

"Honey, you can't ignore us. We're not going away."

She hummed.

They retaliated. Lips traced her features, brushing across her forehead, eyes, the tip of her nose, across her lips to her cheeks then back to nibble at her lower lip.

She might have fought the allure, but Kendrick, damn him, found the sweet spot at her nape. Her body betrayed her. Heat pooled in her sex, moistened it, and they knew. They smelled it, sensed it, or something, because Joel chuckled against her mouth, pressed insistently with his tongue against her sealed lips.

He almost gained entry too.

"You might not want to do that here," a voice interrupted. "Come. I have a place for you that isn't too far."

Ruth pried open her eyes and ignored Joel's smug grin. "I'm not done arguing."

"We'll see about that," he quipped, helping her to her feet. Forget escape, though, Joel swung her up into his arms, his naked chest pressing against her. Spotting Kendrick over his shoulder, she realized they were both still naked. *Oh God.* She focused on the man leading them. The guy who'd held her back at the fight, a man she now recognized as the shock wore off. "You're Carlie's other husband. Where's my sister? What have you done to her?"

"Acat has her. He is most displeased that she helped you escape."

"He's not going to hurt her, is he?"

"Oh, she'll probably cry out," Chaob replied ominously. "In pleasure. Eventually. First, we shall have to extract her promise to obey."

Ruth's cheeks flushed, but at the same time, the husky way Chaob said it made her peek sideways at Kendrick. *What do they plan to do to me?*

Would she fight it? Embrace it? Embrace both of them? Entering a hut, Joel's grip not loosening on her as he strode toward a hammock-type bed, she wondered if she'd even get a choice. *Let them seduce me.* It seemed in this tribe, ménages were the norm. She could worry about the guilt later.

"There is food and drink on the table, should you need it. Have fun. I know I shall," Chaob said, leaving them with a parting wink.

But his mention of beverage reminded her of Carlie's parting words. *Is this the part where they now try to turn me into a monster too?* "He's gone, you can put me down now," she muttered. A finger tilted her chin up.

"And if I prefer to keep you in my arms?"

"Then you'll be sore in the morning. I'm not a lightweight."

"Light enough," Joel replied, hefting her up and down a few times.

"Are you thirsty?" Kendrick asked as he held up a cup and the jug.

Carlie's words came back to haunt her and she flailed in Joel's grip until he set her down. "No!"

"What's wrong? Why are so pale and fearful all of a sudden?"

She backed away from them, eyeing the carved urn and goblet. "I won't let you turn me into an animal. I know it's what you want and what they did to my sister, but I like being human."

"And we like you being human, too. We have no intention of changing that," Kendrick replied softly, putting down the items before moving away from the table.

"You do?"

"We do," Joel affirmed. "We already told them to keep their magic mumbo jumbo away from you. No one is doing anything to you that you don't want."

The tension in her eased. Perhaps it was foolish of her, but she believed them. "So now what? Are we escaping? Walking out the front door? What's next?"

"Next, you get naked."

"What for?" she squeaked.

"I'd hate to tear your only clothes by accident, especially since we don't know where any of our gear is."

She peered down at the rags left to her. "And why would my clothes get torn?" Because surely they didn't truly intend to have sex now? They were in the moon jaguar's camp, prisoners or something. Now wasn't the time for hanky panky. Or so she thought. Judging by the way they advanced on her, their bodies still naked from the fight and unmistakably aroused, it seemed they had different ideas.

"Strip, Ruth."

She shook her head. "We should be escaping."

"Not tonight, we aren't. So get naked."

"This isn't the time or place."

"There's a bed. We have time." Kendrick stood only a step away, Joel across from him. She retreated, her knees hitting the swaying hammock.

"You don't really want me. You're just high from the fight."

"Honey, I want you so bad I'm not going to be able to wait and taste you like I'm dying to."

"He's right," Joel agreed with a nod of his head. "But don't worry, we'll make sure you enjoy it."

"Oh, yes, we will."

"What happened to not doing anything I don't want?" She hugged her arms around her upper body, lest they see her nipples wanted attention.

"Oh, you want this, honey," Kendrick drawled in a low, sexy voice. "Just so you know, we can smell your desire. It's been torture traveling with you, knowing you wanted us."

"Then why didn't you do something?"

"We tried. But you kept rebuffing our advances."

Because she didn't believe they wanted her. She still didn't.

"Stop arguing, *querida*, and remove your clothes." Joel reached out and tugged at her shirt; the ripping sound of fabric giving made her gasp. Apparently, they meant what they said. They wanted her. Now. Oh God, did they suspect, or worse, smell how much that turned her on?

"I'm dirty," she argued.

"Then we'll shower."

Shower? Kendrick moved aside to show a primitive outdoor shower. One without a door, but with the lure of cleanliness, Ruth gave in and stripped, eyes down, cheeks flushes, nipples hard, and her cleft much too wet. Who was she to keep fighting what they all obviously wanted? Time enough for regret later when she got back to the real world. For now, she'd take what they offered and enjoy it.

Hands helped her divest her clothing, agile masculine fingers touching and caressing as her garments disappeared from her body, leaving her pale skin to gleam in the feeble light cast by a source she'd not yet spotted. She kept her eyes downcast as they guided her into the shower and via the pull of a rope, water gushed from the wooden shower head. Tepid and with little pressure, it still made her sigh in pleasure. She quickly scrubbed, aided by too many hands, aroused as heated skin brushed hers. All too soon, the water petered out, but not before they'd all three rinsed the sweat of their travels from their bodies.

Nude, yet not chilled, surrounded as she was by male flesh, hands roamed her skin, teased her flesh. Lips tasted her skin, licked it, set it tingling. Eyes closed, she couldn't see who possessed her mouth, but she still knew. Kendrick, his lips and kisses hard and demanding whereas Joel devoured her. He took her mouth like a man starving, his passion so contagious.

When the mouths began to wander, though, *oh my*. Her eyes closed as they both settled on a breast; it was the height of decadence, especially since she couldn't really differentiate between them, not when they seemed intent on mimicking each other in their torture of her nipples.

Lick. Blow on the wet skin. Suck. Nip. And repeat. Rough hands, the calloused grip of men who used their fingers to work, played with her small breasts, kneading her flesh as they worshipped with their mouths. All too soon she found herself on a swaying bed, naked bodies on either side. Her legs were splayed, a heavy thigh pinning her left leg, an ankle hooked around her right. Fingers tickled up a thigh, others ran lightly back and forth at the top of her mound.

Lips sought hers for a hungry kiss. She opened her mouth wide and let Joel in, eager for his passion. Fingers, whose she didn't know, sought entry into her sex. *About time.* She wiggled her hips eagerly, mewling in need when they only toyed, rubbing around her lower lips.

"Hold onto that thought, *querida*, because I want to feel that orgasm around my cock."

Why did she have to wait? She opened eyes heavy with passion to see Joel rolling off the swaying hammock. With a little more manipulation, Kendrick helping Joel to position her, she found herself sideways, her head pillowed on Kendrick's hard abs, his cock peeking to her left, his body curved around her so he could watch as Joel held her thighs apart.

The look he bestowed upon her splayed sex made her blush right down to her toes.

"Oh, *querida*, if you knew how I love it when you do that," he murmured. He brought his cock close to the core of her, one hand stroking its length. Her pussy twitched in response. She remembered the feel of him inside, so long and curved at the tip.

Her breathing hitched as he rubbed his swollen head across her clit. Shuddered. "I can't resist," he groaned. He dropped to his knees and a moment later, his tongue ran across her sex. Ruth groaned, then groaned again as he plied her with his tongue, flicking it across her swollen little nub, quick strokes that had her reaching for his hair as she panted, "Yes, yes, oh yes."

Not to be left out, Kendrick toyed with her nipples, and she blindly turned to find his cock, releasing one hand to grasp at it and bring it to her mouth. She sucked him as Joel tongued her, moaning her pleasure, body shuddering and shivering at all the pleasurable sensations. Her orgasm coiled inside, an ever tightening spring. When Joel tore his mouth from her, she yelled around the dick in her mouth, "Don't stop!"

Joel sank his cock into her pussy. Deep. Hard. She cried out, moaned as he dragged it back, then slammed it home. Each of the strokes brought forth a sound, and those hums of delight vibrated the shaft she still sucked.

"Oh fuck, go faster, Joel," Kendrick panted. "I can't hold on much longer."

And the pace quickened. Joel's fingers dug into her ass cheeks, holding her slightly up and off the bed, all the better to slam his cock into her. The fleshy sound of smacking bodies competed with the pants and moans. Kendrick matched the pace, his hips thrusting into her mouth. Faster, oh God. Deeper. Thank goodness for the hand she wrapped around the base of the dick in her mouth, because he'd gotten so thick. But she couldn't get enough of the one further below. With each delicious stroke, Joel hit her sweet spot. Over and over again. Dear God, the sensation proved almost painful in its exquisiteness.

Kendrick pulled free a moment before her teeth came perilously close to clamping down. A good thing too, because a moment later, she came, rode a wave of pleasure as Joel pistoned into her, his mouth on the skin of her breast. He grunted her name, "Ruth!" as he thrust one final time into her, and his climax must have been as good as hers because he bit her with enough pressure to cause a painful pinch. She yelled, but then moaned as he sucked at her abused spot, his hips grinding against her, drawing out her orgasm.

Forget passing out, though. Kendrick's cock returned to her mouth, insistent and determined for its grand finale.

Better able to concentrate with her body cooling down, she gripped him above the sac and sucked him, marveling at his thickness, a pulsing width that just grazed past her teeth. But he wasn't content to just let her play. With a little shifting, his cock hung suspended above her as Kendrick rolled to his knees on the hammock, rocking them, but she didn't fear falling as Joel steadied them with firm hands.

Kendrick grunted as he thrust into her mouth and she savored him, sucking him deep, then letting her teeth rub along his smooth length when he pulled out.

Something warm trickled over her pussy and she squeaked.

"Easy, honey," Kendrick shushed. "Joel's just cleaning you off so I can enjoy you."

Surely he didn't plan to … Oh God, he did. Somehow managing a sixty-nine on the hammock, Kendrick lowered his head to her cleaned pussy and licked. She bucked. Moaned. Dug her nails into his hard thighs as she siphoned him. Kendrick toyed even more with her hyper-sensitized clit, and as if that weren't enough, Joel thrust his fingers into her. Her body, still coming down from its orgasmic high, approved of this, and the desire she'd thought sated roared back to life. Kendrick murmured his enjoyment against her mound and his cock grew impossibly thicker.

"I want you to come all over my cock, honey," he murmured against her skin. "I'm going to slip my fat dick inside you and fuck you so hard. And you're going to tremble for me."

True to his word, he flipped off the hammock, leaving her panting and aching for him. He flipped her onto her stomach, spread her legs, grabbed her by the waist to hike her up, and plowed into her. Drove his dick into her quivering pussy and fucked her hard. It sounded so vulgar to even think it, but it wasn't gentle, not the way he thrust into her. Best of all, Ruth loved it. He slammed into her body – a body already softened by Joel's initial foray, and she took it, with short pants of bliss. Her climax tumbled free, a soul-searing, blindness-inducing, limb-jolting pleasure, and Kendrick roared. He curved his body over her, his hips grinding so fast against her buttocks, and as he came, he bit her on the back of the shoulder. But the pain sent her spiraling again, a pleasure so intense, so perfect, she collapsed.

Were intense orgasms like that a werewolf thing? Did they plan to infect her? Did she care at the moment? Given the fact she couldn't open her eyes or move a limb, sated beyond words, she'd worry about it in the morning.

Maybe after they tried that again a time or two, possibly three.

Chapter Sixteen

Ruth stirred, the morning light bugging her closed eyes.

"About time you woke up, Ruthie."

"Carlie. Is that you? I had the strangest dream," she murmured, turning on her lumpy mattress. God, she needed to shop for a new one. "I dreamt you were lost in the jungle and…" She didn't finish her sentence. Why would she when her fluttering eyes spotted the green canopy overhead?

"It wasn't a dream," Carlie replied.

"Apparently. But this also isn't the hut I went to sleep in."

"You call that sleep?" Carlie snickered.

Ruth didn't bother blushing. Not with her sister. "More like a climax coma then. How long was I out? And where are we?" she asked, peeking around at the trees and flora surrounding them.

"Almost back to the real world. Here, drink this. It will help clear your head."

"Are you sure? It's not, you know, poisoned or anything, is it?"

Carlie laughed. "No. Your humanity is safe."

Taking the cup, Ruth drank the cool liquid within, fresh water with a hint of honey. "Where are Kendrick and Joel?"

"Your mates? Male bonding with mine and a few others over there."

"Mates? No. We didn't get married like you." But they'd sure whooped it up. Wow. Even remembering brought a tingle. "I can't believe I slept with them both at once."

"Way to go, little sister. I wouldn't have thought you had it in you."

"I did. Times two." Ruth giggled, a tad hysterically. "Oh my God, I slept with werewolves. Does this mean I'm going to turn shaggy on the full moon and crave Scooby snacks?"

Her sister's lips twitched. "Sorry to disappoint, but no, lycanthropy is not contagious. You're still one hundred percent human."

"I'm sorry, I didn't mean to make you feel bad."

"Bad about what? That I can change into the first golden jaguar to ever join the tribe? I actually like it more and more every day."

"So, that's it? You're going to be catwoman for life?"

"As far as I know."

"You know, most families have a black sheep."

Carlie tossed her head. "I always did like to do things a little different."

"That you do, but if you think I'm cleaning out any litter boxes …"

A laugh bubbled out of her sister. "Don't you dare start getting me catnip for Christmas."

A mischievous grin pulled at Ruth's lips. "How about a windup mouse?"

"Seriously, though, I know this is a lot to take."

"You're telling me. How am I supposed to explain this to Mom and Dad without them having kittens?"

Carlie winced at the pun. "About Mom and Dad – they can't know."

"You have to tell them something, or are you going to let them think you're dead?"

"Of course not!"

"Then what?"

"I don't know. Just tell them that I love them. That I'm okay, and I'll be visiting them soon. Tell them I'm documenting the traditions and whatnot of jungle men and will be back in a few weeks."

"Traditions?" Ruth snickered. "Is that what you're calling sex with them? I think you like them more than you want to admit."

"I don't love them if that's what you're implying. Lust after their bodies, yes, but I don't love those manipulative jerks."

"Says the girl who would rather stay with them than come home."

"Like I said, it's complicated. There are things I need to learn. Things I need to know. But rest assured, I will be in touch."

"She will be safe with us," Acat stated, coming up on them silently.

"I'm gonna put a bell on you," Carlie snarled.

"I'd like to see you try," Acat replied.

"I'll help," Chaob chimed in, also appearing suddenly. "It is time for us to leave, *datura*. We've come as far as we can with them."

With a sigh, Carlie stood, flanked by men who, by their very stance, let it be known they'd defend her with their lives, and in their eyes, Ruth saw they did it because they cared for her. *She's in good hands.* It still made Ruth cry to know her sister was staying behind, because despite Carlie's claim, she could tell her sister loved them.

Final hugs and kisses were exchanged, then Ruth cringed as she watched Carlie's face contort, part rictus of pain, part holy-freakn' shit as her bones literally melted and reshaped until standing before her was a golden freakn' feline.

"Meowr?" The cat cocked its head and Ruth smiled.

"You make a beautiful kitty," she told her sister. With a sniff and twitch of her tail, her furry sibling bounded off, a pair of sleek jaguars shadowing her.

Tears still ran down her cheeks when Kendrick and Joel came up behind her. Kendrick's arms wrapped around her body and hugged her tight. "It's alright, honey. Much as I hate to say it, she's in good hands."

"You mean paws."

"Whatever. Let's get out of here. While we slept, drugged again somehow, those furry bastards had us transported back to the edge of civilization. We're apparently only a few hours away from running water and a bed."

And they were, too, along with their bags. It seemed their slumber after the extreme sex fest in the jungle wasn't one hundred percent natural. Ruth didn't know how many days they lay unconscious, but it proved enough to get them back to a remote village on the other side of the jungle.

Emerging from the green world she'd gotten used to felt surreal. The tiny village they arrived in – not the same one they'd embarked from – seemed noisy and chaotic after the naturalness of the forest. So much had happened. So many things churned in her mind – and her heart. She already missed her sister desperately, but at the same time, she envied her.

Carlie would get to live the dream. Live with and love two men – once she allowed herself – without fear of persecution, and if they spoke truly, for life.

What did Ruth get to look forward to? Going back to her boring life. A mundane existence that didn't include the two hunks who taught her what passion simmered below her surface. Who introduced her to a world of pleasure. Who would now get on with their lives in Canada while she went back to hers.

But they didn't dump her right away, much to her surprise, especially given the interested looks they got from the local girls. To their credit, Kendrick and Joel didn't pay the flirtation any mind, showering her with affection at every turn. She didn't read too much into it. She knew them well enough to know they'd not disrespect her in that fashion.

As they traveled, they hovered close by, Joel or Kendrick guiding her along the rutted paths of the villages with a hand in the middle of her back. Not willing to wait on the bus and their wonky schedules, they quickly made arrangements for a drive into town. A luxurious one too, in the back of a pickup truck that probably owed its existence to the duct tape holding the rotting body together. Nestled between her men – *my men for now* – she didn't speak much, the rushing wind and the missing tailpipe making it too hard to converse. She leaned her head on one brawny shoulder, and just enjoyed the simple pleasure of touching them. They each linked a hand with hers, fingers meshed, and she fell asleep.

The noise of the city roused her and she lifted her head to peer around with bleary eyes. Joel leaned close and shouted in her ear, "We're almost at the hotel, *querida*. Just a little bit longer and you can have a shower and real food."

It seemed even the rumble of the missing muffler couldn't camouflage her sigh of pleasure because Joel laughed and brushed her cheek. The jalopy pulled to a stop in front of a building with a cloud of dust. Coughing and choking, Ruth's eyes watered and she couldn't protest as Kendrick swung her into his arms to carry her inside. While Joel took care of their driver and other arrangements, Kendrick, keys dangling from his mouth, took the stairs two at a time with Ruth protesting faintly she could manage them on their own.

"I know you can, honey, but I'd rather you save that energy for later. Do you know how long I've fantasized about you in a bed?"

"Not until after a shower."

His lips quirked. "Nice to know hot water wins over my technique."

Hmmm, she almost changed her mind, especially when he kissed her before setting her down. But, he broke away while she was still debating, and a moment later, she heard the sound of running water.

She practically shoved him in her haste to get into the stall.

"Easy, honey."

Already naked and under the lukewarm spray, she sighed happily, then squealed as someone crowded her space.

"Hey," she protested.

"Didn't your mother teach you to share?" Kendrick asked with a grin when she opened her eyes to glare at him.

"My water," she growled.

"But I have soap," he offered, proving it by sliding slippery hands up her body. Sudsy hands gliding over her skin in light, tantalizing circles? Mmm. Heavenly.

"You can stay, but on that side," she ordered, hogging the spray. Yeah, so sue her for having a selfish moment. She'd earned it. Besides, judging by the hardness poking her, he didn't mind.

"Is there room for one more?" Joel called out from the other room.

"No," they both shouted.

Ruth giggled as Joel poked his head around the curtain and stuck his tongue out to catch some drops.

"She doesn't like to share her hot water," Kendrick told him in a solemn voice.

"Good thing I got adjoining rooms so we won't get too crowded then," Joel announced. "I'll see you both in a minute after I'm clean." He winked and left.

"Personally, I'll take no water if I get you to myself for a minute," Kendrick admitted, resuming his slow, relaxing circles, his sensual version of cleaning.

He'd just gotten to a very dirty part of her anatomy when a brisk knocking came at their door. Cursing up a streak, Kendrick exited the shower and stole the only towel to answer. A moment later, he returned.

"I've got to go meet with the organizers of our trip, honey."

"Now? But we just got here."

"I know. But, they want the letters the tribe gave us and are demanding a report while everything is fresh. Joel and I should only be gone a few hours."

"Do you want me to come with you?"

"No. This is pack business. You rest up for later." Dressing quickly after giving Joel the news, they both gave her a hot and passionate kiss before leaving.

However, despite their instructions to get some sleep, she found herself wide awake. Alone for the first time in forever, doubt assailed her and reality finally came whooshing in.

What am I doing? Shacked up with two men, in a relationship that would go nowhere, did she really want to drag things out, waiting for the final goodbye?

It was coming. She knew it. They belonged to different worlds. *I'm human. They're werewolves.* Exactly what did she think would happen? Unlike Carlie who ended up a jaguar like her lovers, Ruth made it clear she had no interest in changing. Not that Joel or Kendrick ever spoke about anything more permanent. As a matter of fact, they'd never had a chance to speak of the future at all. A future she doubted included her.

Sticking around for one final round wouldn't make going their separate ways any easier. And she feared begging them for a crumb when the time for goodbye came around. *Oh God, I don't want to be one of those girls who breaks down and begs them not to let me go.* Because, somehow, somewhere along the line, she'd fallen in love with them. Fallen in love with an impossibility.

Forget the confidence she'd gained on her travels. The way they made her feel. A lifetime of self-doubt came back to haunt her.

There was an alternative to an ugly scene. She could make it easier on everyone and get out while the memories were still happy ones. They'd probably breathe a sigh of relief when they saw she'd made the break-up easy.

Tears rolling down her cheeks, she packed her meager possessions, left them a note, a short one when she realized anything longer than *thank you* sounded too clingy. With a heavy sigh and even heavier heart, she made her way downstairs. She ran into Peter who tried to stop her, but she wouldn't listen to anything he had to say. A lifetime of experience had taught her what to expect, despite what Peter seemed to think.

She refused to listen when he talked of them taking her as mate. Surely she'd know if Joel and Kendrick married her even a la werewolf? Surely they would have said something? They hadn't, though. No declarations of love, or happily-ever-afters. And Ruth found she had too much pride, a pride they'd help her find in the jungle, to beg.

She took a cab to the airport and booked the first flight out. Lucky her, it left within the hour. With her passport a little worse for wear, but usable, Ruth boarded a plane for home – via three connecting flights – alone. And without saying goodbye. What was there left to say?

Thanks, but we all knew it was only temporary. Even if her heart hoped otherwise. Even if she loved them. It hurt, but Ruth was a realist. Outside of the jungle, back in the real world, what did she have to keep two men like Kendrick and Joel at her side? She'd lost some weight in her travels, but she'd never end up petite or truly skinny. Heck, she'd gain back the pounds she lost in no time at all. They lived in different countries. Came from different backgrounds. She didn't howl at the moon. Heck, she didn't even like dogs, although, she would have made an exception for them.

She'd enjoyed herself during the time they had. Found pleasure beyond belief. And now the real world called, a world without the hunks she'd come to think of as her own. Where was some Prozac when you needed it?

Chapter Seventeen

"What do you mean she's gone?" Joel's heart stopped.

Peter lifted his shoulders in a helpless shrug. "I tried to convince her to stay when I ran into her in the lobby. I told her to talk to you guys, but she kept saying something about not being one of those desperate girls."

"That doesn't make any sense."

"She seemed to think what you had wasn't permanent," Peter clarified.

Kendrick's brows shot up. "We marked her? How much more permanent could we get?"

"Did you tell her what the biting meant?"

"Of course not. She's human."

"She's your mate. And she suffers from low self-esteem."

"About what?" Joel asked, puzzled.

"Her weight."

"What about it? She's perfect."

"To you and Joel, but in her mind, she's not. She seems to think you pity fucked her because there was nothing better around."

"Of all the stupid things," Kendrick growled. "I thought she'd gotten over that."

"I'm with you this time. How could she think we didn't worship her body?"

"And yet, you didn't tell her this. Apparently, from what I could make out of her babbling, she thought you'd ditch her like a hot potato once you got to civilization. She decided to avoid it by running away."

"To where?" Kendrick asked.

Peter groaned. "God, I hope I never get mated. I swear it makes you dumber than a rock. She went back home, dumbasses, where else?"

Joel punched a wall, unable to contain his anger – and heartache. Abandoned. Again. By a woman who was supposed to love him. He wanted to howl with the unfairness of it. "I knew this would happen. Without the mating bond, she doesn't need us. We should have changed her when we had the chance."

Kendrick paced the tight confines of the hotel hall. "I'm sorry. I didn't think she'd do this to us. I really thought she cared. I never expected her to ditch us like this, without even giving us a chance."

"Oh would you get off your drama horse," Peter barked, exasperation clear in his tone. "Ruth loves you. It's why she left."

"Gee, that makes me so much happier." Joel shot him a dark look.

"Love or not, it doesn't change the fact she's gone," Kendrick added, his expression morose.

"Doesn't change it, no, but it means something because, don't you get it? She didn't want to let you go. She left because she was afraid of rejection."

"So she rejected us instead." Joel sulked.

"And I took you for fighters," Peter muttered in disgust.

"What's that supposed to mean?" Kendrick snarled.

"Figure it out. I'm done talking to you boneheads. Maybe she is better off without you." Peter stalked off while Kendrick muttered.

Joel, however, looking past his hurt, grasped what Peter meant. Why was he giving up? He wasn't his father. And Ruth cared for him. He knew it. So why was he indulging in a pity fest instead of going after the woman he loved?

Fight for our mate? His wolf's query made Joel want to smack himself. Even his inner beast knew better than to throw in the towel without a fight. "We need to get her back."

"Agreed. Peter is right. We're obviously not thinking straight. Since when are we cowards? We just need to convince her that we're serious about her. Serious about having a relationship."

"And if she still says no?"

"We persevere. We can't let her walk away, Joel. She's our mate. The woman we need."

"The woman we love." Loved more than his pride. Hell, he'd beg her on his knees if he had to. Anything to have her give him a chance to prove his worth, and his love.

"You book the flight," Kendrick ordered. "I'll get our luggage."

"On it. Got a plan for when we get there?" Joel asked.

"Actually, I do. I think it's time we took a page from our new tribal friends and kidnap our bride."

Kidnap her, make love to her, and tell her in every way imaginable how much he cared and wanted to spend his life with her. He'd let nothing stand in his way to her heart—well, nothing except customs, which seemed determined to drive him mental.

Joel sighed as he slumped in the hard plastic chair of the customs office. Funny how when he watched those romantic comedies, the heroes never had to wait hours to get off the damned plane and find the woman he loved. He just hoped the guy snapping on latex gloves wasn't coming for him, because there was no way he'd allow a full cavity search. Shudder.

*

Only back a few hours and already Ruth regretted it. Regretted the adventure ever had to end. Regretted not giving in to temptation one more time. Almost regretted her choice to get involved in the first place.

But how was I to know I'd fall in love, and with two men? She'd not set out expecting to meet such great guys, or to indulge in the most mind-blowing sex imaginable. Now, however, after having tasted and experienced male perfection, how the hell would she ever date again? And a better question, how would she make it through the rest of her life never seeing Joel or Kendrick again?

Tears tracked down her cheeks. She scrubbed at them, furious at herself. She knew this might happen. Warned herself not to get emotionally involved. To not fall for their pretty words and promises – sensual touches and kisses – knowing men would do or say anything for sex.

They seemed so sincere though. Sniffle.

With Carlie gone, it was up to Ruth to keep her spirits up and not let momentary jungle madness turn her into a depressed woman who ended up with a houseful of cats. Stupid, hairball-puking things. She decided in that moment she much preferred dogs. Big overgrown ones with washboard abs.

Sigh. Funny how the whole werewolf thing didn't bother her at all. So what if they turned hairy and howled at the moon? She'd gladly invest in lint rollers if it meant keeping them in her life.

Washing her face with cold water again, she knew what she needed. Cherry cheesecake ice cream in a waffle bowl. With extra cherries. Lots of whipped cream. And maybe some caramel sauce. Lots of caramel sauce.

Grabbing her purse, Ruth ignored her still packed luggage and dusty apartment with its dying plants. The local ice cream parlor called, and she intended to answer.

An hour later, belly full of ice cream, not feeling any happier, she returned home. She tossed down her purse, kicked off her shoes, and headed for bed.

She stopped dead in the doorway, fingers frozen on the light switch. What the heck was on her comforter? Blinking, she noted the pile of bills – in a variety of colors she recognized as Canadian currency – didn't diminish.

"Is that enough?" purred a familiar voice.

"Joel?" She whirled to see him leaning on the wall across her bedroom door. "Where did you come from? How did you get in here?"

"Hello, *querida*. Your building security sucks."

"Apparently," was her dry reply. "You still haven't said what you're here for?"

"Don't you know? That wasn't very nice of you, to leave without even saying goodbye." Kendrick chided her.

She raised her chin. "I did what was best, and thought you'd appreciate it, too. Don't most guys hate messy scenes?"

"We do, but we hate it even more when our woman tries to run without even giving us a kiss goodbye or a chance to make her stay," Joel growled in a low voice.

"I didn't want to miss my flight," she lied.

"You shouldn't have left without us."

Why did Joel seem so angry? And not just angry, but livid – and she caught glimpses of hurt – that she'd slipped away without facing him. Cowardly, yes, but she'd hoped to avoid anything unpleasant, preferring to end things on an amicable note. But it seemed she might have misjudged Joel. Did he actually care for her? Want her? Oh God, recalling how his mother abandoned him, had she hurt him? She never meant to do that. What about Kendrick? Was he upset too? Or, her practical side snidely interrupted, was there something about the rescue mission that required her attention? "What are you doing here?"

"*We* came to find you since you so erroneously thought to escape us. We weren't done yet. Not by a long shot," Kendrick murmured, startling her as he snuck up from behind. Once there, he seemed determined to let her know he wasn't going anywhere, or so she assumed as he pressed into her back, his familiar hard body molding intimately to hers. Oh sweet God, how she missed that in the day they spent apart. Her body responded to his closeness by heating instantly. Every nerve ending came to life and practically swooned in ecstasy, especially when Joel closed in from the front.

She licked her lips, a motion avidly tracked by his eyes. The small laugh she attempted emerged breathy and weak, weak like her knees, which buckled when Kendrick nuzzled her neck. She didn't slump, but only because four hands grabbed her. She tried to answer despite her mind already going fuzzy. "Of course we're done. The mission was over. The girls didn't want to come back. We brought the letters and videos, which I might add were a nice touch. No mission, no reason for me to stay. Sorry if I didn't say goodbye in person, but you know me, I hate confrontation." She shrugged her shoulders. Joel's brows arched and his lips curved in amusement.

Kendrick snorted. "Hate confrontation? Since when? You've gone toe-to-toe with me since the first time we met."

"Did not," she retorted.

"You did and still are," Joel agreed, his vivid gaze latched onto hers.

"Well, it's only because you're bossy. Most of the time I'm a really meek girl."

"Ha." Joel snickered.

"I am not bossy," Kendrick retorted. "I acted that way because I cared."

"Funny way of showing it," she muttered.

"Yes, but what can I say? You bring out the savage in me," he agreed. "I see you and I just want to wrap you up and keep you safe."

"Not at first," she reminded.

"No, but only because you scared me. Scared both of us."

"I scared you?" Ruth laughed. "Now that's priceless."

"But true. We didn't go to the jungle expecting to find you," Kendrick replied.

"I'm aware I ruined your all-boys trip. Too bad. So sad."

"See? There goes that saucy tongue of hers again," Kendrick replied, his breath fanning the lobe of her ear. "You know, I can think of much better uses for that tongue."

A shiver went down her spine as she flashed to his meaning, more specifically, the time she ran it down Kendrick's more-than-perfect chest.

Joel inched closer, his lips close enough to touch if she leaned just a little forward. "I can't believe you still don't get it. You didn't ruin anything. As a matter of fact, you are the best thing that happened to us on that trip."

"Forget trip, best thing to happen to us ever," Kendrick amended.

Only someone made of stone wouldn't have felt her heart flutter at such a speech. But it seemed too grandiose. "Did you borrow one of Joel's corny lines?"

Joel rolled his eyes at her weak joke. "So smart most of the time, and yet so freakn' clueless." He shook his head.

"Is this an ego thing? Because if it is, too bad. I'm not stupid. We all knew this wasn't going anywhere."

"And that was your first mistake, *querida*. Did you really think Kendrick and I took up with you just to scratch an itch?"

"We do have more self-control than that, you know," Kendrick added. "Or did, until we met you. See, from the first moment we met, we knew you were the one."

"One what?" Her heart refused to beat, as if it sensed something momentous playing out. The one second in time that would decide her future – and happiness. If she managed to stop arguing with them that was. Why did she keep denying what they seemed determined to say? Why did she keep denying the evidence? *Because it scares me.* Scared the hell right out of her because when it came right down to it, she loved them both. But whoever heard of a forever after with two men? *The moon ghost jaguars, that's who.*

"You are the one woman made for us," Joel murmured, his lips dancing across her neck, his breath warm and shiver-inducing.

Kendrick, not to be forgotten, rubbed his mouth over her nape in a way she enjoyed all too much. "We tried to fight it at first, not wanting to share, dealing with jealousy, dealing with our secret and your humanity."

"We worried we would hurt you, which by the way, will never happen. You mean too much to us."

"You mean the world," Kendrick whispered against her skin. "You are our world. Every tough, woman-of-the-jungle, inch of you."

"You're beautiful. Brave."

"Sexy, and smart. Everything a man, or two, could want in a mate."

The words spun around Ruth, teasing her with hope and warmth. But what they seemed to suggest? The two of them, plus her, living a forever after? She needed to hear it in black and white. Needed to be sure. "What do you want from me?"

"Forever."

"And ever."

"The whole nine yards."

"Until death do us part."

"The three of us, though? What will people think?" Did she care? Could she truly say she'd find happiness if she had to choose between the two? She loved them both so much. *And hey, there's always the jungle.* So long as she had them, did anything else matter?

"Who cares what they think? Let them envy you as the luckiest woman alive." Kendrick kissed her neck, softly, sensually. A shiver rolled down her body.

How could I ever say no? "Forever, huh?"

"And an eternity. I love you." Joel slid his lips across hers.

"Love you so much, we'll even put up with the fact your comforter is pink." Kendrick sounded so pained.

She giggled. "My sheets are flowered."

He groaned. "My masculinity is shot. Quick, Joel, we need to do something to assert ourselves."

"Then we'll need her in less clothes."

"Hey, I never said yes," she protested feebly as hands tore at her garments, stripping her in record time.

"We won't let you say no," Joel murmured before claiming her lips in a scorching kiss.

"And don't forget, we bought you fair and square," Kendrick said in a light voice, nipping her ear.

So that explained the pile of money. Did Carlie tell them about her secret fantasy? "But you didn't abduct me," she managed to gasp between tugs of her lower lip by Joel.

"Easily arranged. Consider yourself our prisoner bride," Kendrick growled, but she heard the sensual hunger and didn't fear. She floated on a cloud as they carried her to the bed and placed her upon it, the bills fluttering around them like colorful leaves.

Joel grasped her wrists in one of his hands and pulled them over her head, stretching her torso for his smoldering gaze.

"I have missed seeing this," he breathed, his eyes reverent. "Perfection."

"Delicious," Kendrick added, dipping his head to flick a tongue against a straining peak as his hands spread her thighs.

"And in need of a proper ravishing as our prisoner," Joel concluded, angling himself over her upper body so that his cock lined up with her lips. He stroked it in front of her as he kept her hands pulled taut over her head. She ached for a taste. Ached for him, as a matter of fact. Kendrick too. "You will promise us, right now, to never ever leave us again."

"Or if you're mad or unsure – anything – at least talk to us first." Kendrick accented his demand with a pinch to her erect nub.

"I promise. What about you? Are you going to promise the same thing?"

"Of course." Joel slapped his cock off her lips as if indignant at her request.

Kendrick chuckled. "Honey, you are stuck with us for life."

"Don't you know wolves only mate with one woman? One very special woman."

"You've had sex with others," she retorted, jealousy making her sound angrier than she was.

"Sex, yes, but only one bears our mark."

"Mark?" Her eyes widened as she recalled the ring of teeth on her breast she'd seen when dressing and the ridge on the back of her shoulder. "You mean the bites?"

Joel nodded. "Even though we know you are the only one for us, and a human, we still claimed you. This is forever, *querida*."

She frowned. "But I never bit you back. Don't the legends have it going both ways?"

"You're human. We can make exceptions."

Or, she could give them what they needed, once they got in reach. Joel still teased her, his hand lightly stroking his rigid length, the tip of it pearled and tempting.

Lips traveled down her belly and despite the room he created between her thighs, Kendrick made sure he dragged his erect shaft down her leg, the heat and hardness of him bringing an answering moisture between her thighs. Oh, how he liked that, she judged when Kendrick growled against her mound, the vibration making her sigh in delight. Then like planned dual attacks, Kendrick speared her with his tongue while Joel filled her mouth with his cock.

Oh dear God. It seemed the time to talk was over and she was in such delicious trouble. With so many sensations happening at once, it proved hard to remember her plan, but when Joel pulled out of her mouth, she struck, nipping his upper thigh, pinching tight with her teeth. Joel cried out and his fingers tangled in her hair, pressing her mouth for a moment against the small bite mark she made. And then she had no time to wonder if she'd done it right, because they shifted her body and prepared her for something she'd read of. Wondered about. Fantasized. *The question is, can I handle it?* Handle both of them at once. God, she hoped so.

Chapter Eighteen

Kendrick wanted to howl for joy, but contained himself, not wanting to do anything to jeopardize the understanding they'd finally achieved with Ruth. Farfetched as it seemed, she'd truly not understood how much she meant to them. Their fault, really, for not explaining more plainly how they felt. *What idiot doesn't tell his mate he loves her?* He wouldn't make that mistake again. He'd tell her and show her a hundred times a day if that was all it took to make her happy.

And he'd also make sure to taste her decadent honey as often as possible, because damn, she possessed the sweetest flavor he'd ever known. Or would ever know again.

He tongued her with all of his passion unleashed. He didn't hold back as he lashed across her clit, bathing it, caressing it, feeling her twitch and tremble under his oral assault.

When he peered up, he tensed for a moment, frightened he'd get turned off by Joel getting sucked by her, but despite the fact he had no interest in Joel as a sexual partner, he couldn't deny the erotic pleasure of watching Ruth devour his friend's prick. His mouth busy with her pussy, Kendrick watched as her lips slid back and forth across Joel's long dick. Felt his balls tighten and his cock pulse as she strained and pulled, her body heaving but held down both by Joel and his handcuff of her hands, and Kendrick, whose heavy body trapped her legs open.

He began to see the merit in what Fernando suggested so many days ago in the jungle. Perhaps they'd have use for the lube he'd brought after all, which currently dug into his thigh from where he'd placed it earlier on the bed. He let his tongue travel downwards, but didn't leave her hungry channel completely bereft. He slid two fingers in, gasping at the molten heat of her, his hips twitching in response to her sex's convulsive squeeze of them. Damn, he couldn't wait to slip into her decadent heat. Her tightness.

But, this time, he wouldn't take her alone.

His tongue probed at her rosette, flicking against it, pleased when she didn't flinch or shy away, too caught up in the moment to notice his actions. But when he replaced his tongue with the tip of his lubed finger, she roused herself enough to yelp, "What are you doing?"

"Trust me," Kendrick murmured, moving his tongue back to her clit, leaving his finger inserted in the tight ring.

"We'd never hurt you," Joel whispered. Shifting his weight, Joel took his cock away from her mouth and began to kiss her, and stroke her perfect tits with his hands while Kendrick flicked his tongue on her nub. Slowly, she relaxed, and his finger eased in deeper. He grasped the lube and dribbled some more between her cheeks and this time, she didn't tense at all when he slid a second finger into her. On the contrary, she moaned. She was ready, he hoped, but not for him. For this virgin voyage, Joel with his slimmer, if longer cock would go first.

He signaled to his friend, and with one last, probing kiss, Joel pulled away and lay on his back. Joel pulled her atop his frame, Kendrick guiding her so she sat on Joel's lower stomach, Joel's cock jutting in front of her.

A little close for comfort, but redeemed by her gleaming wet pussy. Kendrick dribbled lube onto his friend's dick, and Ruth, watching with heavy-lidded eyes, immediately grasped it, stroking the hard length. Damn but it was an erotic sight.

"We won't do this if you're not ready," Kendrick stated.

"I've read about this," she admitted shyly. "And while I won't lie and say it doesn't scare me, I'm willing to try."

She knelt up and over Joel's cock, her teeth worrying her lower lip. Slowly, she lowered herself. Stopped as the head of his cock butted against her virgin passage. Kendrick reached out and stroked her clit, thrumming his thumb across it.

With a sigh of pleasure, she sank down and Joel went still as she took just the tip of him in with a gasp.

"Is it too much?" Joel asked through gritted teeth.

"Yes. Maybe. I don't know." She squeezed her eyes tight, body trembling as she hovered.

Without even thinking, Kendrick leaned forward and let his tongue lap her clit while he thrust his fingers into her. A cry left her, then another, and each time, she sank down further and further onto Joel's cock. But what truly excited Kendrick was her reaction. Her pussy clenched, every muscle tightening and ready. He wanted in there when she exploded.

Quickly, he moved, leaning her back enough to give him access, then thrusting into her. Holy. Freakn' Hell. He'd never felt anything so tight in his life. And when she immediately came? Her channel convulsed in tortuous waves and he almost passed out.

He definitely yelled her name, but it was nothing compared to how it felt when he began to move. Thrusting into her, jaw gritted at the exquisiteness of the action, his mouth found hers for a frantic kiss. Oh how she took control of that, sucking on his tongue, moaning into his mouth. And when she came again, biting the skin at his neck hard enough to draw blood? He not only exploded, but his soul touched hers in a way he never expected, but cherished.

*

Joel held on by the barest thread. And he didn't know how because encased in Ruth's hot flesh, knowing she loved him, knowing she wanted him, made him the happiest man alive.

And then it got better. Kendrick joined the circle, thrusting into her, and for a moment, as they both rested inside her body, her climaxing body, Joel felt something happen in him; something unfurled and reached out to touch … their souls? He couldn't have said. But he wanted to keep touching it for as long as possible. His hands on her hips began to move her, sliding her back and forth on his cock, alternating his thrusts with Kendrick's, seesawing her sweet body as she gasped and moaned, her body caught in a climactic loop, a never-ending orgasm that had his hips pistoning faster and faster, his heart pounding too quick to count, then his whole world exploding.

"I love you." He yelled it. Or thought it. It didn't matter, he knew she heard him. And returned it with a pulsing warmth of her own, a wave of affection that transcended words.

Human or not, Ruth had managed to mate bond with them. If he'd possessed the strength, or the breath, Joel would have laughed. Here he'd worried about her humanity being the barrier to keep them apart. Worried about gaining her trust and love. And when he finally decided he didn't need some esoteric force to keep them together, it happened. For better or worse, they were mated. Blood, heart, and soul.

And he couldn't have been freakn' happier.

Epilogue

"Holy shit. I still can't believe they exist." Stu slapped the dining room table as Kendrick's mother cleared the dessert dishes – Ruth and the other girls in the family giving her a hand.

"Oh, they exist all right. Darned woman-stealing perverts," Joel muttered.

"I told you!" his mother shouted from the kitchen with her impeccable hearing, eavesdropping as usual.

"So what's going to happen to Ruth's sister?" his dad asked.

A sister they were sworn to secrecy about. Kendrick couldn't blame the Moon Ghosts for not wanting the knowledge they could change humans to get out. God only knew what someone with the wrong intentions would do with that little tidbit. Kendrick shrugged. "She keeps saying she's getting a divorce. And their response is to just toss her over a shoulder and make her take it back." He grinned. "I think they might have bitten off more than they expected when they stole her as their jungle freakn' bride."

"I am just happy my parents swallowed her story about staying with the other girls and documenting the tribe they found." Fingers slid around his neck and a sweet perfume enveloped him as Ruth rejoined them. It didn't take her long once she met Naomi and her mates to realize her relationship with him and Joel wouldn't raise any eyebrows.

Convincing her to come meet his family, though, that took a lot of work. Thankfully, they all reaped the benefit of that endeavor. He grabbed her hand and kissed the palm. She giggled, which tickled him, but not as much as knowing he possessed her panties in his pocket. God, just the thought of her naked under the long skirt …

"If anyone can get them to change their dating rituals, it's her. Although I can see the merit," Ruth said, hinting at how they'd kept her captive in her apartment for three whole days, extracting promises to love them forever, among other things.

"Hmmm, hot Tarzan-like men? I can see a whole lot of merit," Naomi remarked.

"In little loin cloths," Ruth reminded.

"We should make some," Francine mused aloud.

"Over my dead body," Mitchell growled.

"You and me both," Kendrick added. "Come here, mischief maker." Kendrick snagged and dragged Ruth onto his lap. She resisted at first, her body stiff. Public gestures of affection still made her blush. However, he already knew for a fact she enjoyed it, so he kept practicing on her. Of course, when she did relax, her bottom nestled against his groin in a much-too-pleasant fashion, making it a form of torture for him. Or, as he liked to call it, foreplay.

Seated on his left side, Joel's hand splayed possessively along her nearest thigh, but it didn't bother him. Not when he knew how much she liked it when they both touched her at the same time. Truth was, he loved it too. Loved watching her face as she gave in to the extreme pleasure they delighted in. A pleasure he wasn't getting enough of currently. Dammit.

Mated or not, his woman refused to have sex with him and Joel while she was staying under his parents' roof. Blushing and stammering, she could only mutter it wasn't decent. Determined, he and Joel took her to a motel, but it only took one complaint of late-night screaming to put a halt to that. No sex until they got their own place. He and Joel took her house shopping the next day. Vacant ones only so they could count on a quick closing.

She leaned close to whisper to him, and he thanked God she didn't know everyone in the room could still hear her. He'd kill them if they breathed a word. "I hear the Holiday Inn over in Kanata has sound proof walls."

God, could she be more freakn' perfect?

*

Damn, I love her.

Joel couldn't help the smile on his lips every time he looked, saw, or smelled his mate. Human or not, he wouldn't change a freakn' thing about Ruth. While his love for her might have started because of a chemical reaction exclusive to his kind, hers evolved out of a genuine like of him for him. To a boy, now a man, who fought for acceptance his whole life, the trust she placed in him, the love she sent his way, melted the ice he'd encased around his heart.

His dad was still a dick. His mother still abandoned him. But someone loved him. Loved him and wanted him just the way he was.

Screw fate. This was what love was all about. Acceptance, laughter, and trust. With a healthy dose of sex.

"I'm not wearing underwear," she whispered in his ear.

When the laughter erupted and Ruth realized her hushed comment greeted more ears than expected, she only turned three shades of red as she grumbled, "Darned wolves. I am so getting you all flea collars for your birthdays."

Had he mentioned how much he loved this freakn' woman? And no matter what challenges life threw their way, he'd do his best to meet them and to cherish what he'd found so he could stay in her life, forever and ever.

He was just lifting her fingers to his lips when the doorbell rang. Given the family all sat around the massive dining room table, no one paid it any mind except for Geoffrey, the family patriarch, who answered the door.

A moment later, a blonde RCMP officer entered the room. Was someone in trouble?

"Patricia, grab a seat," Meredith yelled, recognizing her scent, even from the kitchen.

"I can't. I'm here on business. I'm looking for Stu Grayson."

Kendrick's brother pushed back from the table and stood. "That's me. What can I do for you, doll?"

"Stu Grayson, I'm placing you under arrest." Patricia dangled a set of metal cuffs and jaws all over the place dropped. Except for Chris'. He laughed his face off as he shouted, "About time you came for him. Remember not to bend over in the slammer, big bro."

And that was when the family dinner devolved into chaos. As usual.

(The End...only of this story)

The fun continues in the Freakn' Shifter series with:
Delicate Freakn' Flower, Already Freakn' Mated, Human and Freakn', Jungle Freakn' Bride, Freakn' Cougar, Freakn' Out

See EveLanglais.com for more details.

www.ingramcontent.com/pod-product-compliance
Lightning Source LLC
LaVergne TN
LVHW012035070526
838202LV00056B/5513